Texas... because I ... hailing anoth... I was thinki... he back to the...

G... on following... , where she st... he had ever s... hway.

Sh... n chariot. "V...

Our **Giggle** Guarantee

We're so sure our books will make you smile, giggle, or laugh out loud that we're putting our "giggle guarantee" behind each one. If this book fails to tickle your funny bone, return it to your local bookstore and exchange it for another in our *"A Time for Laughter...and Romance"* line.

Comments?
We'd love to hear from you!
Write to:
Lisa Bergren, Executive Editor
WaterBrook Press
5446 N. Academy, #200
Colorado Springs, CO 80918

The Double Heart Diner

Route 66 Series

Book 1: The Double Heart Diner

Book 2: Cupid's Corner
   (Available October 1999)

Book 3: Lost Romance Ranch
   (Available June 2000)

The Double Heart Diner

ANNIE JONES

WATERBROOK
PRESS

F
Jon

THE DOUBLE HEART DINER
PUBLISHED BY WATERBROOK PRESS
5446 North Academy Boulevard, Suite 200
Colorado Springs, Colorado 80918
A division of Random House, Inc.

The characters and events in this book are fictional,
and any resemblance to actual persons or events is coincidental.

Scripture taken from the Holy Bible, New International Version®.
NIV®. Copyright © 1973, 1978, 1984 by International Bible Society.
Used by permission of Zondervan Publishing House.
All rights reserved.

ISBN 1-57856-133-7

Printed in the United States of America
1999—First Edition

10 9 8 7 6 5 4 3 2 1

1

So, this was it. The Double Heart Diner. The quest had taken only three days—and an entire lifetime.

"Doesn't it just figure?" Jett Murphy muttered to himself. He climbed out of the rented car that had brought him from St. Louis and folded his arms over his dusty blue work shirt. He tipped his head back farther, then farther still, to take in the whole sight before him. If he hadn't been headed for this very spot all along he would have suspected that he'd fallen into some kind of time warp or twilight zone, or that this was a mirage.

No, he decided after a moment's consideration, even mirages had their limits. Something this tacky had to be the work of men. Very *strange* men. Men with little sense of taste and way too much time on their hands. Only such a person could have constructed this eyesore, this monument to commercialism and bad roadside cuisine that jutted against the stark Texas sunset.

For a fact, the shabby Route 66 café wasn't the strangest thing he'd seen on his trek from Chicago to this deserted stretch of Texas panhandle. But it was certainly in the running.

Route 66. The Mother Road. That's what they'd called it way back when. The legendary expanse—now miles of convoluted connections, broken bridges, and busted-up concrete with grass growing in the cracks—was famous for just this kind of odd and amazing attraction. Once the principal route for those traveling between Chicago and L.A., it had become unnecessary after the construction of several interstates and was now preserved primarily by dreamers and nostalgia buffs.

Yet it remained functional. It had brought him here . . . or rather, she—Georgia Darling—had. The road, or the bits that remained of it, had not been the real lure any more than this place had been, this diner he had come to care about even though he had never seen it.

She was to blame for that too.

Thoughts of Georgia invaded Jett's mind. *Invaded,* now there was a good word for what she had done. She had taken over his heart, and even his best defenses had been unable to keep her out. He smiled ruefully at the image of the petite redhead with a mind like a steel trap—and a tongue with almost as much bite—having that kind of effect on him, a successful CEO with a reputation for an almost stoic detachment regarding both his work and personal life.

In her efforts to save this café, Georgia had gotten in over her head, then she'd gotten under his skin. Now she was inside his mind, behind his actions, and most especially on his heart. How did all that happen in just three days? Only a woman like Georgia Darling could pull off something like that. Only a woman like that could have brought the leader of the Padgett Group to this lonesome smudge-in-the-road called the Double Heart Diner.

Jett shook his head as he scanned the structure looming before him—a building in the shape of two hearts side by side, overlapping just a bit. The stuccolike surface of the first heart was painted a pinkish-grape color in contrast to the second, which was more of a grapish-pink. And running through them both, designed to be seen from the now-almost-forgotten strip of Route 66, was a vivid, reddish-orange neon arrow.

Didn't it just figure, he thought, irony twisting the proverbial knife low in his gut, that what had become his spiritual journey, his great adventure in search of love and meaning, had ended in a place like *this?*

The Double Heart Diner. Smack-dab in the epicenter of absolute nowhere. He gritted his teeth and huffed out a hard laugh that had nothing to do with seeing the humor in the situation.

His rental car rocked gently as he pushed off from it and started toward the glass front door with the tattered "Yes, We're Open" sign hanging askew in the window. He'd made it this far, and he'd promised himself—not to mention a certain wonderful redhead—that he'd go the distance. If nothing else, he was a man of his word.

Jett had long taken pride in the fact that he was neither a bellyacher nor a crybaby. Rarely did he take his problems to an authority higher than his own God-given horse sense. But tonight he had bowed his head, folded his hands, and asked the Lord what he should do.

In his heart, he had his answer. What he was about to do might not bring Georgia back into his life, but he wasn't doing it with that hope in mind. He was coming here, finishing his quest, because it was the right thing to do. Whatever the outcome, he would be able to live with his actions for the rest of his life. That should give him some consolation, even if he never saw the amazing, funny, sweet, sharp—and exasperating—Georgia Darling again.

Jett straightened his back and jerked his chin to one side, making his neck pop. Then he gritted his teeth and drew in the now-familiar smells of greasy cooking, car exhaust, and fresh air. In a few long strides he was at the door and pushing his way inside.

Bells jangled, hard and jarring, as the door swung open, and old-style, metal venetian blinds banged against the glass. It took a second for his eyes to adjust to the murky dimness after his time under the graying sky, streaked with natural light and the twinkling of the evening's first stars.

The diner wasn't as forbidding or gloomy a place as he'd expected. On the contrary, with its chrome and mirrors and ribbon of neon color that flowed along the top of the walls in one unending wave, it seemed to bid him welcome. A big jukebox—the kind that looked like it still played records, though it clearly advertised it featured CDs—stood at one end of the building, like the guardian of some portal to the past.

None of the handful of patrons sitting at the booths even looked up when he entered, nor did the lone man, dressed all in black, sitting hunched at the end of the long lunch counter.

Jett breathed in the aroma of slap-in-the-face-strong coffee brewing and cheeseburgers frying. And onion rings. He sniffed again. And . . . what was that other smell? He couldn't quite identify it.

He thought of the splintered-wood-and-natural-stone sign, beside the road about a half-mile back, that had once encouraged tourists to stop at the diner by promising "We put a Double helping of Heart in every serving!" Someone, years ago by the look of it, had carved an addition, big and bold, so that the board now read: "We put a Double helping of Heart*burn* in every serving."

Jett took another deep breath and needed nothing more than the smell of the food to convince him of the correction's accuracy. Not that he would mind a good case of heartburn. It sure had heart*ache* beat by a mile. If he could forget that miserable feeling, even for a little while, that would do him just fine. He took a seat and tried not to look at the silver-haired man—the *prematurely* silver-haired man, he corrected himself—looking back at him from the mirror.

The cook, visible through a pair of swinging doors propped open, slapped another burger on the old-style grill. Jett watched as he pressed down hard with his narrow spatula until grease oozed out around the edges, hissing and popping.

Might as well order himself one of those, he thought. Flipping open the menu, he searched for what he expected could most aptly be named "The Double Heart Attack on a Platter."

"Why, hi, sweet-thing. I don't believe I've ever seen you in here before." Jett looked up as a waitress, with black hair that looked as if it had been inflated by a tire pump, stuck her hand across the counter. "Starla Mae Jenkins at your service, sassy waitress with a heart of gold—and they ain't a dime a dozen. Remember that when figuring your tip, now. And you are . . . ?"

Jett sniffed the air. "Bubblegum."

The waitress cocked her head at him. "How's that again?"

"The smell. A minute ago, I was trying to figure out what it was. I just realized: It's bubblegum." He laughed to himself. "I knew it was familiar. I just couldn't quite put my finger on it."

"Oh, now, you don't want to go and do that."

"Do what?"

"Put your finger on my bubblegum." She blinked at him as if he was a total idiot, then blew a small bubble and let it pop pale pink against her bright red lips.

"No, I . . . that is . . . " Jett sighed and shut his eyes, feeling worn down without having actually done anything. "So, you're Starla Mae Jenkins, huh? You're not exactly what I expected. Or maybe you're everything I expected and then some."

Starla Mae laughed. It was a far more amiable laugh than he had expected would come out of someone who, he happened to know, worked hard just to scrape by as owner of this nearly bankrupt diner. He liked the sound of it, warm and genuine. "And you're . . . ?"

Jett paused. "Does the name 'Padgett Group' mean anything to you?"

"Ahhh," Starla smacked her gum again. "So you've come to see the place for yourself then?"

So he had, but not for the reasons she'd suspect. He looked at Starla for a long moment. His stomach grumbled. "Can we postpone talk about business for a while? I've been driving all day and haven't eaten. What I'd really like to do now is just order."

"Nobody 'just orders' at the Double Heart Diner, sweetthing. Ain't that right, y'all?"

One man at a booth by the window grunted agreement while another customer mumbled his support. The fellow at the end of the counter took his time to straighten, then made a half-spin on his stool, faced Jett, and curled his lip up in a snarl. His eyes were hooded as he growled a husky "That's right, darlin'."

Jett let the menu in his hands fall to the countertop. "That . . . that looks like—"

"Yep." Starla leaned closer. "The ghost of Elvis. He haunts the Double Heart Diner on lonely summer nights like these. Just sits there all alone at the end of the counter until a stranger, like you, spots him and then . . . "

"And then?" Jett didn't believe a word of it, but he found himself drawn in by Starla Mae's intense, sparkling eyes and hushed tone.

"Pffft."

"Pffft?"

Starla Mae snapped her fingers, setting off a ripple effect that had her bracelets clattering. "He's gone—leaving nothing but the key to a pink Cadillac and the footprints of his blue suede shoes."

"Huh?" Jett knew his mouth was hanging open, but he couldn't seem to make it stay shut.

Starla Mae grinned. "And if you swallow that, let me get you one of our twenty-dollar milkshakes to wash it down with."

"Twenty dollars?" Jett blinked, then it all fell into place for him and he joined the waitress in a "gotcha" chuckle.

"Elvis, hon, come on over here and be sociable." She motioned to the man in black, who slid down until only one stool separated him from Jett. "This is my baby brother, Elvis—"

"You mean he impersonates Elvis," Jett ventured, still trying to make sense of what he was seeing and hearing.

"*Young* Elvis," the man emphasized.

"Yes, he does impersonate him. And quite well too. It's just one of his many, many talents." Starla Mae beamed with pride. "And his name happens to be Elvis, as well. Ain't that a hoot?"

"You took the words right out of my mouth, ma'am. A hoot." Jett wondered what his old Ivy League professors and current Fortune 500 business colleagues would think of that assessment. He extended his hand to the young man. "Good getup. You had me going for a second."

"Thank you. Thank you very much." Elvis shook Jett's hand but turned to his sister and cocked one eyebrow knowingly.

"Don't you even go there with me, Elvis Arnold Jenkins!" she said. "I know for a fact that you've earned your way through college by doing your summer gigs. I also know that while you're very good at doing Elvis, you'd make an even better lawyer."

"A lawyer?" Jett eyed the man again.

"Yep." Starla Mae nodded. "He'd make a fine one too; his pre-law professors all say so. And he's been accepted into a fine school, to start next fall—"

"But law school costs money," Elvis said directly to Starla Mae. "Impersonating Elvis in summer hot spots up and down Route 66—that *earns* money. I'm afraid I'm going to have to do a lot more of the latter before I can even hope to begin the former."

"See? Don't he talk like a lawyer already?" Starla Mae's eyes sparkled with pride. "Trouble is, as part-owner of this diner—our folks left it to both of us—he didn't qualify for any financial aid. And we can't convince anyone in charge that this diner isn't capable of supporting itself *and* a law student. Elvis won't take a loan—"

"Honey, we've lived most of our lives in debt. I'm not adding to it. When I've set back enough money, I'll go to law school."

Starla Mae looked at him, her heart in her eyes. She didn't say a word. But Jett got the distinct idea that if she did, it would be about taking risks in order to better oneself and warning against putting off dreams for too long. He imagined she had once given Georgia Darling, in Georgia's high school and college days as a waitress in this very place, the same kind of advice.

The reminder of Georgia made his throat constrict, which put an edge to his tone as he shifted on the counter stool and said, "If it's your dream to become a lawyer, son, you ought to follow it. It might not be as impossible as you think—"

Elvis eyed him warily. "I don't think I caught your name, mister."

"Oh! This is . . . " Starla Mae extended her hand, palm up, toward Jett. "Well, toss me off the rooftop and call me flighty, but I don't believe I ever got your name either."

"Jett," he said, smiling, despite himself, at her interesting way of putting things. "Jett Murphy."

"Jett," Elvis said. "Jett Murphy. I like that name; I like it very much."

"It's a . . . it's a nickname," Jett felt compelled to add. "My given name is Padgett."

"Well, welcome to our diner, Mr. Padgett—Jett—Murphy." Starla Mae finally succeeded in latching on to his hand and giving it a firm shake. "'Least it's still 'our diner' for a little while yet, before the bank comes and takes it over, that is. Are you ready to order now?"

"I thought you said nobody comes to this place and 'just orders'?" He sounded a bit more testy than he felt.

"They don't. Or that's how the saying goes," she replied.

"Ah, 'the saying.'" He narrowed his eyes at her.

"You've heard it?" She cocked her head

He had heard this "famous" saying—from Georgia Darling. In fact, he had probably taken it more to heart than he wanted to admit. Still, somehow he felt driven to hear it from the scarlet lips of Starla Mae Jenkins herself. "I have. Why don't you tell it to me, though, just to make sure I've got it right."

"That I can do." She popped a bubble, grinned, and gave

him a wink. "'Anyone cruising Route 66 who has lost their love or lost their way will eventually find themselves at the Double Heart Diner.'"

"Hmmm. That's just a bit different than I learned it." Jett narrowed his eyes. "So tell me, do you mean 'find themselves' as in find their way or find their love, or 'find themselves' as in just end up here?"

Starla Mae blew a bubble and shrugged her shoulders.

Something in the kitchen sizzled.

Jett bowed his head and snorted out a humorless laugh. "Guess it doesn't matter. Especially since I have lost my love and I sure enough did end up right here. Guess that proves the saying true."

"Unless you take it the other way," Elvis muttered.

"What?" Jett brushed his fingertips over his faded jeans.

"He means, if you take it that you find yourself—as in find what you're searching for—then you haven't proven the saying right. Not yet." Starla Mae plopped her chin in her hand.

"Not yet, indeed. But if you knew how badly I've messed things up, you'd settle for the looser interpretation," Jett told her. "I don't see how I could ever fix this—or find the love I lost—here tonight."

"What's the matter?" Starla Mae cocked her head, her chin still resting in her palm. "Don't you have any faith?"

"In what? A saying? In a peculiar roadside diner on old Route 66?" He shook his head. "My faith is in something else entirely." Only God could help him now, though goodness knows he didn't deserve it.

"Then all the more reason never to give up," she said quietly.

Jett held her gaze, fighting the urge to get up, drive back the way he came, and forget everything that had happened these last few days—forget that pretty little redheaded Georgia Darling, who had turned his world upside down, then walked out on him. But this waitress's one solemn statement had him fixed in his seat. If he had faith, he could not simply give up. He had come here to finish something, and even though she didn't know it, that something would be every bit as beneficial to Starla Mae and her diner as it would be to him.

"Why don't you tell us about it?" Starla Mae finally suggested after several seconds of silence.

"Why?" he asked dully.

"Why not?" she answered.

"Well, you've got me there." He laughed, though he was not particularly amused with himself. "I did pray about coming here and felt led to do it. It only seems fitting, after everything I've been through this week, that I'd end up telling my sad story to a waitress named Starla Mae Jenkins and the ghost of Elvis—"

"*Young* Elvis."

Jett nodded to the man in black, conceding, "*Young* Elvis—would-be lawyer—in a place called the Double Heart Diner."

2

"No good deed goes unpunished." Jett Murphy stood silhouetted against the backdrop of the Chicago skyline that filled the expanse of windows in his plush office. "That's going to be our new company motto. Write it down, Miss Sorenson."

"No good deed goes . . . " Jett's secretary, on her very first day of work, pressed her pen so hard to her steno pad that Jett wondered that the end didn't snap off—it, and the tip of her tongue, which protruded from between her teeth just enough to give her the appearance of a first-grader concentrating on an assignment.

He had not intended for her to actually write down what he had said, of course, but when he saw her attacking the task with such intensity he didn't have the heart to stop her. That was his downfall, he decided, grinding his fist into the palm of his hand and gritting his teeth. He was just too nice a guy for his own good. And it cost him. Oh boy, did it cost him.

He thought of his current predicament and suddenly the impulse to change the company motto didn't seem all that wild after all. What a mess he was in. All because he wanted to buy a crummy little Texas diner—helping the owner out of a financial jam in the process, no less—and turn the property over at a reasonable profit. What was so wrong about that?

Miss Sorenson's pen popped with finality against the thin paper as she finished writing down what Jett had dictated in sarcasm. She stood and looked at him, her glasses askew and her salt-and-pepper hair sticking up on one side—the after-effect of running one hand through it in her frantic search for the pen she had earlier tucked behind one ear.

Jett resisted the temptation to smile at his employee. On another day he probably would have done just that, but his mood would not allow it today. Being too nice to employees—that's what had landed him in this mess in the first place. The sound of his pulse rushed in his ears as his emotions cranked up another notch.

"No good deed goes unpunished," he echoed quietly, muttering more to himself than to his secretary. He turned to gaze out the window once more. "Commit the phrase to memory, Miss Sorenson. Answer the phone with it. In fact, maybe you should check into the cost of having it printed on all our business cards, promotional materials, and letter-heads."

"Yes. Yes, sir."

A soft clattering noise caught Jett's attention, and he turned to see that his secretary had backed up against the door—perhaps to escape his tirade—turned the knob in silence, and started to slip out.

Jett drew a bead on her with one eye shut and shook his finger in single-minded warning. "And should anyone ask you why we've chosen as our motto this cynical but sadly necessary reminder of the world we live in, you look that person right in the eye, Miss Sorenson, and utter two words—"

He glanced down at his massive mahogany desk and

snatched up a simple note scrawled under the letterhead of his own company: the Padgett Group.

Miss Sorenson blinked behind her rimless glasses, wearing an expression not of fear but of a person witnessing a collision in which pieces are sent flying in every direction. She blinked again, obviously waiting for the last chunk of vital information to fall from his lips.

"Georgia Darling," Jett ground out between clenched teeth. "That's what you tell them, Miss Sorenson. Georgia Darling."

"Yes, sir." She took another step backward.

"What's this? You scaring off another secretary, pal?" The deep, reasoned tones of Jett's uncle, the company's principal attorney, drifted in from the hallway. Lou Murphy pushed the door open for Miss Sorensen. He both greeted her and granted her leave with a curt bow of his head that did not cause a single one of the few strands of hair he had left to waft out of place. Uncle Lou came from the side of the family in which one's hair fell out instead of going silver before one's thirtieth birthday. Of the two options, Jett often thanked the Lord for the distinguished coloring—and thickness—of his hair.

"So, you heard all that?" Jett waved his hand to indicate his uncle should have a seat.

"People in Canada heard that hullabaloo, my friend." Lou dropped the black leather luggage he'd carted in as the door shut with Miss Sorenson safely on the other side. "And let me tell you, it is not the way a man of your standing should be talking—especially while in the midst of such . . . delicate negotiations." His uncle, for all his education and success, had an accent like a Chicago gangster in a low-budget black-and-white movie. That always made Jett smile.

"I can't help it, Uncle Lou." He slumped into his leather

chair. "People like this Georgia Darling—loose cannons—make me crazy."

"Yes. Yes. I imagine they would. People you can't control, people whose actions don't make perfect sense to you, would tend to set a fellow like you on edge."

Jett decided to ignore the "fellow like you" remark. His uncle had been a part of the company since the Padgett Group was first established. He knew better than anyone else how Jett had arrived at his cautious, detached style. In fact, Uncle Lou had been one of the initial investors who almost lost everything when Jett had let personal feelings about a project affect his judgment.

It had happened simply enough; Jett had liked the principals involved in one early buyout. Thinking that he could help them as well as those involved with the Padgett Group, he'd been freer with information than he should have been. To his own and his partners' horror, that tiny gesture had nearly cost them the entire deal and, potentially, the future of the company. Since then Jett had carefully cultivated an approach to business that, in time, had spilled over into his personal life: one of tight-lipped control and reserved detachment. It galled him to think that this woman was threatening to do the one thing he had always guarded against—let her emotions lead her to say too much, too soon, to too many people.

"You saw the note she sent with her resignation." Jett shut his eyes and could still see the words on the page. "You know what she says. She's got the press involved now. It's the last straw, I tell you. The last straw."

"So one self-righteous bean counter doesn't like the terms of one of your business deals. Says she holds dear this particular business you're trying to buy up, the one you plan to resell to developers at a substantial profit. She says she's fed up with the way we do things here in Chicago and wants to go back to her beloved Texas. So she gets all worked up and resigns over it. What are you going to do about it?"

Do? The single word hit Jett like a sucker punch. "Doing" things was not his area—he hired others to do things for him.

"She's not a bean counter," Jett corrected, evading the question. "She's an acquisitions accountant."

"She's a nut." Uncle Lou stood up, wandered the room, and then perched on the arm of his chair. "And she's the worst kind of nut; she's a nut with a plan of action."

A plan of action. The words resonated within Jett. It had been so long since he had done anything, since he himself had had a plan of action. He didn't want to admit it out loud, but he held a grudging admiration for this woman who was willing to do something, to take action, to further her cause.

"I ask you again, son: What are you going to do?" But Lou didn't give Jett the chance to answer. Instead he leaned forward and gestured assertively as he laid out the situation for his nephew and client. "You want to buy this diner that's out in the middle of nowhere, right?"

Jett nodded.

"Because we know it's one of three sites under consideration for an expensive new land development deal, right?"

"Right."

"So the Padgett Group plans to buy the dump, clear the land to make it more desirable for development, and resell it at a handy profit, right?"

Jett hedged.

"Right?" Lou barked.

"Well, technically . . . "

"That's what you do, isn't it? Buy low, sell high. Stay one step ahead of everybody else so that when it's time to pay the piper"—Lou arched one eyebrow and tipped his head downward just enough to double the folds in his already double chin—"well, when it's time to pay the piper, that piper is you, my friend."

Hearing his life's work put into such harsh terms made Jett squirm. If this was his public image, no wonder this Georgia Darling had gotten herself worked up enough to quit and go back to a place she felt represented gentler attitudes. At this moment, Jett wasn't exactly crazy about being associated with the Padgett Group himself.

Lou ruffled his red tie with the orange-and-green flower pattern on it. "So, this nut—um, bean counter—er, acquisitions accountant—happens to know something about this diner. It's some kind of old broken-down ruin . . . where?"

"Old Route 66," Jett filled in.

"That's right. That's right." For just a moment Uncle Lou got a faraway look in his eye. "Did I ever tell you about the time your dad and I—now this was before you were born, before your folks were even married, see—did I ever tell you about our little Route 66 adventure?"

"You and Dad? Really?" An image from an old black-and-white photo of his father and Uncle Lou—a pair of skinny young fellows with heads of wavy, dark hair and a fearless gleam in their eyes—formed in Jett's mind.

"I'd just come home from a stint in Korea and I'd bought this slick roadster—turquoise blue and white with lots of chrome. Your dad had just graduated from high school and had some extra folding money burning a hole in his pocket. So we hit 66 just after Memorial Day. We didn't have to be anywhere until he went off to college and me to law school that September—"

"Yeah?" Jett folded his arms on the desk, fascinated, wanting to hear more about the two brothers' exploits.

"Point is, it was a once-in-a-lifetime trip. I'd recommend it to anyone, if it were even possible anymore." Lou suddenly frowned, cleared his throat, and shifted his bulky shoulders. "But the old Mother Road exists only in people's memories nowadays. What's left of it isn't fit for commerce. There's not much of anything still out there, and what *is* left is done for."

"But you said it was a once-in-a-lifetime trip. Did you go all the way to Los Angeles?"

"And back." Lou grinned like a schoolboy.

"Did you see the diner this woman is so set on saving?"

"The . . . ? No. Nope. Our specs say the building on the Texas property went up in '61. Never saw the place." Lou sucked his teeth and gazed off into nowhere. For a moment, Jett could imagine Lou as that young man with a buzz cut, toothpick in his mouth, and one arm out the car window— the whole world laid out in front of him. "I saw some things, though, let me tell you."

"Yeah?" The lure of Lou's words drew Jett physically forward in his seat.

"Yeah." Lou chuckled.

Jett spread out his hands in a gesture of open-mindedness. "So maybe we should consider not tearing down this place after all." The words sounded strange in his own ears. He couldn't believe he was saying them. But after all Lou had said about the Padgett Group, about Jett specifically, and now about Route 66, he felt more open to reconsidering his decision.

"Naw, that's dreamer talk!" Lou scoffed. "Sure, it was a special place. But that doesn't mean we need to go making monuments out of every tourist trap and greasy spoon ever built along that stretch of road."

"We're not talking about every—"

"It's ridiculous. What you are going to do with that land

is far more beneficial to the people who live nearby than that diner will ever be. You've seen the stats on this place, son. It barely breaks even and only does that because the folks who own it do most of the work and don't take home a dime more than they need just to scrape by. Why, you'd be doing them a favor to buy it."

Jett had made that same argument to himself time and again, and not just over this project. But for some reason, he wasn't sure he believed it anymore. For too long he'd felt empty and restless and caught in his own trap, a point that had been hammered home by Georgia Darling's indignation and Uncle Lou's talk of traveling the legendary road.

"Now, this . . . this nut who's decided to spoil your deal by alerting the media to the potential sale of this diner, she doesn't see the big picture," Lou went on.

"Doesn't she?" Jett murmured.

"My job is to make sure she does—or, barring that, to stop her."

"How?" Jett sat up straight.

"Well, she gives us no choice. In her resignation letter, she says that, if she doesn't receive official notice from the Padgett Group that the sale is not going through, she's meeting a reporter at noon today and spilling her guts. You know how volatile information about a sale can be, son, especially at this stage of negotiations. Until we have signatures on paper, we're vulnerable."

Jett scowled. "People just don't realize how a single piece of information can undo months of work and cost everyone involved a lot of money."

"And then there's your old buddy," Lou said sarcastically, "the business columnist who has never gotten a real scoop on the Padgett Group and would love to make you the focus of a whole series of none-too-favorable columns."

"Rod Campbell," Jett muttered.

"He can't accept that you've succeeded without shady ethics." Lou scowled like a bulldog. "You gall his reporter's sensibilities. Getting dirt on a company like the Padgett Group is the stuff of a nationally syndicated newspaper series, and you won't cooperate. You know he'd love to get something on you to further his own career. The fact that you're so elusive and stay out of the public eye doesn't help Campbell's mind-set either." Lou thought for a moment. "Maybe you should—"

"Oh no. No way. I've been down that press-the-flesh, see-and-be-seen path before." Jett did not need to remind his uncle how his openness and trust had nearly cost them everything.

"Now, this woman who's had access to your financial records is threatening to say who-knows-what to anyone who'll listen, unless we bow to her demands."

"Man, that's not good," Jett muttered.

"Not good?" Lou scrunched his face up and shook his pudgy finger at Jett. "That's blackmail, my friend, pure and simple."

"It sure sounds that way when you describe it. But in her letter it really isn't like that—"

"Exactly. That's why we need this." Lou patted the smaller of the two black bags by his side.

"What's that?"

"Video camera and tape recorder—both state of the art. It's everything I'm going to need to get her on record, attempting to blackmail the Padgett Group."

"You? How are you going to do that?"

"We know where she's meeting this reporter fellow."

"We do?" Jett smelled a rat, which, he thought, would have been an improvement over Uncle Lou's pungent cologne. The whole situation felt like a setup. "Tell me, Uncle Lou, how do we know that?"

"Just a matter of a few phone calls, that's all. The city editor seemed to find the entire scenario pretty intriguing . . . "

"In other words, he's setting her up—" Jett paused. "No, wait. We're all setting her up?"

"No. I have no intention of playing into some reporter's hands just to make his job easier and his story juicier. I do happen to know the location of a meeting between Ms. Darling and a certain reporter, and I plan to be there a little ahead of time to have a word with this rabble-rousing redhead."

Jett blinked. "How could you know she has red hair?"

"Guess the question is, how could you not? She works for *you*, pal."

"Hired by my highly competent personnel director, Uncle Lou. You know I don't oversee that kind of thing myself. I do hire all my top people personally, but then I trust them to do their jobs."

"Yeah, I know—professional detachment." Lou shook his head. "Way I see it, you've *detached* yourself from just about everything that really matters, son. What do you do with your time anyway?"

"I work." Jett felt the muscles clamp tight between his shoulders.

"Yeah, but what do you *do*?"

He cleared his throat. "You know—handle paperwork, make conference calls, go over proposals and plans . . . work."

Lou grunted.

"I thought we were talking about this Georgia Darling anyway. How did you say you knew she had red hair?"

"Got a description of her from her employee file. Petite

22

thing, red hair, about eight years younger than you, graduate of Texas Christian University, if that matters."

Jett looked up. "Well, maybe it does."

"What do you mean?"

Was he wrong, or was there a gleam in Uncle Lou's eyes? Jett stood. He picked up the note handwritten by Georgia Darling and studied the swirls and angles of her graceful writing. "You've painted an awfully hard picture of a young woman that neither of us really knows, Uncle Lou."

"Might I remind you that she's done the same about you?"

Jett considered this. It was true. But the picture Lou had just painted of him wasn't much better. That kind of thing had to make a man think.

"Based on one business deal," Lou went on, "this woman who worked for your company only a few months has drawn some pretty ugly conclusions. As far as I can tell, she's not aware of how much you donate to charity, nor does she know how many scholarships you support. And then there are your generous contributions to your church—"

"I don't do any of that for recognition. I've been blessed, and giving some back is the very least I can do." Jett felt his back muscles knot at the truth of that statement. Giving money was the *least* he could do; he just didn't know how to do more. His commitment to his work simply did not allow for anything else, or so he told himself and his pastor.

"Well, you give plenty," Uncle Lou insisted. "But does this nut recognize any of that? Will that make it into her media moment? Not likely. She doesn't know you from Adam, yet she's decided it's her place to paint you publicly as a—what did she call you in that letter? 'A money-grubbing—'"

Jett picked up the note and read from it precisely. "'A

money-hungry, insensitive, heartless, land-grubbing, gravy-guzzling pig.' And I have to admit, that 'gravy-guzzling' part really hurt."

"You laugh now, but when you see yourself portrayed as a villain in the press you won't think it's so clever—especially when they seek you out for comments."

Jett shrugged. "I have no intention of wallowing around in the media mud with this woman. I'm not going to play dueling sound bites."

"Of course not. You're too smart for that. Which brings me to Part Two of my plan." Lou patted the bigger suitcase.

"I'm afraid to ask—"

"I've taken the liberty of having a few things packed for you. I also have things all set up for your stay in the family cabin," Lou said, referring to the Padgett vacation home in Wisconsin. "Your plane tickets are in here. Flight leaves at six-thirty. Take a cab—I'll look after your car."

"Lou—" Jett stepped forward in protest.

"We sign the papers in five days," Lou interrupted. "That's as fast as we can get them drawn up. We can't let our competitors know what property we're going for, or they may sweeten their deals to secure the buyers and knock us out of the running. But if we can keep you out of the public eye—and *her* out of the papers—for a few days, we'll have it made."

"Just how are you going to keep her out of the papers?" Jett definitely didn't like the way that sounded—not that he thought any harm would come to the lady. His uncle might talk like a gangster, but he was a law-abiding citizen: a letter-of-the-law–abiding citizen with the kind of legal knowledge to be up to something. "What, specifically, is your plan, Uncle Lou?"

"I'm going to talk to this young lady."

"Just talk?"

He nodded. "I'll try to convince her that you and the Padgett Group are not corrupt."

"And if that fails?"

"I'll get her on tape saying outright what she implies in her letter, that she is employing extortion as a means of getting her way." Lou's expression was bland. "Then one phone call to the police and she's detained."

"You'd have her arrested?" Jett came around his desk, his stride purposeful but not threatening.

"Hey, she's the one breaking the law, not me." The sparkle in his uncle's eye suggested teasing, but his words were carefully chosen to provoke a reaction and Jett could not help but respond.

"No! No way. I won't be a part of it, and I won't let my lawyer—or my family—be a part of it either." Jett turned to look out at the city, pushing back the folds of his suit jacket to place his hands on his hips. "I don't want to operate like that. I won't."

"But she's the one—" There was a lilt to his uncle's voice, like that of one child trying to draw another into mischief.

"There is no way you are going to convince me, Uncle Lou, that this person really intends blackmail. I doubt she even realizes it sounds like that."

If Uncle Lou had been baiting him, Jett realized, he had gladly obliged. He had been transformed from a man who wanted this woman publicly fingered as the cause of his problems to a man who was actually defending her. He'd gone from not wanting to get involved to wondering what action would be the right one to take.

"Poor kid, she's not even savvy enough to understand that she's being undercut and manipulated by some reporter. And you."

"But that letter, her demands—"

"She's riled up. She's homesick. She's feeling wronged. She's found something she cares passionately about and is willing to do something to help her cause." His pulse picked up as he spoke, and when he turned to confront Uncle Lou, it felt as though something almost electric was racing in his veins. "As someone who hasn't had that feeling in a very long time, and who suddenly realizes that I miss it more than I can comprehend, I am not going to let anyone punish her for that."

"Then what are you going to do?"

"I'm going to talk to her," he said quietly, his course set in that single instant.

"Talk?" Lou half grinned.

"Why not? That's what you were going to do." He ground his back teeth together for a moment and looked into the distance, putting his thoughts in order. "Yes, that's what I'm going to do. You yourself said she'd made up her mind to do all this without ever speaking to me, without knowing me. So who better to talk her out of this whole thing than me?"

"Well, at least take this." Lou held out the bag with the video and audio equipment in it.

"I won't need that." He bent down to pick up the bag filled with clothes. "But I will take this and your advice to make myself scarce until the sale goes through. I'll have Miss Sorenson cancel my appointments, and I'll call in regularly to keep in touch. Are there jeans in here? I'd like to change before I meet this woman. I don't want to come in looking like I'm trying to intimidate her in a suit that cost more than she makes in a single paycheck."

"There are jeans and T-shirts, sweats, that kind of thing. A regular blend-into-the-crowd wardrobe."

"Good." He slipped into the washroom and quickly traded his suit and tie for a much more casual look.

"Where'd you get these clothes?" he asked as he stepped back into the office. He tucked in the pocket on the faded jeans.

"I borrowed them from your cousin. You know, my son, the I'm-not-in-this-for-monetary-rewards minister. In the meantime, he can wear some of your things. Maybe he'll get used to it and get a real job."

"He has a real job, Uncle Lou. He's my pastor and I rely on him, as do a lot of other folks who otherwise might completely lose their way in life."

"You don't look lost to me."

"Looks can be deceiving." He held his arms out to his sides, offering his new look as evidence even a lawyer could not refute. "And I happen to know you are very proud of your son."

Lou grinned. "So sue me; it's true. He's a good man, and so are you. The fact that you care enough to take this on yourself, against your learned lawyer's advice, proves it."

"Yeah, yeah." Jett again picked up the bag with his cousin's clothes in it.

"Take this," Lou commanded. He stood and thrust the smaller bag toward Jett. "I'm speaking as your uncle now, as much as I am speaking as your lawyer. I care about you, son, and I don't think you realize the repercussions that could follow if this talk you have should go awry, or if this Darling woman is really capable of extortion. That 'very least' you think you do by helping others financially could be lost to you through lawsuits and a ruined reputation."

"I really do not believe she is the type—"

"But you don't know now, do you?" He pushed the bag toward Jett again. "The directions to this place where she wants to meet the reporter are in there anyway. Might as well take the whole thing."

"That's a pretty sorry excuse to get me to take it."

"You're being stubborn; you don't deserve a good excuse."

This time he took the bag, if only to satisfy Uncle Lou. "Okay, I've got to get going. I probably should run by the apartment—"

"Why?" Lou snorted. "You haven't got a wife or family to kiss good-bye—you haven't even got a goldfish that needs feeding. Nobody's going to miss you if you don't go by the apartment. Time's running out. Just go."

Lou's assessment cut Jett deep, though he knew it was not meant as a criticism or to wound. It was the truth, plain and simple. He'd made a life for himself in which his employees did the real work of his business and his money did his charity work. As long as he was in control and signing the checks, nobody really knew or cared who he was or why he did what he did.

Except Georgia Darling. She was the first person in a long time to actually challenge him, and with good cause— or so she thought. He left his office, actually looking forward to meeting her face to face.

• • •

Georgia Darling hooked her finger over the nosepiece of her dark glasses and tugged them down so she could peer over the top of the rims. She scanned the crowd of diners at Lou Mitchell's restaurant, a Chicago landmark since the 1940s, for the man she had arranged to meet. She fidgeted with a small box of Milk Duds given to her by the host before she was seated, a longstanding tradition at the restaurant that marked the beginning of Route 66.

She tapped the floor with the toes of her favorite cowboy

boots, the turquoise ones with the leather broken in just right, and bit her lip. Where was that reporter anyway? Georgia shut her eyes and tried to calm herself. She was doing this for all the right reasons, wasn't she? *Wasn't she?*

When she'd written her resignation letter, she'd felt so sure of her actions, just as she had been since the day she'd first seen the figures that pertained to buying a certain property in the Texas panhandle. She was working for the company that was going to buy the famous Double Heart Diner!

Georgia knew the landmark and its owner well, and she loved them both. As soon as she'd seen that her company meant to buy the old place, she called her friend Starla Mae Jenkins and learned as much as Starla Mae could offer. Much as she hated to sell the property, Starla Mae realized she could not continue to run it on her own. It wasn't a financial fiasco, but neither did it provide the kind of security Starla Mae knew she needed to get her younger brother through law school. Starla Mae knew that once she sold the diner it might well be done for, or at the very least be made over into something unrecognizable to anyone who'd loved it for the past thirty-odd years. But Starla Mae had made her peace with that. Georgia would have liked to have done the same, and perhaps she could have if the sale had meant merely a facelift or a name change for the property. But Georgia had seen the financial files on the Double Heart purchase.

The computations and estimates did not lie. That's one reason Georgia liked numbers: They were reliable and honest, unlike many people she'd come across in her life. And this time those numbers—the quotes and projected costs—all said something that Georgia could not bear to believe: The Padgett Group was going to level the Double Heart for no other reason than to make this spot more alluring to some snobby land developers.

When she'd realized that was their plan, she'd written a simple note to the never-seen CEO of the company—a Mr. Murphy—explaining why this was an unconscionable action. There had been no reply.

Time passed. More feasibility studies and cost estimates crossed her desk. She tried several times to make an appointment with this Murphy fellow, feeling that a personal appeal could affect everything. He always declined to meet, however, and nothing changed.

In the meantime, she'd found herself missing Texas more and more, and the Chicago winter did nothing to inspire any change of loyalties. She had few friends here. In truth, she had few friends anywhere. No family either. She'd always been a loner. In Texas, however, she at least had a few people who cared what happened to her—and those people owned the Double Heart.

Time began to run out for that diner. So she asked herself, as she tried to whenever faced with a tough situation: "What would God have me do?" The answer was, of course, "the right thing." And Georgia felt that for her, the right thing was to resign from the company that could destroy such a wonderful place, leave the city where she felt so ill at ease, and go home to try and save the Double Heart by whatever measures she could.

Before she left, though, she felt she had to offer the Padgett Group, quite calmly in her resignation letter, one last chance to listen to her. If they chose not to do so, she would turn to the media for help.

That was what had brought her to Lou Mitchell's today and what had her all on edge. Had she really done the right thing, or had she done the easy thing? Had she followed her conscience, or had she done what everyone seemed to do these days when they didn't get their way—find a mouthpiece through which to cry foul and start a finger-pointing campaign?

She slipped off her dark glasses and folded in the ear-pieces, realization hitting her. What was she doing here? Espionage? She shook her head. This big-hearted Texas gal was about as well-suited to that as she was to living in this vast, cold city, working as an acquisitions accountant. She'd fooled herself to think otherwise, and she'd fooled herself to think she could actually go through with trashing her former employer just because his actions had struck a sentimental nerve.

Luckily, she arrived at this conclusion before the reporter arrived. Georgia tucked her glasses into her T-shirt pocket, stood to leave, and began making her way toward the door before she remembered something.

If she hadn't paused to retrieve her Milk Duds she might never have spotted him. But by the time she had her candy in hand and had turned around, there he was: the reporter. She knew it was him by the black camera bag over his shoulder and the fact that he marched up to the host with total confidence and started asking questions.

Georgia had told the city editor she had red hair, and she knew that the moment the reporter stopped asking his questions the host would point directly at her. She couldn't let that happen. No, sir. She knew herself well enough to know that her feelings about the Double Heart could make her do and say things that she had already decided not to. If that reporter made contact with her, he just might tap into that. She might blurt out something that she would later regret. Better to evade him than to risk it. But how?

Georgia began to walk toward the back of the restaurant, hoping the eclectic crowd would provide some kind of cover. Even as she did, she realized that the clutter of people in business suits and men with leather vests and tattoos would never provide a means of blending in.

She knew God wanted her to do the right thing, and she was trying to. But she was sunk. In that moment, Georgia found herself asking *another* question that all too often she proposed in silence: "What would Lucy Ricardo do in a situation like this?"

She glanced around, frantically wondering how to make herself disappear. She considered for one fleeting moment sliding into a booth and pretending to be a member of someone's family but discarded that idea as she'd simply draw more attention to herself when the family protested. She scanned the room again, realizing now that the host was pointing to the table where she had been sitting. She had to find a way to become invisible to this man so she could quietly slip away. She noticed that the only people who seemed to have that kind of uniformity in this place were the workers.

Georgia froze. Why not? An impulsive action had gotten her into this, after all. Why not let another rash impulse get her out, she reasoned.

"Okay," she admitted to herself in a flash of insight as she bunched up her shoulders and rushed toward the kitchen, poking her Milk Duds into her waist pack. "A girl has to do what a girl has to do."

3

Less than three frenetic minutes and two shorthand accounts of her predicament later—in which she explained to the staff her goal of dressing like a busboy and getting to the front of the building—Georgia peered out from the swinging kitchen door. There he sat: the reporter. She didn't know his name—the city editor hadn't been sure who would be available, or so he'd told her. But there the man was, waiting in the booth where she had been sitting minutes before.

"Oh, great," she muttered to the busboy who had suddenly become her shadow. "He probably caught a glimpse of me dodging this direction and figured I ran to the rest room or something. He clearly thinks I'm coming back."

"Yeah, lady. That's bad news. If he's seen you already, that disguise won't fool him. It wouldn't fool *no* one. You gotta cover up that hair."

"Hmmm." He had a point; her hair definitely would give her away. She would have to have something to disguise it too. Georgia glanced around the warm, damp kitchen. Her gaze landed on a gleaming wire shelf stocked with supplies. "Don't y'all have a hair net I can borrow?"

"Not just laying around, lady."

"What about those?"

"What?"

She pointed to a box of something that looked like shower caps.

"Those? Those are disposable bowl covers, lady. What are you going to do with those?"

Georgia snatched one out of the carton. The clear plastic, ringed with elastic, was dotted with tiny, white triangles. It would not conceal her hair, but it would certainly tone it down a bit. She jerked the cover down over her head. "What do you think? Would you pick me out of that crowd?"

"Not on purpose, lady." He gawked at her as if she had lost her mind along with most of her dignity.

"Well, that's another way to go then." She straightened the long, white—or rather *formerly* white—apron that covered her from collarbone to mid-shin and adjusted her oversize, yellow dishwashing gloves. "Even if he did recognize me, he'd never have the nerve to print anything I might tell him."

"You got that right."

"Good." She slid her sunglasses back on, gave the busboy a snappy salute, and headed toward the dining room. "I'm going in . . . er, out."

"Use the cart there for cover," he called as she pushed through the door and into the chaotic eating area.

Without missing a beat, she snagged the handle of the bus cart and began to push it across the room, her eyes glued to the front door. The wheels wobbled and squeaked, but she pushed on. When a waitress stepped into her path, Georgia pulled back and came to a stop. She hoped the dishes clattering in her gray plastic tub did not draw too much attention to her.

She checked on the reporter from the corner of her eye. Was he looking? She paused. No, he wasn't looking—but he sure was *good*-looking! She'd been too nervous to notice before, but she did now, as she was forced to stand still while the waitress took an order directly in front of her cart.

Distinguished, that's the word she'd use. Despite his casual dress, or maybe in part because of it, the man had what in Texas they would call appeal "as big as all outdoors." And when you were talking "outdoors" in Texas . . . well, that translated to more appeal than any one man ought to have.

She stole another glance over the top of her glasses. He had a good face, she decided: honest and lightly lined, particularly around the eyes. That meant he smiled often and freely, she concluded. And his hair. Gray? No, silver—dark beneath and at the collar, giving it the look of tarnished sterling, though he certainly didn't seem old enough to have earned the coloring.

He strummed his thumb over the menu, then laid one hand on his camera bag. He had strong hands with long fingers, she noted. She heard herself sighing and quickly shook off the impulse to go over and tell the man she'd changed her mind. She didn't dare. She'd seen *60 Minutes*. She knew how these fellows operated. If they wanted a story they went after it. Best simply never to give him that chance.

Besides, this was an attractive man, a compelling man. She, on the other hand, was a Lucy Ricardo–wannabe wearing a disposable bowl cover on her head.

As the waitress slipped past her, Georgia hunched her shoulders and pushed forward once again. The sooner she escaped, the better.

"Miss? Oh, Miss?"

Georgia plowed on.

"You with the cart!" Georgia found herself being waved at by one woman in a cluster of elderly ladies standing next to a recently vacated booth. "Can you take away these dishes please?"

"We'd like to sit here," another explained, gesturing broadly at the table still piled with plates. "If you'd be so kind as to clear all this away."

Georgia glanced up to see if the reporter had noticed the tiny fracas.

He kept his head down.

The ladies apparently took her rubbernecking as evidence that she simply could not spot them in their pink and purple stretch pants, flowing tops adorned with flowers not found in nature, and perfectly rounded perms with a decidedly bluish cast. Soon they were all attempting to get her attention.

"Over here, dear!"

She stared at the sea of waving hands and gently flapping upper arms, which continued to flap for a few seconds after the waving had stopped.

The reporter did not even lift his eyes.

Georgia relaxed. If she was quick enough, she could whisk away those dishes, push the cart a few feet closer to the door, then make a mad dash for it.

"Whoo-hoo! Here, dear. Here!"

"I'm coming," Georgia muttered through clenched teeth. "I'm coming."

Her cart rattled to a stop.

"Isn't that nice, dear?"

"Isn't that sweet?"

"That's right, dear. Get that cup and saucer too."

"Careful not to drip, drip, drip!"

The ladies offered direction and encouragement like coaches cheering on an Olympic hopeful. She suspected with a cringe that they would surely bring the attention of her reporter—as well as everyone else in the place.

Her reporter? She stopped with a glass of icy slush and soda in one hand and a wobbling bowl of lime Jell-O in the other. Just when had he become *her* reporter, she wondered? She glanced his way again.

The party of old ladies began to seat themselves; the unnatural surfaces of their oversize handbags squeaked against the vinyl booth as, one by one, they scooted themselves around the horseshoe-shaped bench.

The reporter had buried his nose in the menu as though it revealed the path to a vast treasure.

Three ladies had been seated, and now the last was about to squeeze in. *Squeeze* being the operative word, as this woman was the most . . . well, the least likely to fit herself neatly within the confines of the space between bench and table. Georgia nudged her cart over as far as the space would allow to give the woman more room, then turned her attention back to the man. That man. That apparently arrogant, self-absorbed, wouldn't-know-his-news-story-if-it-rolled-a-pushcart-over-his-toe man.

Crazy as it seemed, it pricked her ego to realize this gorgeous reporter had not even looked her way, not once. She dumped the Jell-O into the dishpan with indignation.

Snob, she thought. *One of many media elitists who think they decide what's important. Can't even be bothered to pay attention to what's going on right under his—*

WHAM!

The last of the ladies gave a final mighty heave and landed in the seat with such force that her leg shot up in the air. Her foot shoved into one side of Georgia's behind . . . and kept right on pushing.

Georgia's head jerked backward, then snapped forward—an action that would surely result in one dandy case of whiplash. She heard herself gasping and shrieking just as the sticky-sweet ice and slush from the plastic glass in her hand hit her neck and throat. Her lower body slammed into the pushcart, which decided at this precise moment to get in touch with its inner go-cart and went rocketing off toward another table filled with enough food for a large family of lumberjacks.

Flapjacks flopped into two diners' laps. Milk and juice slopped right and left. An entire stack of buttered toast fell to the floor—every piece landing butter-side down with deceptively delicate little *plop plop plops*.

Georgia lurched forward, the slush dripping down her front and onto the floor. Too late to try to prevent the mayhem, in that instant she suddenly remembered why she hardly ever wore her cowboy boots in Chicago: no traction in slippery conditions.

Another yelp tore from her lips. Her feet flew out from under her; her arms and legs flailed like those of a person drowning. She hit the floor with enough force to actually shake loose the bowl cover on her head, the elastic slowly tightening and taking most of her hair up into a tuft, as if she'd blown a big bubble from the top of her head.

The tumbler that had been in her hand, true to its name, went somersaulting high into the air. An instant later it landed on the hard floor, complete with cartoonlike bouncing sounds. As the last *boing* resounded in what was now an otherwise deathly silent restaurant, Georgia had just one thought on her mind: Ego aside, she really hadn't wanted that reporter's attention *this* badly.

Escape was her only recourse. With as much dignity as any person could muster in such a situation, she whisked off her bowl cover, kept her body low, and began to quietly crawl toward the front door: one knee after the other, one yellow-gloved hand then the next leading the way.

To get out—that became her focus. She heard the scuffling of feet on either side of her, heard the murmuring start as she crept past the crowd of patrons. *Don't look up,* she warned herself. If she looked up, she'd meet someone's eyes. Then she'd have to acknowledge this whole fiasco. If she could just get to the door without having to do that, she could slip out into the fresh summer air and be left alone to nurse her aching backside and smarting pride.

"Just a few more feet . . . " she muttered through clenched teeth, egging herself on. "Maybe three or even just—"

A pair of well-worn tennis shoes and faded blue jeans blocked her getaway path.

"Two," she concluded with a sigh. *Caught.* As if humiliation at her own hands weren't enough, now she'd be publicly berated by the manager or some security person. *Perfect,* she thought, *just perfect.*

"C'mon, we've got to get out of here." Firm but gentle hands wrapped around her upper arms and tugged her upright.

The momentum caused her boots to go skating in two different directions—but since she was being held in place, she managed simply to skid nearer to the person trying to steady her. She shut her eyes to prepare for the collision, which was quickly over with a thud and a groan.

* * *

A nut, Jett thought to himself. Georgia Darling was a cute nut with a strangely compelling air about her, a sort of bumbling sweetness that just cried out for a man like him to step in and help her out, protect her, guide her. But she was, just as his uncle had predicted, a nut just the same, a nut he had to get out of this restaurant before the reporter showed up and took the chance to portray her as a complete buffoon. That helping her also meant helping *himself* a smart businessman like Jett could not dismiss.

But whether he was motivated more by a protective bent toward the girl or by a desire for self-preservation, Jett did not have time to analyze. Instead, he grabbed her by the shoulders to keep her upright and looked her in the eyes. "I know I'm not what you expected, Miss Darling—you are Miss Darling, aren't you? Georgia Darling?"

She nodded, batting a wayward red curl away from her face.

Nice face, he thought—*for a nut.* He shifted the weight of the bags slung over his shoulders and nodded back. "I thought so. As I said, I know this isn't the meeting you expected, Miss Darling, but then, it isn't exactly going as I'd envisioned it either."

"I'll bet it isn't." She motioned helplessly to her drenched apron, her huge gloves making a blubbering sound with what otherwise might have been a graceful gesture.

"Listen, we don't have time to talk now. We've got to get out of here."

"Gee, I don't know. My next show is in ten minutes," she joked. "If I left, what would everyone here do for entertainment?"

"I'm not worried about everyone here. I'm worried about you." He meant that; he was genuinely worried about how easily a crafty journalist might tear this trusting woman to bits for his own agenda. Goodness, she couldn't even hold her own against a pushcart and a plump grandma. "C'mon, let's get out of here before your contact shows up and spots us together."

He began to propel her toward the front door.

She dug in her heels—as much as cowboy-boot heels

could dig in on a wet tile floor. "My what? Aren't you my contact?"

"As it turns out, yes. That's my plan, at least. Now stop dragging your feet. We've got only a few seconds to make a clean break for it." They passed the host's stand, and Jett reached into his pocket to retrieve a wad of bills. "This is most of the cash I have. I think it should cover any damage. I'm sorry about everything."

"Hey, you can't do that!" Georgia pulled back with even more tenacity. "I pay my own way in life." She thrust her hand into her own pocket and produced some money, which she counted out slowly.

Jett grabbed what she had and threw it on the counter with his offer. "No time for that, Miss Darling. We've got to get while the getting is—" He stole one hard, assessing glance toward the door, then muttered in recognition, "Rod Campbell."

"Who?" She craned her neck to see.

"Rod Campbell. I call his weekly *Business Alert* column *Business Assault*. He's trying to get a story on me."

"Why? What have you done?"

"Succeeded and stayed out of the public eye while doing it. Let's get out of here." He started to shepherd her off.

"B-but you just handed that man most of my traveling money!" Georgia made a grab, but Jett intercepted it.

"Forget the money." He turned his back to the front door, which put him face to face with her. "And consider this my two cents worth of good advice, free of charge: Make an about-face and run for it."

"What?"

"Look, we don't have time for another argument or floor show. You have to trust me—you can do that, can't you?— just for the next five minutes or so."

She studied his face. In a split second she had made up her mind and nodded her head. "I believe . . . I believe I can."

"Then do as I say: Turn around and go!"

"Where to?"

"Let's try the kitchen; I'm sure it'll have an exit."

"The kitchen?" She winced like someone swallowing a lemon. "I can't believe I never thought to ask them for another exit! I just barged in with one thought on my mind, told them I had to get to the front door—and I could have just ducked out the back of the kitchen!"

"The beauty is, you still can. Let's go."

Georgia threw one last glance over her shoulder—sizing him up—drew in a deep breath, then plowed ahead. People made room for them to get through, probably partly out of self-defense, considering her last exploit, and partly out of sheer curiosity about what she might do next.

"Murphy!"

Jett tensed at Rod's angry shout.

Georgia froze in her steps and gazed back at him, her eyes huge. "Murphy? You? You're *Padgett* Murphy?"

"I thought you knew." Jett tried to urge her forward.

She took a few halfhearted steps. "Well, I didn't. I assumed you were someone sent by him. Everyone knows Murphy never does his own dirty work! But now that I do know who you are—"

"Now that you do, you finally have the opportunity to do what you say you've wanted to do all along: discuss with me my company's plans regarding the Double Heart Diner, right?"

"Um . . . " She wet her lips and took a few more steps. They were almost within arm's reach of the kitchen door. "Right. I guess, right."

"You guess right, indeed. But we won't get the chance to discuss it if that fellow back there gets his way."

"Hold it right there, Murphy!" came a shout from behind them. "I should have known you would get to her before I did. Well, it won't work, you hear me?"

Georgia scowled at Jett, her forward movement halted.

"Look, Miss Darling," he said quickly, "that reporter and city editor set you up. They invited my lawyer here to catch you in the act of extortion just in case your story didn't prove newsworthy enough for their purposes."

"Extortion? I never—"

"I don't have time to explain this to you." He pushed forward but met her shoulder—an immovable object. He sighed. "You made an implied threat, Miss Darling, to go to the media if you didn't get what you wanted from our corporation. A lot of folks would see that as a form of blackmail."

She gulped. Her lip trembled. She swiped at her nose with one quivering yellow glove the size of a bear's paw.

Jett laughed.

"Don't laugh at me!" she demanded.

"I'm sorry, but you just look so . . . laughable. And without guile. And like you really need a knight in shining armor to rescue you from this mess."

"You're going to rescue me?" Georgia's eyes lit up. "Does that mean you'll reconsider destroying the diner?"

"Can we just get out of here," he asked, "and talk this whole thing out later?"

"Oh yes. Yes! Let's go. I'll lead the way."

Behind them Rod continued to bellow. But the crowd, having closed back in to better watch Jett and Georgia's retreat, kept him from catching up with them.

"I swear to you, Murphy, I'm not done with this story.

Not by a long shot!" he shouted angrily after them.

Jett pushed open the kitchen door for Georgia. She looked back in Rod Campbell's direction.

A camera's flash went off.

Jett looked back as well.

Another flash.

"C'mon, let's go," she whispered, hurrying ahead.

"You haven't seen the last of me, Murphy." Rod took another picture, then another. "You can't duck out, stealing the best source ever to come forward with information on you, and think I'll just let it go. Don't get too cocky just because you bought off my source this time."

"Bought me off? Me?" Georgia squawked.

Jett smiled.

"You better have some terrific hiding place, Murphy," Rod continued to yell. "Because I'm coming after you, and I'm going to expose you both for what you really are!" If he explained further what he thought they really were, they didn't hear as they plunged into the hot, aromatic kitchen and let the door fall shut with a *whoosh* behind them.

"That man is so . . . so . . . not nice," Georgia hissed as Jett shepherded her through the kitchen toward a door marked "Exit."

"And that's the fellow you wanted to champion your cause of saving the Double Heart Diner."

At the mention of the diner she loved, Georgia straightened like a soldier called to duty. Her pace became more lively, her face flushed. "Let's get out of this place."

"Getting out of this place won't be enough, I'm afraid, Miss Darling. You heard Rod Campbell. He won't quit until he's shed an unflattering light on me and my business. Not only that, he could cost me a lot of money by tipping off competitors to my next move. And if Campbell has to cast your reputation in shadows as well to get the story, I doubt he'll mind a bit."

"Don't you worry about my reputation, Mr. Murphy. It can stand the glare." She pulled off the apron and threw down her dishwashing gloves. "I only hope you can say as much for your own."

He met the challenge in her tone and posture with confidence. "I can."

"Good. Then let's go." She hit the back door and stepped into a shaft of sunlight in the otherwise dark alley.

"Go where?"

"Don't you worry about that, Mr. Murphy. You are now in the company of a girl with a plan. Just follow me." She grinned at him.

Jett stopped short.

"Well, are you coming or not?"

Reluctantly, he started up again. "I'm coming. But I have to tell you, I don't like the idea of someone else taking control of my situation, Miss Darling. And when I see that glint in those eyes of yours, I suddenly have this feeling that I have just jumped from the frying pan into the fire."

4

Jett could not believe his ears.

"Texas? I only agreed to follow you to your vehicle because I took a cab over, and standing in the street hailing another one might just draw too much attention." Jett switched the now-heavy bags to his other shoulder and tried to keep up with Georgia. "I was thinking we could ditch Campbell, then go back to my office, where we could discuss this mess."

Georgia just kept on moving, and Jett kept right on following. Finally, they reached a discount parking lot, where she stopped at the most pathetic excuse for a vehicle he had ever seen that wasn't abandoned alongside some highway.

She swept out one hand as if offering him a golden chariot. "Well? You coming or not?"

"Coming? To Texas?" He laughed. "I can't go to Texas! I've got to catch a flight to Wisconsin!"

Georgia narrowed one eye at him and plumped her fists on her hips. "Why not? Is there a warrant out for your arrest in that state or something?"

"You don't have a very high opinion of me, do you?"

She reached into the truck bed and flung back a black plastic tarp. Beneath it, a cache of luggage sat next to stacks of boxes all neatly marked with words like *Kitchen, Office,*

Books, and *Bedroom.* "Toss your stuff back here. It'll be fine once it's covered up."

He hesitated.

"Look, Mr. Murphy. I know you don't owe me this, but I owe it to myself—and to the people who own the Double Heart Diner—to try to change your mind about tearing it down. That place is a part of me. It's part of a lot of people, good people. If you tear it down you'll be destroying something that can never be replaced. You won't just be getting rid of a struggling business, Mr. Murphy; you'll be destroying the only home I've ever really known." Tears welled up in her eyes.

Jett felt like a heel. He never wanted to destroy anyone's home.

"Back at Lou Mitchell's you told me you wanted to rescue me. Well, I don't need rescuing, but the Double Heart Diner does. You want to be a knight in shining armor, Mr. Murphy? Then come to Texas with me."

Jett met her gaze and in it found more compassion, honesty, and desperation than he had seen in years. He had cut himself off from other people so he would never make the fatal mistake of giving away too much control. And now a simple, heartfelt request for him to come and see the impact of his actions was wearing him down. The grudging admiration he had felt for Georgia earlier in his office grew as he watched her lay herself on the line for a cause she truly believed in.

Without saying a word, he slung his belongings into the back of the pickup. The impact of his bag landing in the bed made the whole vehicle jounce, telling him that the sad, old, once-red truck—which the sun had faded to the color of tomato soup—probably had at least one broken shock absorber. "For the record, I'm not the sort who has warrants sworn out for his arrest, and I think you know that."

"You're not the sort who can take a joke either, it seems." She chuckled, seemingly to herself, as she walked around her truck to wrestle open the driver's side door.

"I can take a joke," he told her across the sun-scorched hood. He gave her a hint of a smile as she continued to yank on the handle. "When I hear a joke, that is. But don't forget: I'm dealing with someone who's already made up her mind that I'm a landmark-leveling villain."

"Well," Georgia said grudgingly, "I can certainly see why your sense of humor might be, um, stretched a bit thin today." Finally, after much maneuvering, her door popped open. Jett's, on the other hand, fell wide open at his slightest touch, creaking and swinging like a busted saloon door in a B-Western movie.

He climbed in and settled on the faux lambskin seat covers, shifting his back from right to left to scratch the immediate itch the fabric raised. Wincing, he just had to say something. "I don't recall what I pay you—what I used to pay you before you resigned, that is—but I imagine it was enough for you to afford a much better class of transportation than this, Miss Darling."

"What's your point, Mr. Murphy?"

"My point is, you've made assumptions time and again about what kind of man I am. But what sort of girl are you, that you'd prefer to drive a beat-up old truck like this around Chicago?"

She met his gaze dead on. "The kind of girl who does not belong in Chicago."

"You belong in Texas, right?"

"That's the conclusion I've reached. Why else would I resign and make setting things right for the Double Heart my parting shot?"

"So you didn't resign just over the Double Heart." He hadn't thought so, but her hair-trigger impulsiveness made him want to ask.

"Now you're the one who doesn't think too highly of me." She narrowed her green eyes at him, but he could still see the glimmer of mischief sparking in them. "I'm passionate about my causes, I will give you that. But I wouldn't quit over something like this. No, it'd be more my style to hang tough, to try to change things from the inside. If I truly believed that were possible . . . "

"But you don't?"

"No, sir."

Sir? From anyone else he would have taken that simply as a sign of respect. He was her employer, after all.

Oops. *Had been* her employer. This woman had no reason to show him any deference now, nothing to gain by it, really. No, when he heard her use the word *sir* in reference to him, he recognized it as a kind of verbal shove—a means of showing their divisions. He was on one side: the side of "yes, sir" and "no, sir" and "whatever you say, sir." She was on the side of "right." That's how she'd see it, of course. The challenge in her tone, in her careful selection of how she addressed him, spelled that out for him loud and clear.

"So you've pretty much given up on me doing the right thing—as you see it—regarding this Double Heart Diner?"

"Now I didn't say that." She smiled. And what a smile. Seeing it warmed him in ways he'd long forgotten. The instant the expression faded from her face, Jett wished he could see it again.

"So I'm not beyond hope?"

"I don't think anyone is beyond hope."

"Not even a 'gravy-guzzling pig'?"

Instead of the humbling chuckle he expected, Jett saw

Georgia tense. Her gaze clapped on the rearview mirror and her jaw stiffened. "No, not even a 'money-hungry, insensitive, heartless, land-grubbing, gravy-guzzling pig.'"

He tried not to laugh at the exact quote from her letter.

Then she quietly added between clenched teeth, "Sir."

There it was again. Sir. It put a distance between them. Drew a line. Yet when he looked across the seat at this Texas wildcat of a woman, whose determination was as plain as her innocence, distance was the last thing on his mind.

"So you haven't given up on me yet, but you don't think you can work to change my mind from inside my operation? That means the only place from which you think you can change me is . . . where? In Texas—or, more precisely, at the Double Heart Diner itself?" He leaned his shoulder toward her and lowered his voice to gently growl out, "Georgia?"

So much for keeping distance.

She cast him a sidelong glance, her mouth set in a way that conveyed her agreement with his assertion without stooping to his level and playing his game. She jammed the key into the ignition and cranked it until the engine sputtered, then coughed.

"C'mon, Truvie, you can do this. Do it for me, hon."

"Do what for who?" This woman either had all the makings of a lovely, compelling-though-quirky innocent who needed a little guidance or else she was a total wacko. Until he could be sure which it was, he had to keep his guard up. "Who are you talking to?"

"To Truvie," she said with a matter-of-factness that implied only a moron would ask such a thing.

"Um, who is—?"

"Truvie? She's my truck." Georgia cranked the engine once more. Again, it convulsed, but did not start.

"You've named your truck?"

"Of course!" She scowled, rubbed her fingers together, then grabbed the key again. "I had to have something to call her. After all, she has more personality than most people I've run across. C'mon, old girl, you can do this. Do it for me and Texas . . . and the good ol' Double Heart."

She tried again. This time the engine roared to life, then began to positively purr.

"Good girl." Georgia patted the dusty dash. She backed out of her parking space. The truck lurched forward, shifted, lurched again. Georgia then guided Truvie out of the lot, cruising toward the road that once had been the beginning of the legendary old Route 66.

Jett didn't say anything more.

Georgia drove on as if the matter of this impromptu road trip had been settled. Her silence only gave Jett more time to concentrate on how much his back itched and how little reason he had to be in this situation in the first place. They'd given Rod the slip. Now, if Jett just disappeared until the sale went through, the reporter would have no reason to hype the small incident into anything more than smoke and speculation. And Georgia could not play on his sympathies or try to convince him to do something falsely heroic and foolhardy. Of course, she could still take her case to the media and blow the deal before any papers were signed.

He stole a peek at her from the corners of his eyes. The set of her jaw and death grip on the steering wheel made her look all the more like the hapless underdog ready to take on the heartless bully.

That bully being him.

Discomfort at that analogy made him squirm—or was that just the seat cover? He looked at her again and knew the feeling had nothing to do with man-made fabrics. He had to say something, anything, to break the tense silence.

"Texas, huh?" *No way,* he thought. He was headed for his family cabin up north, not for some reckless adventure that, in the end, would change nothing.

"Yep, Texas." Eyes on the road, she jutted her chin forward in a show of bravery that the slight tremble of her lower lip did not bear out. "If there's any hope of changing your mind, that's where it lies."

"Pretty long way to go for a hopeless cause," he muttered.

"'Bout eleven hundred miles."

He blew out a long whistle.

"Why?" She glanced his way, with the serene expression of one who knew she was in the right. "Do you have a limit to how far you'll go for your causes?"

"Every reasonable person has his or her limits." That was not only a very earnest claim, but Jett hoped it served as a warning that she had not won him over to this plan of hers. "Even you, I'm sure."

"I'm guided by my faith in those matters."

"Faith in?"

"God, myself, and others."

"'Others' being me?"

She didn't answer, just guided the truck through Chicago traffic with the ease and confidence of someone gliding along on sanctified wings.

He wanted to tell her to give it up. The deal was as good as done. He'd have the deed to that diner in hand by the end of the week. A trip to Texas wouldn't change that. Nor would her high ideals, her fly-in-the-face-of-reality passion, or her damsel-in-distress charm.

That's what he should have told her.

Instead, he snatched up his safety belt and jabbed it into place with a metallic clack. "Eleven hundred miles?"

"About that."

"How long would a trip like that take? A week?"

"More like three days, allowing."

"Allowing?"

"For sticking to the two-lane tidbits of old Route 66. It's tricky maneuvering at times: an awful lot of forgotten back ways, long stretches without seeing anyone else. Sometimes there's no option but to take the interstates. Throw in stops at some of the famous sites and a couple of overnight stays so I'm not too exhausted to drive safely, and there you go. Of course, if we didn't stop at all and stuck to the interstates with the new higher speed limit, we could do it in about seventeen hours. But then we'd miss the whole point."

"The point being kidnapping?"

"Kidnapping?" She laughed sharp and loud. "Yeah, right. Like anyone on earth would believe someone like me could kidnap a man like you."

"Well, I am here against my better judgment."

"Better judgment?"

"Yeah, judgment—ever heard of it?" He tapped his temple.

"Following your heart." She tapped the left side of her chest. "Ever hear of *that*?"

He tightened his jaw. A trickle of sweat snaked down his spine where it pressed against the coarse seat cover.

Georgia turned her attention back to the road and the task of piloting them through the outskirts of the city.

He didn't have time for this, Jett told himself.

We sign the papers on the diner in five days. If we can keep you out of the public eye for a few days—and her out of the papers—we'll have it made. Uncle Lou's words came back to haunt him. Right behind it came Rod's promise to ferret him out and paint this routine business transaction as something ugly and mean-spirited. Sitting next to him in this truck, he realized, was the very person who could help Rod accomplish that goal.

Jett not only had the time; he needed the time. And he needed it with Georgia.

"Texas?" He was not committing to the ludicrous idea. The skin on his back prickled. Between the irritation of the seat cover and the agitation all the feelings this woman's nearness raised in him, he doubted he'd last through rural southern Illinois. "You think the state is big enough for the two of us?"

"It's always been big enough for me," she muttered. "You should fit fine, yourself, once we knock a little air out of that overinflated ego of yours."

Well, if anyone could do just that . . . , he thought. What he said, though, was, "One day."

"What?"

He held up his index finger. "I'll give you one day to change my mind regarding this venture, then it's back to Chicago." That should give him enough time to figure out if she would do anything to ruin the deal. Besides, he was a man who had made quite a successful living out of negotiations. The key to negotiation was to stay in control. Even if he could or would give her more time, he did not have to tell her that. By setting a limit like this, he kept the upper hand—and at the same time reminded himself not to risk his objectivity by getting too carried away with this wild idea.

"But it's a three-day drive to the diner trying to follow Route 66. Otherwise, I have to take interstates and drive like a maniac."

"Well, if anybody can . . . "

The truck squawked in protest as Georgia slowed to take a turn.

"One day isn't enough. I need three." Her brows pressed downward, distress troubling her clear eyes. "I don't know how else to convince you without showing you the place you're determined to destroy."

Jett fixed his gaze out the window, determined not to cave in to a pretty woman's pleading expression—especially when it came to something as serious as his livelihood. He drew in the smell of the musty truck and the sweet fragrance of the suburban summer air, courtesy of the window that would not quite shut.

"Then I'd say you have your work cut out for you."

• • •

"Hey! Hey, you!"

"Who? Me?" Lou Murphy recognized Rod Campbell from the picture they ran with his column in the paper. But Lou figured the troublemaking jerk did not have to know this right off.

"Yeah, you." Rod crossed the parking lot of the pancake house, as if led by the accusing finger he kept trained at the dead center of Lou's chest. When he got near enough, he stabbed that finger right into Lou's favorite tie. "You're Murphy's attorney, aren't you?"

"Hey! Careful there, buddy." Lou swatted the other man's hand away. "I'll thank you to keep your hands off my person, and most especially off this tie. It happens to be a very classy piece of apparel, given to me by my son, the minister."

That caught the fellow off guard enough to make him stop and actually consider the piece of red, orange, and green silk held in place with an onyx-and-diamond tie stud.

Style, Lou thought, *it gets 'em every time*. He stepped back and took advantage of the moment to fish his car keys out of his pocket. The jangling of his weighty key ring had an awakening effect on Campbell, who shook his head and scowled.

"Yeah, you're a lawyer all right." Campbell sneered. "Always quick to find a way to avoid a direct question."

"Hey, I wasn't avoiding nothing." Lou held his hands out. "Just asking you to show a little respect. Extend some common courtesy, as it were. Maybe that's how people can tell you are a reporter—because you ain't got no manners at all. No offense."

"None take—hey, I never said I was a reporter!"

"Lucky guess, then, huh?" Lou grinned and twirled his keys around his index finger.

"Oh there was nothing lucky about it—just like there was nothing lucky about Murphy showing up here five minutes before I did and tearing out of here with my source."

"Maybe your editor tipped him off."

"My editor didn't even want me to come here. He wasn't even going to tell me about that woman's far-fetched ploy, except he got a tip that Murphy himself would be showing up. That was worth a shot, even though we figured it probably was a hoax."

"Hoax?" Lou puffed up at the inference. "What about the tipster who made your editor think it was a hoax?"

"Oh no. I'm not going to give you any information that might help you find the leak in your organization, counselor. Let's just say that no one at the paper expected the man to come down in person. Murphy never does anything himself."

"Yes, that has been true in the past." Lou nodded, then drummed his fingers over his belt buckle. "But maybe that's all about to change."

"I'd ask what you meant by that cryptic remark, but I don't get the feeling you'd tell me."

"That ain't gonna happen, my friend." Lou laughed. He'd already spent far more time with this bozo than he should have, but he couldn't help it; he felt magnanimous. He could afford to feel that way today. After all, his plan was beginning to work. There was nothing left to do now but put on the finishing touches, set the thing fully in motion, and get out of the way.

"I got nothing to say to the press." Lou flipped his keys into the palm of his hand. Satisfied that he'd gotten Jett more personally involved in the affairs of his company—and in life overall—he was ready to hightail it out of there himself. "In other words, no comment."

He sauntered deliberately over to the car, aware of the reporter's seething glare fixed on his back the whole time.

Popping open the door, Lou took a long, measured beat, then looked up with a taunting smirk. "You know what 'no comment' means, don't you, my friend?"

"I personally think it means your client's got something to hide."

Lou shook his head and clucked his tongue. "Such a suspicious mind."

"Make cracks all you want. I am going to find out what Murphy is up to. Mark my words."

"You're wasting your efforts, my friend." Lou threw out the bait, knowing he needed Campbell's cooperation if he hoped to accomplish his goal. "He and the girl are probably well on their way to—Oops!"

"Where? Look, it's obvious you're trying to feed me some information. Why don't you do us both a favor and just say it outright?"

"Tick-a-lock." Grinning broadly, Lou feigned sealing his lips with an invisible key, which he then tossed over his left shoulder.

"Oh, for . . . I'll find him myself. I'm not without my resources, man. I can think of a dozen places to start searching out that rat."

Lou nodded, patted his fingers together, and waited for Rod to turn away, then dropped one last hint from the corner of his supposedly latched lips. "Maybe you should try thinking of sixty-six places . . . as in Route 66."

Rod squinted over his shoulder at Lou. "There isn't such a thing anymore. It's all busted up."

"Oh, the Mother Road still exists, my friend—in people's memories and in their hearts." Lou grinned, then tossed out one last tidbit for the man to grab. "There's also enough of the real route left to serve as a guide to get a certain person where he or she might want to go . . . if you catch my drift."

"Hey, I have no interest in chasing this guy all over the country. I want the story and I want it bad, but there's only so much I can do."

Feeling certain that he'd given the man enough to keep his nephew running, but not nearly enough to jeopardize the deal, Lou climbed into the car, smoothed his silk tie, and leaned out to give Campbell a conspiratory wink. "Then I guess you'd better get going before they get out of the state entirely."

• • •

The Illinois countryside blurred in Georgia's side window. Chicago lay behind them and the open road ahead. She'd done it. This morning she had promised herself she would do something to take charge of her future, something bold: She would at least try to stand up for her ideals and change the fate of the Double Heart. She'd accomplished that—even if she'd acted like a big old clown in front of Murphy to get it done.

There was no point in dwelling on that, Georgia told

herself, not when she had so little time to redeem herself in this man's eyes. But redeem herself she would. He'd given her a day—in her book that meant twenty-four hours. As much as she hated to leave Route 66 behind, she'd have to take the interstate to make it in time. The nearest junction was twenty miles away. They'd part ways with the Mother Road there.

Breakfast in Lou Mitchell's this morning and in the Double Heart tomorrow—that was her goal. Once she got Padgett Murphy through those doors—once he met the people who ran the landmark café and the folks drawn to it—he'd change his mind about tearing it down.

Anyone cruising Route 66 who's lost his love or lost his way will eventually find himself at the Double Heart Diner. That's what they said. It had been true for Georgia, who had found kindness and friendship and someone willing to take a chance on her there. She'd spent plenty of hours working at the café, often talking over the meaning of life with Starla Mae Jenkins. The waitress with a heart of gold, who liked to remind everyone those weren't a dime a dozen, had made sure Georgia got through high school. She'd also talked the young girl into going to church and convinced everyone Georgia could make something of her life.

Georgia had waitressed at the Double Heart through high school and college, often getting her only real meals of the day there, meals she never once was allowed to pay for. No one went hungry at Starla Mae's place, not physically or spiritually. Places like that, where a kid like her with no real family or roots could feel at home, were a vanishing phenomenon that deserved protection. The Double Heart Diner was more than a café, and even a man like Murphy would understand that if he ever climbed out of his ivory tower long enough to see for himself.

Suddenly she felt like Don Quixote, tilting at windmills, and the image made her proud. A giggle bubbled up in her chest. She was really doing it. She was really on her way home with the best chance for saving the landmark sitting right next to her in her pickup truck.

Georgia waggled her shoulders and jounced on the seat. "If I were a dog I'd be wagging my tail!"

"I beg your pardon?"

"Oh my!" Her heart raced and her cheeks warmed. "Did I say that aloud?"

"Yes." His lips twitched into a skewed smile. "You did."

"I . . . uh . . . " So much for redeeming herself. "I just meant that . . . um—"

"That you're excited to be headed home? I can certainly understand that."

"Thanks."

"For what?"

"For not laughing at me." She wondered if he picked up the petulance of her tone. She had wanted to impress him with her words and actions, not win him over by default— no matter how gracious he was about it. She put aside the urge to sulk and plastered on what she hoped passed for a mature, detached expression. "Heaven knows, I've done enough today to cause a granite statue to bust out in a belly laugh."

"And the day's not half over yet."

Georgia hadn't intended to laugh, but he caught her off guard with his easy charm and she chuckled.

"Don't worry about it," he told her. "You haven't exactly seen me at my best this morning either."

Something in her wanted to protest. She hadn't said she was not at her best today. In fact, she thought she'd been rather quick and clever and resourceful in a highly stressful situation, and in the end, she'd triumphed. Unconventional, yes, but not at her best? She'd beg to differ . . . that is, if he were any other man on the face of the planet. Because, while she might differ with this man until the cows came home, there was one thing she would never do—and that was beg anything of him.

Besides, begging was definitely not her style. Wheedling. Negotiating. Steely-eyed standoffs or improvised action. Those were her forte. Begging meant showing weakness, and if Georgia had learned anything in her lonesome life as a young girl sent to live in foster care after the death of her parents, it was that showing weakness only made a person vulnerable. She would not let herself be vulnerable to anyone. Especially not Padgett Murphy.

She sighed and stole a sidelong glance at the man. For the first time she really had the luxury of studying him. No surprise, he looked even better sitting there, all rugged and tousled, than he did back at the restaurant, viewed through the confusion of people while the sweat caused by the plastic bowl cover on her head stung her eyes.

Padgett "Jett" Murphy. The boss. The big cheese.

She stole another glimpse.

Georgia, honey, she said to herself, *there ain't nothing cheesy about that man.* Even in the roomy cab of her truck, his long legs could not quite stretch out straight. His shoulders rose above the back of the seat. There seemed to be no place for him to put his large hands. They moved from resting atop his legs to dangling between his knees, then he braced them against the torn dash.

Who would have expected a man like this to have such strong hands? Pale hands with manicured nails buffed to a shine and almost delicate fingers, more accustomed to gripping a pen than to taking real issues in hand—that's what she'd expected. What she saw, however—long, blunt fingers with tanned skin and sparse coils of coarse black hair—made her think of a man equally adept at holding that pen or a tool, caressing a woman's cheek, or even lifting a baby up in the air. Jett Murphy exuded just that kind of capable masculine presence, from his fingertips to his posture to his sly grin and sparkling eyes. Just looking at him made her feel . . . safe.

She hated that about him.

This man was the enemy, Georgia reminded herself. Jett Murphy was the faceless giant behind the heartless corporation that wanted to destroy the Double Heart Diner. He was Goliath to her David. Just because he had the most gorgeous eyes she'd ever seen, that did not mean she was going to suddenly stop aiming the truth smack-dab between them. To do that, and to be taken seriously, she had to prove to him she wasn't a bona fide flake.

"Look, Mr. Murphy, if we want to make this a pleasant and productive trip, we should probably lay down some ground rules right here at the start." She used her most take-charge voice. "Beginning with some personal guidelines."

"Okay by me."

"It's very important to me that you understand this is strictly business. I am not the kind of girl who up and runs off with a man for dubious purposes. I want it acknowledged up front that the only thing that will be going on between you and me during this trip is . . . maple syrup!"

"Nothing dubious about that, all right." He waggled his eyebrows at her.

"Kindly knock off the sarcastic leering and look out the window." She jabbed her finger toward a white sign in the shape of an arrow with faded black letters on it and read aloud: "Maple sirup."

"They misspelled *syrup*."

"Of course they did; it's a classic Route 66 road sign. It means Funk's Grove, this place famous for its maple syrup, is coming up. You've heard of Funk's Grove, right?"

He frowned.

"The Dixie Truckers Home?"

His brows pleated down over his eyes.

"The Pig-Hip Restaurant?"

He winced.

Georgia sighed and shook her head. "You are really not into the whole Route 66 experience at all, are you?"

He shrugged, but had the good manners to look sheepish instead of glib about it. Then he feigned a lost-puppy look that was belied by the twinkle in his eyes and said, "Guess you'll have to forgive me. I've led a very sheltered life."

"You say that as a big joke. But let me tell you, Mr. Murphy. From what I've seen of you—or more to the point, from what I haven't seen of you, in the papers or in your workplace—and from what I know of your business dealings, I tend to agree with that assessment. You do lead a very sheltered life. The problem with that is, if you're always in the shelter, you never see the sunlight."

"And you hope this little trip is going to change that, don't you?"

"Well, I wouldn't presume to—"

"Oh c'mon. You can admit it. It's just the two of us here now. When you wrote that letter, you thought that you were the one who could personally show me the error of my ways. That's why you jumped at the idea of hauling me off in your truck to—"

"I did not haul you off," she protested.

"You did, and you loved it." He grinned like the cat who ate the canary. "And now you're offering to be my own personal ray of sunshine, to show me the way, aren't you, Georgia Darling?"

He wasn't the first man to say her last name like an obvious endearment. But from him it sounded honestly spoken, not like teasing or like some slick come-on.

"I . . . um . . . I did hope . . . " Her gaze trained on him, she batted her eyes, not to flirt, but because her mind could not seem to take in anything but his smile and his nearness. No words sprang to her rescue. What words were there? She could not lie to the man; it wasn't her nature. She *did* think that she alone could change his mind and his dealings regarding the Double Heart.

"Well?" He crossed his arms over his broad chest. His smile didn't waver as he prodded, "You hoped what?"

"It's not that I . . . but more like . . . " Think, Georgia. *Think!*

Not only did she have to come up with an answer that was neither a lie nor a confession that, yes, she'd been just that sappy about this whole situation, she had to do it fast. The man she'd coaxed along with her on this adventure, whom she hoped to influence to her way of thinking—the man she absolutely had to show that she was a savvy and responsible woman—was waiting.

Georgia gritted her teeth and shut her eyes for an instant. She eased off the gas, letting Truvie roll gently along the deserted strip of narrow road. All her attention was riveted on the task of wowing Jett Murphy. She had to find something sure and sane and downright dazzling to say to him and she had to do it now.

He tapped his foot.

She swallowed hard.

He shifted again.

She opened her mouth to express her thoughts in a brilliant summation . . .

And that's when the truck hit the tree.

5

A re you okay?" Jett reached across the seat to touch Georgia's shoulder. The whole event had amounted to nothing more than a jarring thud as her cumbersome truck rolled to a stop against a crooked tree by the side of the two-lane road. Yet it served as a reminder that his choice of traveling companion left much to be desired.

He looked over at Georgia sitting with her eyes wide and luminous, like a little girl about to burst into tears.

Much to be desired, indeed, he thought, swallowing hard at the impulse to put his arms around her and tell her everything would be fine. Such impulses made it all the more imperative that he get a grip on his emotions. It was one thing to have agreed to go along on this jaunt, even for a day. But to let his interest in this woman take precedence over common sense? Nope. Not him. Not the man who had made a studied practice of staying removed from the messy emotional business of life. His impersonal approach had worked for a long time, and he wasn't about to backslide now—not for Route 66, a dilapidated diner, or even Georgia Darling.

He cleared his throat and, using his most authoritative voice, asked again: "Miss Darling? Are you all right?"

"I'm fine." She put her hand to her forehead. "H-how's Truvie?"

"Truvie?"

"My truck," she reminded him.

"Oh yeah. Your truck. Let's get our priorities straight," he muttered. He glanced out over the sun-bleached hood. "From here it looks like the tree took the worst of the blow, and it seems to have suffered only a little gash. I'd say it's nothing serious."

"Good." She nodded, her teeth sinking into her lower lip as she strained to take a look at the scarred tree trunk herself.

Jett set his jaw. "I'm fine too. Thank you for asking."

"That's goo—oh!" Her hand went to her full lips. "Oh my. I didn't mean—you're okay too, right?"

Though he had no reason to, Jett wished he'd ranked above her truck in her list of concerns. He pressed his fingertips to his temple, then slowly smoothed his open palm back to the nape of his neck. No cuts or lumps, he noted with a little disgust. A head injury, after all, would explain this silly need to have Georgia fret over his welfare. He made a fist and let it drop to his lap. "I'm fine."

"Isn't this just typical?" She shook her head.

"I hope not. Otherwise we'll never get anywhere. Do you have any idea how many trees there are in Illinois alone? If ramming into one every few hours is typical, then one day of travel won't get us very far."

"No, not hitting the tree." She groaned, grimaced, and rolled her eyes. "It's typical that something like this happened, when what I was really trying to do was think of some way to prove to you that I'm not some hare-brained kook!"

He cocked one eyebrow. "And *this* is what you came up with?"

She scowled at him.

He'd wanted a smile. He didn't realize it until she reacted to his jest so negatively, but he definitely had wanted to make her smile. Having seen it only a few times, he already craved witnessing again the way joy and humor entirely took over her beautiful face. Jett told himself she was just startled, perhaps embarrassed. With just a little more gentle joking, he'd win that smile he longed for.

She wrenched open her door and slipped out into the warm afternoon air.

Jett followed suit, enjoying the opportunity for improved circulation in his limbs. "Much as I wouldn't have had you do this for the world, I have to admit I'm glad to get some ground under my feet after two hours of rattling along in that pathetic excuse for a truck."

"Pathetic excuse for a . . . ?" She glared at him. The sunlight made the wind-tossed curls of her red hair shine like a halo around her cocked head. Her boots became two flashes of turquoise color swishing in the tall, dry grass as she quickly stepped around the truck to where its bumper met the tree.

Georgia patted the dull front fender. "Don't you listen to him, Truvie-girl," she said in a soothing tone. "He doesn't know what he's talking about."

"Ha!" Jett strode around the front of the truck, his arms folded firmly over the unfamiliar shirt he'd borrowed from his cousin. The urge to tease her slipped away as he watched her stroke the side of her crummy vehicle instead of trying to appease him. "If this ride doesn't get any smoother, most of my fillings will have vibrated loose before I ever get to sink my teeth into a meal at the Double Heart."

She sneered and crossed her own arms, fire in her eyes. "Oh, yeah? I happen to think the ride was plenty smooth. And just for the record, I've known people who didn't have any teeth at all who had no trouble finding something to fill their stomachs at that very diner."

"I'll just bet you have." Smile? He couldn't have cared less about coaxing one from her now. "Well, maybe you can introduce me when we get there, and one of them can recommend something."

"Maybe I will." She nailed him with an icy stare. "If the diner's still standing by then."

"If it's not, it won't be the fault of my company, Miss Darling." They stood on the side of the road in mirror-image poses—arms knotted over the chest, weight on one straightened leg, chins lowered like bulls about to butt heads. "However, after having seen you in action today, I can't promise that when you get there you won't smash into it and knock down the whole crumbling building yourself."

"Smash? I never—"

He propped the toe of his shoe up on the bumper, beside the crease left by its encounter with the tree.

She clamped her mouth shut.

"And if the place should miraculously survive any of your misguided attempts to park ol' Truvie, heaven help them once you get inside," Jett went on. "Hopefully, their dish carts come with rubber bumpers and their servers are heavily insured."

So much for charming a smile out of her, he thought. Still, his pulse skipped and his breath came a little quicker than usual, and that felt surprisingly good. Even arguing with this woman stirred up feelings in him he'd long thought dead. He braced himself for another go-around.

However, Georgia backed down. Her shoulders slumped slightly forward, her arms falling to her sides as she leaned against the truck and looked at the ground. "You think I'm a lunatic, don't you?" she asked in a soft voice.

Jett felt a twinge in his chest. He considered the image he had of Georgia: first fiery, then humbled; all energy, then quiet contemplation. He thought of her enthusiasm—which she applied equally to escaping the restaurant and to saving the diner—and felt humbled. "No, I don't think you're a lunatic at all. I think you're . . .

Gorgeous. Undisciplined. Passionate. A pain in the neck. He dismissed the descriptions as quickly as they formed in his mind.

"Alive," he finally finished in hushed awe. "I think you are truly alive. I'll have to admit, I really admire that about you."

"Admire what? Being alive?" She snorted, all traces of meekness evaporating. "Which part? The breathing? The talking? The uncanny ability to crash into things?"

"All of it." He chuckled.

"I have to tell you, that is not the most compelling compliment I've ever received, Murphy." She tossed her head.

"It may surprise you to learn, then, that it is one of the most compelling ones I've ever given, *Darling*."

"Oh yeah?"

"Yeah."

Georgia's chin quivered. Her eyes darted right, then left. She cocked her head, and a lock of red hair flicked against her rosy cheek. Pointing at him with one finger, she began to slowly nod her head. "I'm beginning to get to you, aren't I?"

"The way a lone termite gets to a forest." The sun heated the length of his back.

"I thought so."

"But a single termite can't fell an entire forest alone, you know."

"Don't be so sure, Mr. Murphy. This is a Texas termite you're dealing with, after all."

71

"Is that so?" Who did she think she was dealing with? His analogy was a sound one. He and the Padgett Group were like a mighty forest. They'd be standing long after Georgia had gone on to sharpen her teeth on other supposed wrongs in the world. And they'd be none the worse for having tangled with this woman.

"You know it's so, and you know I *am* getting to you."

He opened his mouth to set her straight.

Then she smiled.

At that precise moment Padgett Brennan Murphy knew he was an absolute goner. Which meant he had two choices: Give up the whole idea of buying the diner, or get as far away from this tenacious little termite as possible.

Abandoning the diner deal meant letting down a lot of people who counted on it going through—including all those who stood to gain the jobs and opportunities that the new project represented.

As entertaining as the brief adventure had been, the time had come to bring it to a close.

• • •

"Well, if you're okay and I'm okay, and as long as Truvie looks fine . . . " Georgia bent low to peer under the truck for any signs of leaks or hanging parts. Satisfied that nothing was visibly out of whack, she straightened and slapped her hands together. Her improved mood adding buoyancy and length to her strides, she quickly reached the driver's side door and called out, "Then I guess we can just jump in the truck, back it up and—"

Jett just stood there, the frown on his face as fixed as his feet in the tall, whispering grass.

Georgia swung her arms toward the truck cab to encourage him to move and repeated, "We can just jump in the truck—"

He did not budge.

"We can jump—" This time she added a springing motion with her legs, leaning her torso toward the truck without ever lifting her feet from the ground.

Not lifting his feet from the ground was the only behavior Jett mimicked.

"Fine." Her hands slapped against her thighs. "You don't want to get back in the truck. Would it be too personal if I asked why?"

When he spoke it was to the heavens and not directly to her. "She's driving a truck that she has to sweet-talk into starting, one that has lambskin seat covers that have apparently been manufactured instead out of steel wool and shock absorbers that have—at least on my side of the vehicle—actually deteriorated into shock *inflicters*."

Georgia winced at the truth of his words. She started to launch a justification but paused when she wasn't exactly sure where to aim it.

Jett began to pace and in his calm, powerful voice, railed on. "I've pretty much overlooked all that so far. I didn't even mention that my door is held shut only by a shaky latch and sheer willpower, or that my window will not roll up all the way, creating a wind-tunnel effect perfect for funneling bugs into my right ear."

Georgia cringed, her imagination running amok as she felt some tiny thing tickling her skin near her simple silver earring. She put her finger in her right ear and wiggled it, sighing with the relief that brought.

"But now, as I stand safely out of grips of that torture—out in the middle of nowhere, with the front of said truck physically impaled by a tree—she wants to know why I'm not excited about climbing back into that deathtrap and bumping off down the back roads for more of the same."

"He promised." Georgia opened her arms and turned her face upward too. "He sat right there, knowing all the facts he just mentioned—except the part about us getting impaled on a tree, and who could have known that? I mean if we had known about it, we'd have avoided it. Furthermore, I do think the term 'impaled' is a bit harsh for this circumstance. 'Dinked' is more like it. The truck has dinked a tree. A little, tiny dink, for that matter. An itsy, bitsy—"

Jett cleared his throat.

Georgia flinched, then forced herself back on track, her face turned toward the brilliant sunshine. "The point is, he promised. He sat right in that cab of that truck with his door shuddering and his seat cover scratching and bugs booking their final passage down his ear canal, and he *promised* to give me one day. One day to convince him, to get him to the Double Heart or die trying—"

"That's what I'm afraid of."

She ignored him. "And now he won't get back in the truck."

A short intake of breath from his direction signaled to her that Jett had something more to say on the subject.

"But then," Georgia raised her voice to prevent his intervening, "if his promises don't mean anything, what good would it do for him to get in the truck anyway? A man like that could get all the way down to the café, say anything to appease me, then go right ahead and do whatever despicable thing he'd planned all along."

"Well, then, if we're in agreement on that"—he clapped his hands together—"maybe we can get back in the truck, turn it around, and head home."

The clapping sound gave Georgia a start, but that was nothing compared to the jolt she felt at his reckless disregard for her attack on his honor. In trying to disgrace him into continuing their iffy arrangement, could she actually have pegged him that precisely? That he did not pounce on her supposition or spring to his own defense made her feel as though an icy stone had fallen to the pit of her stomach.

"You . . . you aren't going to argue with me?" She studied his seemingly sincere face for some sign of this more sinister nature.

"Does the forest argue with a termite, Miss Darling?" He smiled. "No. There's no point in it, just as there is no point in me playing into your little shame game. It's a big, fat waste of time."

"Hey, as long as we're using the time you said you'd give me to prove my case, why does that matter to you? Besides, I don't think it's wasted, not if you are a man with any kind of honor at all."

"Only a man with some kind of honor would do what I'm doing right now. To let you go on thinking that your misguided actions here can alter the course of the plans we've laid for that land in Texas—that would be very dishonorable indeed."

"What I think and what I try to accomplish are my concerns, not yours. I'll thank you to stop trying to save me from myself and just live up to your own word. You aren't denying that you gave me one day, are you?"

"No, I won't deny that. I did say you had a day—"

"Aha!" She jabbed an accusing finger his direction.

He eyed her with his face turned slightly away. "But while I did promise you a certain amount of time, I never promised you anything more, especially not that your efforts would change my mind. If anything, what I've seen along the way today has cemented my first opinions even more firmly in my mind."

"Seen?" She kicked up fresh-smelling weeds and grass as

she made her way over to where he stood. "What have you seen so far but miles and miles of empty road?"

"Exactly. When I see what's become of the places where there were once thriving businesses and compare that to the kind of prosperity I know my plan will bring about—"

A shrill chirping sound cut him off.

"What's that?" She looked around them for a phone booth or house with its windows thrown open, something that might account for the muffled but familiar noise.

"Sounds like a phone." He tilted his head.

"Yeah, but where's it coming from?"

It rang again.

He scratched his fingers through the short, black-and-silver hair at his temples. "If I'm not mistaken, it's coming from the bed of your truck. Your cell phone, maybe?"

"Don't have one."

"Hmmm. Then maybe I do." He strode to the back of the truck, tossed back the black tarp, and began foraging through the luggage he'd brought with him to Lou Mitchell's.

"Maybe?" She followed behind him, her thoughts and emotions swirling so that she couldn't focus on any one thing. "You don't know if you have a cell phone or not?"

"My uncle packed some things for me." Digging into the black bag, he pulled out a small video camera and even smaller tape recorder and handed them back to her.

"Your uncle packed these for our meeting?"

He glanced back at her over his shoulder. "He thought you were trying to blackmail me."

She juggled the objects into the crook of her arm. "Not exactly the trusting type, is he?"

Jett shrugged.

The phone rang again.

He returned his attention to the bag, first pulling out a

shirt almost identical to the one he had on, then a large paperback book—greenish blue with gold-and-black lettering on the front.

Georgia draped the shirt over the camera and recorder, then placed the book on top. "The Bible? Hmmm. Maybe I spoke too soon about your uncle."

"The time to make up your mind about people is never."

She bristled against this veiled message about how she had treated him since before they'd even met. "Yeah, well, if we're going to resort to communicating with each other in fortune-cookie sayings, then here's one for you: Actions speak louder than words."

The subdued ringing suddenly came through loud and clear as Jett tugged free a small black object from the bag. He turned to her with the phone in his palm and grinned. "You will meet a tall, handsome stranger who speaks with much wisdom about your future."

"Smart cookies make their own fortunes," she muttered even as he flipped open the small phone.

"Hello?"

She bit her lip to keep herself from spouting more gibberish just to cover her own anxiety.

"Uncle Lou!" He covered the mouthpiece with his fingers. "It's my Uncle Lou."

"Imagine that."

"Will you excuse me a minute?"

She nodded.

He nodded.

She nodded again.

He nodded one more time, only this time it was more of a shooing away with the jerk of his head.

"Oh." She blinked. "Oh you want privacy?"

"Please?"

"Sure." She stubbed the toe of her boot in the dirt as she trudged away from the scene of the man leaning against her truck, which was leaning against a tree, which was now—thanks to her inattentive driving—just plain leaning.

Her heart heavy, she tried in her mind to put the pieces of the last few minutes in order. She'd begun this trip with low expectations of this man's character and high hopes of converting him to her way of thinking. But after spending so much time in his company, she found her opinions starting to shift. While her estimation of Murphy had slowly crept toward the positive, her optimism about the diner situation had begun to wane. After all, was Jett Murphy really going to change his mind about the Double Heart?

"No!" Jett's end of the telephone conversation carried over to her, and while the response obviously was intended for his uncle it also served as her answer.

No. No way. His mind was made up, and there was no hope of her altering it. He obviously had not gone into this development deal blindly. He'd studied the matter, gathered what he deemed necessary input, and had formed what he saw as an educated, considered, and prudent—albeit *wrong, wrong, wrong*—opinion about what was the best course of action. How could she fight that?

"Impossible!"

"Exactly," she mumbled. Men like Murphy did not scrap big money deals because of sentiment or nostalgia. They based their decisions on factors like logic and the greater good and—

"One hundred percent unadulterated lunacy." Jett pushed his free hand back over his head, then dropped it to his hip. "That's what you're proposing, you know. It's insanity, pure and simple."

She knew Jett's protests were meant for his uncle, yet she

could easily apply them to her own proposition. Now, with the realities of Chicago far behind them and the dreams of the Double Heart far beyond her reach, she finally had to admit it: Her cause, though a noble one, was lost. She'd never get Murphy to the diner.

"Never." Jett's one-sided remark echoed own her glum conclusion.

As soon as he hung up the phone, Georgia told herself, she'd let him off the hook.

"Well, thank you." His tone dripped with acid sarcasm. "Thank you very much."

It was over.

"What else can I do?"

She had lost.

"That's it then. It looks like there's no other choice."

Georgia clasped her hands in front of her and threw back her shoulders. If there was one thing she knew how to do, it was suffer defeat and disappointment without revealing her true feelings. Even as a child in foster care who had often been moved from home to home, she had not let anyone see how much each loss had hurt her. Today would be no different.

"If that's the way it has to be, then . . . "

She angled her chin upward and pushed down the burning ache in her heart as her single-minded mission slipped silently from her grasp.

"Okay. Good-bye then."

The cellular phone made a clipped beeping sound as Jett broke the connection. He tossed it back into the bag, then stood for a moment, head down.

She watched him and instinctively knew the inner turmoil that must be playing out within him. He wasn't an ogre, after all. He had feelings. He'd never set out to crush her expectations or foil her fantasies. He was just doing his job.

He sighed, flexed his large hands at his side, then raised his head. The sunlight gleamed across his thick, silver hair, his expression obscured by shadow so that she felt, rather than saw, his eyes on her.

What a good sport, she thought. First, the man who avoided public exposure like the plague—the man who had people just waiting to do to anything he needed for his business, and probably for his personal life as well—had shown up himself to save her from her own naiveté. Then he'd helped her escape a reporter's wrath and had allowed himself to be battered by her truck on a trip that he knew would, for him, come to no productive end. The least she could do in return was to make this easy for him.

He took in a deep breath.

She had to beat him to the draw.

He opened his mouth.

She rushed forward, her own lips parting. Just as her boots scuffed dust up onto his athletic shoes, he reached out to take her by the shoulders.

"We can go back to Chicago now."

Georgia spoke at the exact moment that Jett announced, "Let's get back on the road. Right now Texas looks like my best option."

6

Jett slid behind Truvie's steering wheel and, much to Georgia's chagrin, got the obstinate truck to start right up. Over the next few miles, he filled her in on his conversation with his uncle. By the time they pulled into the Dixie Truckers Home near McClean, Illinois, Georgia still wasn't sure what had hit her.

"If we are in such an all-fired hurry to get out of Illinois now," she said, "we should keep making our way to the interstate. It'll be much faster, and we'll be far more anonymous."

"I told you. Uncle Lou thinks Campbell will take the interstate. If we stick to the two-lane highways, we'll have less chance of running into him. Besides, I thought you wanted to stay as close to the original Route 66 as possible."

"I did. I do. I think." She scrunched up her nose and tried to force her jumbled thoughts to settle. "I don't know anymore."

"You?" He laughed and urged Truvie into a tight parking spot between a local sheriff's cruiser and a plain sedan with a Cubs sticker on the back window. "I thought you had all the answers. What could you possibly not know about?"

"Well, for starters, I don't know why you are so set on running from this Rod Campbell fellow."

He turned his upper body toward her, and the whole truck rocked from the movement.

"You heard the man back at Lou Mitchell's. He's got it in for me, and he isn't going to let little things like the facts or either of our reputations stand in the way of his sharing that opinion with the world. I am a scoop. A story. Someone who can get him the kind of publicity he craves, who can advance his career. Not because I'm so crooked or so fabulous, but because I'm uncharted territory. I haven't done an interview in a decade; I don't like publicity. A decent story about me would do. But if Campbell could come up with something that smacked of impropriety . . . "

"But he's a newspaper man. He has a responsibility to tell the truth."

Jett snorted.

"If he prints any lies about you, at least you'll have legal recourse."

"I couldn't care less what he prints about me. While I have tried to maintain a sense of privacy about my life, I also believe a man should live in such a way that if anything printed about him is a lie, those who know him will know better." Jett opened and closed the fingers of his hands as he gazed out the side window, then turned and focused on her eyes again. "I'm not afraid of any stories a creep like Rod Campbell could concoct about me."

The depth of his conviction raised a lump in Georgia's throat. Still she managed to rasp out, "Then if it's me you're worried about—"

"No. Campbell knows if he went after you or any inno-cent employee—or even an innocent bystander—to try to get to me, I wouldn't let that ride." Jett's eyes were cool but not cold, his voice grim but not threatening. "Somewhere in his pea brain Campbell knows that whether what he believes about me is the truth—that I'd go to any means to get what I want—or what I know about myself is the truth—that I work hard and do the right thing—he has to know that either way, I'd come after him."

"But if what he is willing to write can't touch you, why not just face him down?"

"It's this diner deal, Georgia. It's at a very . . . delicate stage of the negotiations. If the wrong information got out right now . . . " He thumped his closed fist against his knee. "It's timing, you know. If you had started this ball rolling last month or aired your complaints about it next week, I'd be safely tucked away in my apartment—or in my family's cabin, maybe—not dodging renegade trees and rolling into greasy spoons trying to give this jerk the slip."

"You mean if Rod prints the details of your land proposal . . . "

"Details?" Jett smirked. "He doesn't have to have anything as trivial as details . . . or truth. He just needs to cast doubt, throw in a handful of what-ifs, pepper in a few worst-case scenarios. And if he spices it heavily with his personal opinion of me—carefully coated in just the right sugary terms to prevent a slander suit, of course—then the whole deal could be . . . let's say adversely affected."

"Really?" Despite her grudging respect for this man, the notion of his diner-wrecking deal falling by the wayside did not exactly distress Georgia.

As if he could read her mind, Jett leaned forward and looked at her intently. He got so close she could see the pupils of his eyes dilate and feel the warmth of his breath. Her skin tingled at his nearness. She felt her pulse as a faint, quickened patter through her heavy limbs. She found herself drawn toward him, awaiting whatever tidbit of information he had to share.

"And Georgia?"

"Yes," she whispered.

"Before you go getting any bright ideas about how this will further your cause, maybe you should consider this: Just because I might not make this deal, that doesn't mean someone else won't."

She sat back, folded her arms, and pressed her lips together.

He sat back too. "I have to tell you that your original tactic—sticking with me—is still the best one. In fact, it's probably the only viable strategy right now for preserving your precious diner."

"It is?" The seat springs squawked as she suddenly sat bolt upright.

"Right now, there's just one buyer for the diner. But if news breaks about the potential for development of the area, there's no telling what kind of people might be drawn into the bidding."

"Might be better," she insisted, not really feeling it in her gut.

"Might be worse. Much worse."

She looked away from his discerning gaze.

"But as of this moment, the Padgett Group is the only contender to buy the Double Heart." She heard him thrumming his fingers on the steering wheel in what seemed a practiced casualness. "And since I am, in essence, the Padgett Group . . . "

"Since you are the Padgett Group, going along with you in hiding out from Campbell is the best opportunity I'll ever get to affect the outcome of this process," she admitted grudgingly.

"Well, we can give Campbell enough info for a story and see what else comes up. Or you can stick with me, baby."

Georgia sighed. "So you're saying the devil I know is better than the devil I don't know."

"Devil? Me?" He mugged a truly ridiculous choirboy expression. "Why, sweet, lovely Miss Georgia! How you do turn my head with all your flattery."

"And you turn my stomach with yours." She smiled through her wariness.

He laughed. "So it's agreed then? I'll keep heading to Texas with you if you'll help me keep the deal out of Campbell's column?"

Georgia hesitated. "I'm still not convinced you're a better bet than Campbell. After all, isn't he supposed to be some kind of consumer advocate?"

"Corporate adversary is more like it."

"A big-business watchdog," she countered.

"Yeah, a pit bull."

"You're not afraid of a little scrutiny, are you?"

"Have you ever seen a pit bull attack, Georgia? Scrutiny is not high on its list of priorities."

She lowered her chin, her mind on Jett's plans for the Double Heart. "At least pit bulls have priorities."

"Don't start that 'gravy-guzzling pig' routine again," he warned, his eyes teasing.

Before she could respond, he slid from his seat, slammed the truck door behind him, and came around to her side of the vehicle. The moment he touched the handle, her door just fell open.

Georgia sat there, unsure of what he expected.

He extended his hand. "Partners?"

She curled her fingers in a tight ball, reluctant to place her hand in his. She worried as much about the physical connection as she did about the symbolism. It implied a trust and submission she wasn't sure she was ready to give.

They'd been on the road only a few hours and already he'd had more sway over her opinions than she'd had over his. He'd commandeered her truck and made some inroads into her emotions as well. And just when she had decided to turn back and give it all up, he had demanded they press on—and for all the right reasons too: to give the Double Heart its best chance. Now he was asking her to forge a partnership with him, and there was no doubt in her mind whom Jett Murphy saw as the senior partner.

At every turn, Georgia saw herself giving over more control to the man she once thought she could manipulate or beguile or even bully into seeing things her way. If she took his hand now and let him guide her from her own truck, would it signal she had surrendered too much?

She eyed that strong, large hand. Her chest constricted and her thoughts swirled. Something in her actually wanted to place her grip, her trust, and her future squarely in that hand—and to align herself with the man it belonged to. That, more than anything she'd gone through in this long day, truly frightened her. To a woman who went through life on the offensive, never allowing a hint of weakness to show through her veneer, the gesture asked too much.

"And just for your information," Jett said, his hand still open as he waited for her to take it, "I do have my priorities straight. And right now the top one is getting something to eat."

With that, he had clearly drawn a line, indicating that the discussion had ended. He'd won again, and that fact rankled Georgia down to the pointed toes of her turquoise cowboy boots.

"So you're saying you're not a gravy-guzzling pig . . . " She tipped her head to one side, hopped down from the seat of the truck without his assistance, and tossed him an impish but compelling grin. "But you want to be?"

"Well, I don't know about gravy—" He shoved her door shut with a thud.

"Oh, honey, we are at the Dixie Truckers Home." She led the way across the parking lot. "Doing without gravy at a truck stop like this is downright un-American."

"Okay, fine. Gravy it is." He took just two long strides to make up the distance between them. "But help me out here. Do I order it by the cup or by the gallon?"

"Why not just order a tub?" She raised one eyebrow. He had no way of knowing she was angrier at herself than at him when she huffily threw back, "All the better to soak your fat head in."

She marched on past him and did not stop even when she heard his footsteps grow quiet or when he called after her, "What? What? *Now* what did I do?"

* * *

"For a person who's fed up, you're sure packing in the patty melt." Jett swirled his spoon in his coffee cup, one eyebrow raised at the platter of food before her.

"Fed up?" Georgia poked a golden, crisp french fry— glistening with catsup—into her mouth. After savoring the contrast of hot, salty potato and cool, creamy tomato, she inhaled the faint odors of diesel fuel and cigarettes mingling with the delicious aromas wafting from the kitchen. She reached for her frosty chocolate malt to wash down her mouthful. With the ache that came from gulping down the malt too quickly still throbbing behind her eyes, she cocked her head and blinked. "Fed up? Where'd you get the idea I was fed up?"

"That little act of yours out in the parking lot, when you stomped away from me after I explained why I was your best hope for saving your landmark diner."

Act. The single word resonated through her like a harsh chord. He knew. He'd seen through her shallow arrogance and pretense of petty indifference. His calling her on it told her that he knew she was scared, weak, vulnerable.

Georgia had set out this day to show Padgett Murphy something, and that's just what she'd done: She'd shown him the last thing about herself she wanted anyone to see. She pushed away her food, her appetite now vanished, and slumped her shoulders forward with a sigh.

"You've got me there. I was pouting. I was angry. And why wouldn't I be?"

"Why *would* you be?"

"Are you kidding?" She huffed out a hard laugh. "Haven't you been paying attention today? I've made one gaffe after another while you've been the one who's calm, collected . . . in control."

"Ah." He kicked back, stretched his legs out, and placed his elbows on the back of the rounded booth so that both hands dangled down with deceptive nonchalance. "There's the rub: control. When you wrote that letter to me, you felt you were calling the shots. And now . . . "

"And now you're calling all the shots—and using the euphemism 'partners' for something that's just short of a hostage situation."

"Hostage?" His relaxed pose disappeared as he jerked to rigid attention.

Two truckers and a family from Des Moines—or so the father's T-shirt read—lifted their heads to stare.

Jett cast them a benign smile.

Georgia beamed in their direction.

They went back to their meals and menus.

"Hostage?" This time he whispered. "Where do you get that?"

"Okay, maybe *hostage* is a bit extreme, but you have to admit you do not think of us as equal partners in this." She picked up her sandwich, tore off a corner, and popped it into her mouth. She chewed it up, then said, "When you consider your status, your position of power over what happens to the Double Heart, and your connections, things really are weighted in your favor."

"Keep eating like that, and that weight may shift in your direction yet."

She mouthed "ha-ha" and gobbled up another fat, greasy french fry.

"Besides, I don't think you are giving yourself enough credit." He lowered his head and his voice. "I could not make this trip without your help."

"Without my *help* you wouldn't have to make this trip at all," she reminded him.

"You've got a point there." He drummed his fingers on the tabletop.

Georgia wished she had something more to say, but all the ground had been covered . . . and re-covered. She sighed.

His drumming slowed to a rhythmic tap . . . tap . . . tap, like the proverbial Chinese water torture.

Georgia churned her straw in her malt cup. It glopped up and down in the thick drink, making a high-pitched screech each time she pulled it up through the slotted lid.

Tap.

Glop. Glop. Scree-eech.

Tap.

Glop. Scree-eech.

Tap.

Glop. Scree—

"Excuse me?" Georgia was cut off by an itty-bitty waitress with wine-red hair spun high on her head, like cotton candy on a stick. "Mind if I ask you where you two are from?"

"We came fr—"

Jett silenced Georgia with his hand on her shoulder. He scooted forward in the booth with his eyes narrowed at the middle-aged woman. "Why?"

"Well, because there's this fellow wearing a Cubs ball cap that's been asking all the truckers if they've seen a red-headed gal and a gray-haired man in a red pickup with Texas tags—"

"A reporter fellow?" Jett hastened to ask.

"That's what he claims." The waitress scratched at her scalp with the chewed-down nub of her pencil eraser, causing her whole hairdo to wobble back and forth.

Georgia and Jett exchanged looks.

"Uncle Lou says he doesn't think even Campbell would pursue the story if he had to chase us across state lines," Jett murmured. "We've got to get out of Illinois pronto."

"Illinois? First we have to get out of the truck stop, buddy," Georgia shot back.

Even as he nodded his agreement, Jett looked up at the waitress and asked, "Just where is this fellow right now?"

"He went out back to pass the word around among any truckers in the parking lot." She waved her hand toward a row of big rigs.

"Far enough from Truvie to let us make a break for it," Georgia whispered to Jett.

"Provided he stays far," he whispered back.

Georgia wet her lips. "Maybe we could do something to ensure he stays—"

"Oh no!" Jett held up his hand. "I've seen the way you operate, lady. I have no desire to run through the Dixie Truckers Home with a plastic bag on my head, pushing a dish cart, while you throw food and plates as a distraction."

"You underestimate the power of the feminine mind." She tapped her temple, one eye narrowed.

"Don't do that."

"What?"

"That look of yours. It's enough to make a strong man weak in the knees."

She gasped, an almost imperceptible intake of breath, really, but still a purely instinctive response to the idea that anything she did could affect a man like Jett Murphy. The smile that curled slowly over her lips was just as unplanned, and she dipped her gaze demurely. "I make you weak in the knees?"

"I said you could make a strong man weak in the knees," he corrected, his tone gruff. "But *me*—?"

She did not look at him even when he leaned in so close his breath stirred the curls near her ear.

"Me, you obviously make weak in the head—seeing that I am actually considering whatever scheme you're brewing up in that convoluted brain of yours."

She met his gaze with a shift of her eyes and grinned. Glancing up, she gave the waiting waitress the ultra-condensed version of their story, concluding with, "So what do you say? Would you be willing to stall this reporter for a while? Long enough to give us a respectable head start, if nothing else?"

"Well, I don't know . . . " The woman gnawed at the end of her pencil. "I'd like to help you out, your cause being to help the Double Heart and all. Heard of that place, of course. They're good people down that way, I'm sure. But still, if I waste too much time delaying this reporter fellow, I'll lose out on some tips . . . "

"Oh I get it." Jett dug his hand into his pocket to retrieve his wallet, but when he opened it, even Georgia could see his cash supply was running alarmingly low. She made a quick calculation: With what was left, they could pay for dinner and fuel up Truvie once more. Then they'd be broke. Bribery was clearly not within their budget.

Jett inched closer to murmur in Georgia's ear, "I handed most of my cash to the greeter at Lou Mitchell's."

"I got news for you, buddy. You handed him most of mine too. I can use my credit card to get more . . . "

"We don't have time for that, and I don't think they let you put bribes on a credit card." He smiled. "Besides, credit card receipts have your name on them, and if we're not going to leave a trail for Campbell, not handing our names out would be a wise start."

"Good point."

"Guess we'll just have to run for it and hope Campbell doesn't catch up with us." Jett tucked his wallet away again.

Georgia bit her lip. She peered at the waitress with her fanciful hair, beaded earrings, and outfit that clung to every curve—and even created a few curves of its own—and her heart grew buoyant. Finally, she saw a way to contribute to her "partnership" with Jett. She knew what to do to get them out of this. She had the idea, the courage to follow through, and one other thing—or rather, two other things—to make it all happen.

Leaning forward, her spirits soaring, she smiled slyly and asked the waitress, "Ma'am? What size boots do you wear?"

7

Jett paced the distance of the musty motel room, the cell phone pressed to his ear.

"C'mon, Uncle Lou. Pick up."

R-r-inng!

"Nothing," Jett muttered, closing the phone to disconnect the line.

Muffled humming, or perhaps actual singing, drifted from behind the locked door that separated his room from the adjoining one. The sound set his teeth on edge and caused the muscles in the back of his neck to slowly wind into an aching knot.

Georgia Darling. He'd said it this morning, and the day's experiences had served only to confirm his opinion: The girl was trouble.

Of course, this morning he still had the advantage of having never looked into those earnest green eyes or having listened to the passion in her voice as she spoke of the things she cared about most. This morning he'd still been safely ensconced in his well-guarded life. He'd been distant as a monarch from his employees and the people his business affected, well removed from the career he'd chosen.

Now he was in an inexpensive motel room in St. Louis, hoping the city would provide him and Georgia with the kind of anonymity they needed while trying to figure out their next move. He had no cash left. His legs had gone numb from the constant vibration of that rattletrap truck, and the skin on his back felt raw from the scourge of those seat covers.

To make matters worse, he had an angry reporter on his trail and his uncle wasn't answering the phone to give him advice or at least look up some phone numbers. Three hundred miles from his office, Jett could not utilize the numerous contacts that Lou might have sent scurrying to sort out this mess. And he had Georgia Darling to thank for all that.

That and the fact that he hadn't felt so alive and involved in years, he mused.

Yes, Georgia Darling was trouble all right: jaw-clenching, time-consuming, pull-your-hair-out, heartstring-tugging, don't-know-what-he-did-before-he-met-her trouble.

He stared at the closed door.

The humming on the other side grew louder.

He snatched up the TV remote control, aimed it at the small set bolted atop the dresser, and clicked it on. The local news program was just wrapping up the sports segment. Jett checked the red numbers on the bedside clock. Six-twenty-four.

Great. His gaze went to the door, its deep brown, faux wood finish marred by scratches, and its silver knob dulled from countless cleanings. He had a whole evening ahead of him in which to listen to that humming and to think about the day past and the days ahead, always aware that she was in the very next room.

Just thinking of her nearness made his senses percolate. He wished now that he'd taken a room as far down the long row of red doors as possible, or perhaps one on the second floor of the sparse, blocky building painted the color of old-fashioned vanilla ice cream. Even a room in the next closest motel, across the busy four-lane road and down two intersections, would not have been far enough away to keep his mind from straying to thoughts of her.

When she had sat beside him in the truck and at the restaurant—when he could see her face, catch the tantalizing scent of her soap, and hear her laughter—he had not dared let himself dwell too much on his undeniable attraction to her. But now as he stood alone, thinking of her, the explanation that it was purely a primal male urge to protect someone so incapable of taking care of herself just didn't cut it. He wanted to draw her into his arms and reassure her. He wanted to be her hero, the only man who could make her dreams and goals happen. He wanted to kiss Georgia Darling.

He'd never met a woman like her before and, given his lifestyle, probably never would again—unless, of course, he changed his lifestyle. This trip, he thought, stroking his thumb down his bristled cheek, could have just that effect. After this trip, this time with Georgia, nothing about his reserved, detached life would ever be the same.

"Lord, what have I done?" He anchored his feet wide and scrubbed both hands over his face. Not the traditional prayer posture, but Jett did not doubt the Lord heard his words and cared about his questions. "What should I do now?"

A few hours ago he had been so sure of his course of action. The Double Heart Diner was, to him, just another piece of junk real estate. He had been convinced that with his company's intervention, it would better serve its community by making way for fresher opportunities. Now that it felt like a real place, a spot that mattered to people—like Lou Mitchell's and the Dixie Truckers Home—Jett wasn't so sure anymore.

The way to be sure, Jett realized as an answer to his prayer, was to go to Texas and see for himself. That, or hire someone to do it for him and report back.

Who was he kidding? This had become a personal dilemma, and he had to solve it personally. Having arrived at his answer, he sank to the edge of the rock-hard bed and turned up the volume on the TV.

"That story and a final humorous tale from one of our affiliate stations when we return." The newscaster beamed a toothy smile at the camera, then the program cut away to a commercial.

"Mr. Murphy?" Rapid tapping on the door jarred his attention away from the kid hawking lunchmeat.

"What?"

Georgia's voice lilted in from behind the door. "I was just thinking—"

He let out an exaggerated yelp. "You . . . thinking? Heaven help us both!"

His ribbing brought weighty silence from the other room, followed by a droll delivery that left no question as to her opinion of the quality of his humor. "If I tell you I think you're funny, will you open the door so I can talk to you face to face?"

"Well, I guess flattery has opened more than one door in the business world." Jett phrased it that way to remind her— or perhaps himself—that this was still strictly a business situation. "Why not this one?"

Stiff from the ordeal of the ride, he groaned as he got up, started to mute the news program, which had resumed with a report on an upcoming local festival, then decided against it. Having the television blaring in the background would add to the overall informal tone of the meeting. Besides, it would give him something to feign interest in, to help keep him from acting on any of his jumbled emotions.

"Yes?" He pulled the door open, speaking with unprovoked formality. "Did you want something, Miss Darling?"

"I was just *thinking* . . . " She paused and looked up at him, obviously daring him to make a cutting remark to her face.

He declined the unspoken offer with a tip of his head.

"I was just thinking that it's still early. And while I'm not really hungry since I ate so much at the Dixie Truckers Home, I wouldn't mind getting out and hitting Ted Drewes."

"Ted whose?"

"Drewes." She rolled her eyes. "The Custard King?" She said it as if that should mean something to him.

He shook his head. "I didn't even know custard had its own sovereignty, much less any particular ruling royal."

"It's an expression! A made-up title." She laughed and leaned against the door frame. "You know, like the Queen of Mean, the Prince of Chintz . . . "

"The Duke of Earl?"

She pursed her lips at him.

He laughed.

"The thing is, Ted Drewes Frozen Custard is one of the most famous stops on old Route 66 still in operation . . . "

"Tell me, is there anything still on old Route 66 that doesn't revolve around eating?"

"Are you kidding?" Her eyes grew wide and she held up one hand, apparently ready to tick off on her fingers numerous non-food-centered attractions. But before she could, something on the television caught his ear.

"—and now we close with something on the lighter side, from one of our Chicago affiliates. It seems that earlier today at a landmark restaurant, the prominent and usually very reclusive Chicago businessman Padgett Murphy was involved in an incident straight out of a slapstick movie."

He spun around even as Georgia pushed past him, one trembling finger extended toward the screen. "That's . . . that's us!"

Still photo images appeared of the two of them fleeing the scene at Lou Mitchell's, while the anchorwoman read on. "The incident, which included flying food, perplexed patrons, and a bevy of broken dishes, preempted a meeting between a disgruntled ex-employee of Murphy—"

"Disgruntled? I never said I was disgruntled! Look at that face." Georgia jabbed her finger at a photo of herself: yellow-gloved hand raised, red hair stuck straight up after its encounter with the plastic bowl cover, and mouth open. "Now I ask you, is that the face of someone who's disgruntled?"

More like deranged. Jett kept the thought to himself, instead placing his finger on his lips and hissing out a stern "Shhh!"

"—and local business columnist Rod Campbell."

"Did I tell you Campbell was looking to soak up a little publicity, or what?" Jett muttered.

"A spokesperson for Murphy confirmed that his company had already made restitution to the diner, to the satisfaction of the owners and patrons, for damage caused by today's episode."

"Thank you, Uncle Lou, for clearing that up."

"Campbell, however, was less than satisfied, stating: 'That a powerful man like Murphy would go to such lengths to prevent an innocent interview with an ex-employee has to make you wonder. What is he so desperate to hide? And how far is he willing to go to protect his interests?'"

The camera pulled back to show the whole news team, grinning and tapping their papers on the desktop.

"Well that's the news for this evening." The anchor's smile hardly moved as she closed the broadcast. "Be sure to join us at—"

"I can't believe they ended it with Rod's quote like that! It's as good as saying something untoward is going on and that I abducted you to keep you from spilling the beans." Jett clicked the TV off.

"Actually, I think I did spill the beans. And the coffee. And the—"

"Making a joke of this is not going to make it go away, Georgia." He scooped up the cell phone and began punching numbers. "Information? St. Louis, please. I need a listing for Channel—"

"What are you doing?" Georgia grabbed at his forearm, yanking the phone away from his mouth.

"Calling that station."

"What for?"

"To demand a chance to give my rebuttal."

"They aren't interested in your rebuttal. That station doesn't care who you are or what you have to say." Like a bull terrier tugging on a rag, she dug in her heels and held back his arm so he could not raise it again and speak into the phone. Her eyes filled with a mix of soft pleading and commanding common sense. "Even if they did listen to you and run a counter story, the only thing you accomplish is to bring on the very media attention you said you wanted to avoid."

"Hello?" a tinny voice called out from the phone in his white-knuckled grip.

"You think?" he asked, knowing she was right.

She nodded. "All it was to them was a human interest story—fluff, filler. They've already forgotten about it. I mean, it's not like it's even a story they hunted down themselves.

They got it through some service or whatever television stations do. You heard her intro, she said it came from an affiliate station in . . . "

Her words trailed off, and she relinquished her grip on him.

Jett lifted the receiver to his ear and growled out a "Never mind" before hanging up, then tossed the phone on the bed.

"That's probably why Uncle Lou didn't answer. He's been deluged with callers since that story ran back home."

"I am so sorry," she whispered.

"Right now that's worth about as much as my reputation." He pushed his hand back through his hair and shut his eyes. He could not deal with both her contrite expression and his own anger.

"This will all blow over in time." She sounded genuinely convinced of that.

"Yeah, you're probably right." He didn't know which swayed him more: her bright-eyed optimism or the kernel of truth in her words. He cupped his hand to the back of his neck and sighed. "If we don't give Campbell any more fodder, it will all die out."

"So what are you going to do then?"

"Do?" He snorted. "Doing things got me into this fiasco in the first place."

She blinked her thick lashes at him. "I don't understand."

"Well, look at it this way, Miss Darling." He moved toward her as he spoke. "This morning my uncle implied that I did not get personally involved enough in my own business, in my own life, for that matter."

She raised her eyebrows in surprise at the admission, or was it because he was closing in on her?

He kept moving, both verbally and physically. "Around noon, I resolved to remedy that and had a now-infamous run-in with a certain redhead."

She gulped.

He stood close enough now to see the movement in her slender, white throat, to hear her breathing quicken. He crept closer still.

"By midafternoon, I'd dug myself in so deep I was past the point of no return. And now, before sundown, I find my face on the evening news with my carefully cultivated professional image held up to ridicule and question. I think I've done enough for one day, don't you?"

"Um, actually . . . " She bit her lip, twisted her stockinged toe into the carpet and, with her big doe eyes looking up at him sheepishly, said, "I can think of something else you might want to do—"

• • •

"Let's go over this again." Georgia clasped her hands behind her back and strode across the dark green carpet like a general taking command of a war room.

Her initial discouragement, the feeling of being held hostage to this man's decisions, had fallen away. Yes, her confidence had ebbed today. But when she had seized the opportunity to barter her boots for the cooperation of the reticent waitress, that confidence had returned stronger than ever.

Good partnerships came out of a mutual need and exchange of abilities, she reasoned. At first glance, it might seem that an out-of-work gal from Texas, with no kin and no particular prospects for the future, had little to bring to a collaboration with a gorgeous, reclusive entrepreneur. Not true.

Georgia delighted in the realization that she had something to offer Jett Murphy that he simply could not provide for himself. Creative ingenuity, she liked to call it—a certain, classic redhead approach to things. The Lucy Ricardo Factor, the likes of which a man like Murphy could never hope to acquire. And while they might not both achieve their most desired outcome in this matter, if either of them hoped to win at all, they would have to work together.

With that thought feeding her enthusiasm, she spun on her heel and squinted shut one eye so as to look menacingly shrewd. "Our objective now is to get to the Double Heart Diner without further interference from Rod Campbell, and without drawing any attention to ourselves that might cause people involved in the deal to balk. Right?"

"Right." He sat back in the one swivel chair in the room and lifted his feet to the bed, crossing them casually at the ankles.

Georgia didn't have to be a mind reader to know what he was telling her with this purposefully relaxed pose. He was willing to listen to her ideas, but certainly not ready to spring into action solely because of her suggestions. The challenge of that made her smile inwardly. She folded her arms over her chest and studied him down the length of her not-so-lengthy nose.

"Now, we've ruled out flying down to Texas, because that involves passenger lists with ID checks and a car rental in Amarillo to get us to our destination—"

Jett laced his fingers behind his head. "Too much of a paper trail, and it gets us in way too early. My hanging around in advance of the deal would only fuel speculation, with who-knows-what results."

"You do think, however, that your uncle can arrange for there to be a car and cash here in St. Louis for us to pick up in the morning?"

Jett sat forward, swinging his feet to the ground. "I'll try him again on his private line."

Doesn't feel so hot not to be the one in control, does it? Georgia could see he was working hard to shift the balance of power back in his direction. If nothing, else, she supposed, this little adventure would teach them both a lesson in sharing and working with others that they both—especially Jett—sorely needed.

Jett punched a long string of numbers into the phone, which was dwarfed by his large hand. He held the receiver to his ear and even Georgia could hear the muted whir that signaled the ringing of the phone on the other end. She tapped the toe of her shoe on the carpet and waited. One ring. Two.

"Hello? Uncle Lou! I can't believe I finally got through to you." He leaned farther forward and rested one elbow on his knee. "Yes, I suspected that's why you weren't answering the phone."

The expression on his face teetered between angst and resignation. Georgia felt tempted to go to him, rub the back of his neck, and coo soothing words into his ear. *Coo?* She blinked at the peculiar notion, trying to bring herself back to her senses, but the impulse did not abate. She wanted to walk across the room, stand by Jett's side, and do her best to ease his apprehensions with kind words and a tender touch—a purely innocent, understanding touch that would knead away the tension from those broad, muscular shoulders and gently massage the anxiety right out of those worry lines in his forehead.

Yeah. Right. She knotted her arms so tightly over her chest that her fisted hands dug into her ribs. What she wanted, she had to admit to herself, was for Jett Murphy to like her—and not as a business partner. There were only about a thousand reasons why she had to fight that hankering with all her might—not the least of which were her moral convictions.

Traveling across the country with a man she hoped would help her save a landmark was one thing. Traveling with a man she wished would take her in his arms and kiss her? Oh my!

"I saw it on a news program here," Jett told his uncle. "Yes, *here*—in St. Louis. Oh we've stopped for the night in St. Louis."

Maybe if we were smart, we'd stop everything here, she thought. *I shouldn't even be on this trip with Jett—Mr. Murphy,* she corrected herself.

"Look, it's no big deal. We've got everything under control."

Easy for him to say. Georgia glared at her image in the mirror. The odds of a man like that reciprocating her feelings were a million to one. Of course he saw no temptation lurking in their continued association.

"I also need for you to get a comfortable but nondescript car to me here. I can't rent one without giving my name, and since this news piece aired here, why risk it? Oh, and some cash too—traveling money." He listened a moment. "Good, that should do nicely. Yes, we're going to drive on to Texas. I'd like to look around the . . . um . . . property before we finalize the deal."

He smiled up at her, but it looked more like the expression of a man who had just tried to squelch a belch in public and had not quite succeeded.

Oh yeah, this man likes me, her inner voice—which had a wicked way with sarcasm—taunted. *He likes me like the plague.*

"Yes, I think it's the right thing to do too," he went on, this time his gaze decidedly averted from hers. "Since I— she what?"

Georgia jumped, one hand clutching the collar of her T-shirt, the other wadding the soft curls at the side of her head. "Whatever it was, I didn't mean to. And if I did mean to, I had a very good reason."

Jett lowered the mouthpiece, still not looking directly at Georgia. "Not you," he whispered.

"Whew." She let her hand drop from her hair.

His face became a mask of concern as he gathered details from the other end of the line.

"What is it?"

Jett put one hand over the receiver. "My secretary. She's apparently turned up the heat by giving out some misinforma—She said *what?*" He turned back to what his uncle was saying.

"What? What?" Georgia closed in. "What kind of 'misinforma—' did she give out? What did she say?"

"She answered the phone with it?" Jett asked his uncle.

"Yeesh! That can't be good, whatever it is," she muttered.

"And then she told them what?" His face paled.

The suspense was killing her. Georgia's skin practically crawled with the itch to find out how Jett's secretary had answered the phone. She bent low to whisper, "What?"

He held up one finger, asking her to let him hold off his answer a moment longer. "How many people heard this?"

Georgia bit her lip and twisted her fingers together to keep herself from grabbing the phone and getting the scoop directly from good ol' Uncle Lou.

"Well, thank heavens for that, at least."

Georgia pantomimed doing just that: making a shallow curtsy, rolling her eyes upward in her most angelic expression, and mouthing a quick "Thank you" in hopes that her humor would ease Jett's anxiety enough to get him to speak to her.

Her antics did win her a smile—sort of.

"I just can't believe this." He scored his fingers back through his thick hair. "Where on earth did she get an idea to do something that idiotic anyway?"

Georgia tipped her head, as if she also was awaiting Lou's answer.

"Who?" Jett bellowed into the phone.

She held both hands up in the universal gesture of blamelessness. "Hey, I don't even know your secretary."

"Who?" Jett repeated, his face flushed red in the hollows of his lean cheeks.

"Who, already?" Georgia whispered.

"Me!" He bolted up from his chair, thumping his finger into the center of his chest. "Me?"

"You?" She pointed too. "This is very interesting. In fact, if I actually knew what this was about, I bet I'd find it fascinating. Of course, any story in which the infallible Jett Murphy plays the goof-er and not the goof-ee . . . um, I mean, the one upon whom the goof has been perpetrated—"

Jett finally turned his attention to her. "Shh."

"No wonder your secretary ratted you out." She slumped onto the edge of the bed. "You're a grouch."

"Shhh!"

"And on top of that? I think you've sprung a leak!"

"Yes, I understand, Uncle Lou," Jett said back into the phone. "As long as she doesn't intend to do it anymore. She, um, she didn't actually have the company letterhead changed, did she?"

Georgia raised an eyebrow. "Ooh. Sounds like the makings of a corporate takeover. Maybe I should be racing off to Texas with your secretary."

"Now, there's a frightening thought," Jett muttered, holding the phone away from his lips. "Hurricanes have left less

damage in their wake than the pair of you on a slow day."
Before Georgia could make a snappy comeback, he said back
into the receiver: "Yes, sir. You're right. Popping off like that
without taking into account the possible consequences is
what got me into this particular mess to begin with."

"Ha!" Georgia cried triumphantly.

"But the rest of the mess is courtesy of a certain redheaded firebrand," he added through the first real smile
she'd seen from him since the conversation began.

Her stomach lurched in that way it does at the moment
one surrenders to the thrill of rocketing downhill on a roller
coaster. Even her head felt dizzy. As she waited for it to clear,
she heard Jett give his uncle the address of their motel. He
then arranged to collect the car and cash. Someone would
see to Truvie later that evening, then would drive her to
Texas where she and Georgia would be reunited.

Jett sighed, closed his eyes, and set his mouth in a grim
line. "I will," he said into the phone. "Extra careful. I do
understand what's at stake here, Uncle Lou. I'm not sure I
fully understood this morning when I set this traveling circus in motion, but I have a pretty good idea now."

What did he mean by that? Georgia was afraid to ask. If
it was good news, she would not want the added enticement.
She was having a hard enough time keeping her feelings in
check as it was.

And if it was bad news . . . she didn't even want to think
about it.

8

"What were you thinking?" Jett asked his forlorn image in the motel bathroom mirror. A towel lay draped around his shoulders as he awaited Georgia's ministrations.

"You weren't thinking, silly." Standing directly behind him, she met his eyes in the reflection. She yanked into place the finger of what looked like a hand-shaped, plastic sandwich bag. "You were trusting."

"Trusting!" The word leapt from his lips as if forced by a sharp blow, low to his gut. He closed his eyes, but that did not shut out the feelings of dread crowding in on him. "I must be out of my mind."

"No, but you are about to be out of your head"—she leaned on the wooden back of the desk chair she sat on and teased—"out of this head and into a different-looking one."

Jett watched as she snipped a packet here, mixed a concoction there. She waggled her eyebrows at him, tugging at her gloves like a crazy person.

"Now relax. *Relax.* I know we agreed to take some drastic measures to disguise ourselves." It was the "one more thing" she had convinced him he should do. "But you have to know I'd never do anything that might physically hurt you."

He hung his head but kept his eyes fixed on her and his

expression wry. "Let's see, you'd throw yourself on a run-away dish cart, ram your truck into a tree, and walk quickly across a hot gravel parking lot without your cowboy boots. But hurt me? No, I have no reason to think you'd ever do anything to hurt me, Georgia."

She raised up her perfect little chin, the picture of sweet serenity and pride. "Of course not."

"No."

"Besides . . . " She reached down to snatch up a plastic bottle filled with murky liquid, then sealed its tip with one finger and gave it a shake, the end of her tongue pressed to the edge of her white teeth. Her eyes flashed. "I didn't bring my mad scientist equipment with me, so I can only make do with what we found on our trip to the drugstore. *Bwahaha-haha.*" She gave an evil laugh.

"Funny," he deadpanned.

She raised the bottle over his head.

Jett cringed.

She swatted at his shoulder, laughing. "Loosen up, will you?"

"Sorry. I'm just not the type of person who's accustomed to changing his appearance in order to flee the scene."

"Are you implying I am?"

Breaking into his best "gotcha" grin, he played into her perfect setup with a teasing, "Well, if the hair dye fits . . . "

Brrraaappptt. Georgia let the bottle's response speak for her as a great gob of brackish goo went squirting into her palm.

Jett's nostrils burned and twitched as a stinging odor filled the cramped quarters. He jerked his head away from her. "That stuff isn't going to turn my hair green or purple, is it?"

"No. That wouldn't be much of a disguise. And by the

way, my hair isn't dyed." She met his gaze in the mirror.

"I'm sure it's not. It's far too lovely to be anything short of God's own handiwork." He meant that, and he knew it showed in his face and in his tone.

Her expression softened a little.

"I'm sorry if I implied otherwise, I was just joking. Okay?"

"Okay."

"Now can we get this over with?" He tensed just thinking about what he was in for at her hands.

"Sure. Sit still and keep your head up."

His scalp tingled as she sank both hands into his silver hair and began to massage in the pungent foam, her head bowed low over her project. The otherwise garish light caressed the highlights and contrasts of her beautiful curls, while her nimble fingers applied pressure to tilt his head to one side, then the next. His gaze never faltered.

"It really is, you know," he murmured.

"What?" Her features pinched to convey her confusion, but she did not stop kneading the dye into one coarse patch of hair after another.

"Your hair," he rasped with unintended huskiness. "It's truly lovely—just like you."

He craned his neck to look back at her, needing to see her response directly and not through the filtered distance of their reflected images. Their gazes met. Hesitance, warmth, then denial flickered in the depths of Georgia's eyes. She bit her lip.

Jett's interest fell to her mouth, then moved again to her eyes. The typically sophisticated women in his circle would have needed no clearer signal to openly advance. They often needed far less. While his masculine pride had caused him to find some appeal in that, his personal convictions had led him to find only disappointment in the overemphasis on physical interactions between a man and woman. All too often, this happened before, or even at the expense of, spiritual ties. That had worn thin for him a long time ago. He needed more from the kind of woman he would want in his life.

"Keep your head straight or you'll drip and end up all streaky." Georgia gently nudged the side of his head.

He glanced up at the woman fussing over him and grinned. Much as he wanted to pull Georgia close and kiss her, he found far deeper satisfaction in the fact that she would have no part in that behavior.

"There." She swirled her hands over his scalp one last time, then raised her gloved hands like a surgeon fresh from scrubbing up.

"That's it?"

"That's it. Just let it set for . . . " She wrangled with an unruly paper that had been folded into a tiny rectangle in the box of hair coloring. "Hmmm. According to these instructions, we'll need to leave it on for the maximum time suggested to cover the gray."

"Silver."

"What?"

"Gray sounds old. Silver sounds distinguished. I know it's probably silly, but I like to think of my hair as silver." He shrugged.

"Well, for the duration of our little charade, you can just think of it as . . . " Georgia looked at the front of the box. "'Ebony sable.'" She peeled off her gloves and plopped them onto the unfurled instructions sprawled on the sink counter. Then she turned to Jett and made a subtle flourish with her bare hands, as if to present her accomplishment.

He'd stayed so focused on Georgia, Jett suddenly realized, he'd forgotten to keep an eye on what she was up to. Now he almost dreaded what he might find.

She waved her hand again like a model on a game show displaying a "fabulous grand prize!"

Jett steeled himself by gripping the chair arms. He shot her a warning glare.

She merely grinned at him.

He ventured a peek at himself in the huge mirror. "Georgia Darling? What on earth have you done to me?"

"What?"

"It's purple!"

"The color of the dye does not indicate the results you'll see on your hair. It says so right here in the instructions."

"It's p-purple," he sputtered, noting that the color of his face was fast approaching that same shade.

"It's ashy, really, I'd say. Smoky." She put her hand on his shoulder as if that might assuage him.

"Smoky *purple,*" he corrected.

"Oh stop being a baby." Her reassuring pat turned into a jab. "It's going to be fine. It's only a temporary rinse, after all. You just have to wash it five times to get rid of it."

"Five?" He tried to remember if he'd seen one or two travel-size bottles of shampoo packed in his bags.

"Five. No big deal. Honest."

He wanted to believe her, but then he noticed she didn't have any purple sludge smeared all over her gorgeous hair. "Honest?"

"On my honor." She held up her hand by her head, but it sank just a little when she wet her lips, looked away, and murmured, "If my word still means anything to you, Mr. Murphy, after all I've gotten you into . . . "

"It does," he cut her off, not wanting her to think he seriously held anything against her. "And you might as well call me Jett." He glanced again at his reflection in the mirror.

She bit her lip again.

He shrugged. "Once a man has let a woman work his hair into a grapey, gray lather, they ought to be on a first-name basis. That's always been my policy, at least. Okay?"

"Okay . . . Jett." She lowered her eyes just enough to show a shy and demure side of herself that until now Jett had not suspected even existed.

He liked it.

"And you can call me Georgia," she murmured.

"I already do," he reminded her.

"Oh, yeah. Good then. That's good." She started to reach for something on the counter, then altered her movement as if to touch the towel wrapped around his neck. At the last moment she stopped herself and tucked her hands under her folded arms. "Good."

"Good." Their eyes met in the mirror reflecting his froth-covered head.

Georgia smiled.

For that smile, Jett did not care what color his hair ended up. *But please, Lord,* he added in a sudden, silent after-thought prayer, *please . . . not purple.*

• • •

"It's blond."

Georgia cupped her hand along one pale wave on her head. "I know."

He pushed his fingers through the now inky black hair that swept back at his own temple. "Blond. Blond."

"I know. I know."

He looked like he was trying to stifle a sneeze and mouthed the word yet again, "Blond."

She spun around to face the side mirror of the sedan Jett's

uncle had had delivered to the motel the night before. Once Jett's hair had been rinsed and dried, and she'd convinced him she had not permanently stained his scalp or any such thing, he'd seen to the preparations for the rest of their trip. And she'd gone off to her room to tend to her own disguise.

This morning Georgia had gone over some simple instructions with the man in charge of getting Truvie to Texas in a few days. They'd thought it best to park the truck out of sight, at a storage facility, until then. After that she'd grabbed a couple of muffins and coffee at a nearby gas station market. By the time she returned to the motel, Jett was just finishing loading their things into the trunk of the blue rental car his uncle had arranged for them to take the rest of the way. Whose name it was rented under, she did not know and did not ask. As she'd strolled across the lot, Jett had looked up from his task to make his statement of the obvious.

Blond. Like she didn't know the exact shade. In the side mirror she studied her face, framed in pale waves. She never envisioned herself as a baby-doll blond. But she had to admit, the pretend persona did have its appeal.

The idea of playing someone else, someone very unlike herself, intrigued her—especially with Jett Murphy along for the fun. She wondered what type of woman a man like that would go for? The Marilyn Monroe type or the natural, sun-bleached all-American? She pulled at a stray wisp of hair, letting it fall recklessly over one eye. Then she batted her lashes furiously and wet her lips, imagining . . .

"Hey? You okay?" Jett called from the back of the car where he was tussling with the bags to fit them all in the compact trunk space.

"I'm divine," she purred, lashes aflutter. "Thank you ever so much for asking, you big strong man, you."

"Um . . . don't mention it." He stopped to gawk at her. "I . . . uh, you sure you're okay? Because it looks like you've got something in your eye."

She froze mid eye-bat.

"And your voice sounds all kind of . . . breathy." Jett did not even try to conceal his amusement at her display. "Maybe your air conditioning was turned down too low last night. Maybe you're coming down with a cold."

"Keep it up, mister, and I'll show you cold." She sniffed and bent to check the mirror again, rearranging her disheveled bangs. "I was just trying on a personality type to go with my new hair."

"I like your old personality better." He went back to his work, but she heard him grumble from within the shelter of the trunk, "And your old hair."

"Well, I like this new look." She patted the wig into place. "Don't you? Really?"

"Well, yeah, but . . . "

"But what? Too much? It's too much, isn't it?"

"Too much? I didn't know those words were even in your vocabulary." He chuckled, obviously pleased with himself.

"Ha-ha. I think it *may* be too much. Maybe I should have gone with the brown pageboy. Or the black back-comb with a flip. But then our hair would be too much alike . . . "

"Yeah, I hate it when I go off on a cross-country chase and someone in my getaway car has the same hairdo," he deadpanned. "Of course, I wasn't planning on any back-combing, whatever that is, or a . . . flip?"

"Your attitude is flip enough, thank you." She laughed.

"I think the word you're looking for is *charming*."

"Oh, the word I'm looking for is not a word I care to find on my lips at all, so just stop pressing the issue, please. I mean it. Last night you made unkind remarks, implying that my hair is dyed red. Today you don't like it that I've gone blond. What is it with you anyway?"

He pursed his lips, his fingers again raking through his hair.

She wagged her finger and plunged ahead, feeling full of fun and hope—glad for a few moments in the morning sunlight, even if they were in a motel parking lot. "You don't like the way my hair was; you don't like the way my hair *is*. What do you suggest I do? Buy a big ol' beekeeper's hat with netting all around it?"

That said, she snatched at the newly acquired hairline and tugged back, whisking off the hairpiece with bravado.

"A wig?" Jett's repeated finger-combing turned into an undeniable, brisk scratch. "That was a wig?"

"Of course it's a wig." She lifted several strands of her own damp hair, savoring the coolness of the morning air on her scalp. "What did you think?"

"Hmmm, I don't know. Since you insisted that I dye my hair . . . "

"A man can't wear a wig, silly. It would look too phony."

"Oh, and *this*"— he pinched a cool, colored strand of his hair between his thumb and finger—"this is perfectly natural and lifelike?"

"What's wrong with it?"

"Nothing, if you're a Labrador. But for me or anyone else? It's bit drastic."

"What's so wrong with it? Isn't it similar to the color your hair was before it went gr—?"

"Silver," he interjected before she could even get the word out.

"Silver," she corrected.

"And if my hair ever had been this color, I think I'd have

dyed it long before this." He shut the trunk.

"That's good then." She opened her door but did not get in.

"Good?" He went around to his side.

"Yes, good," she echoed. "Because we're trying to hide our identities here. If your hair had once been 'ebony sable,' we would have done nothing but make you look like a much younger version of yourself . . . "

"Hey, my hair has looked like this most of my adult life, including when I was *much younger.* For your information, I went gray while I was still—"

"Silver."

"Hmmm?"

"Silver." She pointed to his hair.

He glared at her for one, two, three seconds, then broke into a grin. "Okay, Okay. Enough. Campbell has sent the word out to look for a petite, wacky redhead and a tall, distinguished gentleman with silver hair." He slid his hand down his T-shirt and jeans as though they were a tuxedo. "I guess this will fool them."

Wacky? Is that all he thought of her? "Wacky? I'll show you wacky—"

"Ah-ah-ah." He shook his head while opening the back door to the car and reaching inside for something. "Remember, we're not supposed to act like ourselves from here on out."

"Oh good." She jerked open her car door and slid inside. "Then that means that from here on out you'll be funny."

"I'll try my best—starting with this." He began to fiddle with a piece of white poster board.

Despite her curiosity, she feigned a total lack of interest. Instead, she slapped her wig back on and began stuffing her red curls beneath their blond counterparts.

A sharp *thwack* of the poster against the backseat made her steal a look in the rearview mirror. "What is that?"

"My idea of a big joke." He chuckled, backed out of the car, then swung the door shut with a *whomp*.

Biting her lip, Georgia strained to read the big, bold letters printed in red on the white background. She concentrated on piecing together the words, reflected up into the back window, trying not to let Jett catch her in the act. He must have suspected what she was doing, though, as he slid behind the steering wheel and she let out an audible gasp.

"And you had the nerve, the unmitigated gall to call *me* wacky?"

"I thought you might like that."

"Like?" The solid click of her seat-belt buckle echoed the sharp tone of her voice. She tried not to give away the sudden mix of excitement, confusion, and fear she felt at seeing what he'd placed in the car window. "*Like* may not be the exact word I'd go for, but we'll leave it at that for now."

He concentrated on pulling the car out of the parking lot, but Georgia could not take her eyes off the sign in the back window—the sign that proclaimed to the world one simple, stunning, red herring of an announcement:

"Just Married."

9

"Haven't you ever heard the expression 'hiding in plain sight'?" Jett maneuvered the car handily along the St. Louis highways. By the time he and Georgia got started that morning, rush-hour traffic had already subsided, making their passing unremarkable.

"Haven't you ever heard the expression 'nutty as a fruit-cake'?" she countered, her eyes twinkling.

"Not usually directed at me, I haven't." He leaned over as if confiding a secret. "How about you?"

She started to say something, must have thought better of it, then tossed her head and looked out the passenger window. That platinum blond mop on her head quivered instead of bouncing as her natural curls would. Jett missed those curls already. He blinked at the multiple lanes in the straight road ahead. He missed Georgia's curls. Now there was something he would not have foreseen himself thinking when he first laid eyes on that redhead less than twenty-four hours ago.

Whoa. Too fast. His mind automatically went on red alert—or was it redhead alert? Detached. That was his style. Make the decisions. Find the right people to carry them out. Give orders. Do not get personally involved.

Yet in less than a day, Georgia had breached the wall he

121

had built around himself. Breached? He'd practically built her a ladder with his own two hands and helped her over.

If he didn't fight against such emotional involvement now, who knew what tomorrow might bring? Would he buy the diner only to decide to refurbish it with his own two hands, then take on the jobs of fry cook, floor-show entertainer, and busboy?

He set his jaw. He certainly wasn't going to let that happen. Better to get things back on course, set an even keel, get on the straight and narrow.

"Would you open the glove compartment, please?" He used his best professional, authoritarian voice, as if directing his secretary to take a letter. "I asked Uncle Lou to provide a few necessities for the trip. You'll find a small manila envelope in there, I'm sure."

"I'm almost afraid of this." Georgia wrestled with the unfamiliar latch for a moment, then the compartment fell open and she pulled out a light brown packet. "After you sprang that crazy sign on me, I'm not sure what else to expect."

"You started the ball rolling with your maniacal makeovers and the idea to go undercover to throw Campbell off our trail," he reminded her gently. "I just took it to the next logical step."

"If posing as a newlywed couple is the next logical step to you, I can't fathom what you might have in store after that." She dropped the envelope onto her lap, shutting the glove compartment soundly. Then she raised her hand and began to tick items off on her fingers as she made a list. "Let's see: Run from Campbell, dye hair, play married couple . . . um, rent a circus wagon? That would really throw him off our track."

"Not if they've seen you in action."

"Hey!"

He laughed. He couldn't help it. She brought out the humor in him. He reached across the seat to tap the bulging envelope on her lap. "I'm just kidding, Georgia. The reality is, Campbell has sent the word out to watch for a . . . what did that St. Louis news anchor call us?"

"A prominent Chicago businessman and a disgruntled employee." She growled out the word *disgruntled* through clenched teeth.

"Yes, 'a prominent businessman and a disgruntled employee.' Campbell implied I'd all but kidnapped you in an attempt to conceal my nefarious deeds. Now, what presents a less disgruntled and desperate picture than a couple on their honeymoon?"

She caught her lip between her teeth and cocked her head. "Is it too late to vote for that circus wagon thing?"

"Yes."

She plucked a piece of nonexistent lint from her pants. She stubbed the toes of her shoes together. She squinted off toward the horizon.

He waited.

She crossed, then uncrossed, her arms. "Okay." She sighed. "Okay, then you have a point."

"And that just kills you, doesn't it?"

"I have no idea what you mean."

"Admitting that I have a point—a very valid point. It kills you, doesn't it?"

She smiled so sweetly he could practically taste the sugar. "Why, Jett, you have many good points. Your generosity, your willingness to see another person's side of things . . . "

"My ability to act like a giant piece of toast."

"Toast?"

"Yes, toast. That must be how you see me. Why else would you be buttering me up like this?" He changed lanes with ease, pretending he didn't know what she was up to. "Unless, of course . . . Why, Georgia, you wouldn't be trying to use flattery to influence my decision about the Double Heart, would you?"

"Would it work?"

He tried unsuccessfully to look imposing and stern as he shook his head.

She laughed. "Okay, so I tried. Not exactly the first time a *wife* tried that tactic to influence matters in her favor."

Wife. The weighted word stilled all lightheartedness within him. He did not want to think of the underlying implications of his and Georgia's playacting, to allow himself even for one moment to picture her as his wife.

"Open the envelope, why don't you?" His suddenly somber tone matched his mood. "There should be some cash, a map, and information on hotel reservations."

She withdrew a computer printout. "Tulsa?"

"What?"

"Your uncle has us stopping at a hotel in Tulsa."

"And?"

"And . . . don't you think we can get a little farther down the road today? Tulsa isn't even a seven-hour drive from St. Louis. I was thinking we'd get at least as far as Oklahoma City."

"Uncle Lou wanted us to take this at a more measured pace, that's all. Use as much control over our actions as possible. That allows him time for damage control. You have to see things from our vantage point, Georgia—get the big picture. He's thinking . . . "

"He's thinking of flying in to Tulsa."

"He is?"

"That's what this note says. 'Will be in Tulsa at six P.M. Meet me,'" she read. "Then he gives the flight information."

"Well." He looked at the clock on the dash. "Looks like we don't have to be in Tulsa until six. That gives us some time to do a little sightseeing along the way."

"That will mean more time on the road." Georgia began unfurling the road map. "More chances to run into people who might have seen that goofy story about us on TV, or truckers who've been alerted by Campbell to look out for us."

"Lucky for us we have our sign then, isn't it?"

"Oh yeah, it's a regular blessing." She rolled her eyes.

For a few minutes, Jett's ears were filled with the muted sounds of the highway and their own car's tires whirring softly over the road. He could tell that she was sulking over this whole sign business, but he had no intention of stirring things up any more than necessary. So he said nothing.

Finally, Georgia shifted in her seat, glanced back at the sign in the rear window, and aimed a questioning gaze at him. "Tell me again why it's a blessing?"

"Think about it." He paused to let her do just that before going on. "If anyone really were trying to track us down, the sign alone might be enough to stave off their close scrutiny. If it keeps a few folks from giving us a second look and connecting us to that story, then it's certainly worth it, don't you think?"

"Oh I think. I think all right. But what I think, I'm not sure you want to know." She thrust out her lower lip like a five-year-old who did not get her way.

Jett held back the urge to burst into a belly laugh. "Stop being so glum, would you? There's no reason to pout. Just because this time I was the one who came up with the . . . um . . . *creative intervention,* shall we say?"

Georgia turned and stared at him. "What did you say?"

"There's no reason to pout?"

"No, the other part."

"Creative interventions?"

"Bingo!"

"Gee, and I didn't even know we were playing. This is great!" Her whole attitude shifted. Her face brightened. Her hands gestured in the air as if she were carrying on a silent inner dialogue: rehearsing it, sorting out her words before she spoke. "If you think about it, it's terrific."

Much as it delighted Jett to see her liven up like this, he had to say, "I don't follow your thinking—"

"Ah, but you do! You *do*. That's what's so great. You are actually beginning to follow my thinking quite well." She wiggled in her seat, like a puppy with a new bone. "Don't you see it? I'll admit, I was feeling badly that I had not come up with the whole plan we're using. Feeling that I hadn't contributed enough to the overall facade I suggested we use. Like I'd only done half the job."

"Uh-huh." Jett said it as if he knew what she meant, even though he had no idea.

"But I really shouldn't feel badly about that at all, because of what it represents."

He was almost afraid to ask. But, then again, he just had to. "What does it represent?"

"The Lucy Factor."

"The what?"

"Lucy Ricardo? *I Love Lucy*?"

He raised one finger. "I've thought a couple times that you remind me of her."

"I'll take that as a compliment." She beamed at him.

He grinned, knowing he probably looked like a big goof and not caring one bit. He was rolling down the Missouri roads with a woman he liked and admired. She loved Lucy and he loved . . . he loved . . .

He loved that she loved Lucy, he quickly intervened in his own thought process. He urged Georgia to continue, unwilling to dwell on the feelings that necessitated his quick mental save. "And?"

"And whenever I get in a jam, I always ask myself two questions. First I ask, What would God have me do? to get my moral grounding before I act. The answer to that one is usually pretty straightforward and obvious, if I put my own wants aside."

He nodded, duly impressed with that approach.

"The next thing I ask, though, doesn't always have the most obvious answer. See, I ask myself, How would Lucy handle this? That question stirs up my imagination and gives me a unique perspective. Does that make any sense to you?"

"It's kind of scary, but in a way it does."

"I knew it!" She clapped her hands.

He flinched. "Knew what?"

She dipped her chin to look at him through her thick lashes. "You're starting to show the effects of exposure to the whirling, churning, ever-active inner processes of my mind."

"Remind me to pick up motion-sickness remedies. Sounds like I'll need them." But the drugstore did not sell any remedies for what really ailed him, Jett realized as he stole another look at the woman sitting next to him. "Now, do you want to explain to me in English for non-redheads, just exactly what it is you think has happened to me?"

Georgia looked at him with such glee in her eyes that he actually felt a gut reaction, even before she rubbed her hands together, gave an exaggerated cackle, and proclaimed, "You, Mr. Padgett Murphy—CEO of the Padgett

Group, prominent and reclusive Chicago businessman, and soon-to-be owner of the Double Heart Diner—are beginning to think like *me!*"

• • •

Georgia, pleased as punch at the turn of events, strolled out from the small roadside store, her purchase in her pocket and her heart light. They'd stopped for gas and she'd made a quick pit stop. Afterward, on her way out of the store, a tacky clutter of souvenirs had caught her eye and captured her imagination. A few moments later, she met Jett as he came around the dingy brick block of a building and presented him with her new twist: her wonderful, brilliant addition to their partnership. "Rings?" Jett yelped.

Georgia frowned at him, wondering if he was a natural-born yelper or if he had just picked up the startling habit in the last day or so. Either way, she decided to offer her explanation in a calm, soothing tone, so as not to inspire any further outbursts. "Watch and learn from the master of alternative interventions and solutions, Mr. . . . um, Jett. If you are going to do something this far-fetched, you for sure had better have all your bases covered. Or, in this case, all your ring fingers."

He stuffed his fingers into his pockets as the warm summer breeze stirred around them. The place, like almost every place they'd chosen to stop, was all but deserted. Still, she kept her voice low and her senses on alert.

"Think about this," she commanded as if talking to a reticent child. "You are the one who chose this particular device, having us play newlyweds, to evade detection. Well, newlyweds have rings. Right?"

"Yeah, I suppose." He scratched a path through his hair with his hand—his right hand—while his left one remained safely confined in his jeans pocket.

Georgia squinted off at the strip of road that disappeared over the gentle hills in the distance. She had a very reasonable addition to this plan, and she would not be deterred.

"Lucy never would have tried to pull off anything this big without the proper costumes." She held up the silver band inlaid with tiny chips of far too blue a shade of turquoise and peered at him through the circle. "Lucy would have had rings."

"Correct me if I'm wrong, but didn't most of Lucy's plans go seriously awry?"

He thinks he's funny, she told herself. *Or worse yet, he knows he's right.* But that reality did not dampen her enthusiasm one iota as she handed him the ring she had picked up in the dusty little shop a few yards away. "Here, just put it on. It'll be a nice touch, you'll see. Wear this ring, please?"

"Why, Georgia, this is all so sudden." He held his hand out, palm up.

She plopped the ring in it, feeling good that he was meeting her halfway on this.

He did not slip it on.

"What do I owe you for this?" He reached for his wallet.

"Don't worry about it," She waved the offer off. "My treat."

"No. I can't accept a ring from a woman I hardly know, it's just not—"

"Quit worrying about it, okay? It's no big deal."

"Yeah, but it's . . . a ring. I can't wear a ring from you without—"

Gee, he sure knows how to make a girl feel wanted, she thought. It was one thing to know there could never be anything more than this peculiar partnership between the two of them. But to hear him rail so forcefully against even the pretense of a deeper relationship with her, especially when that pretense was his idea in the first place? It hurt.

No, wait, she told herself. It can't hurt. If it hurt, that meant he had gotten to her, gotten beneath her guard, and that couldn't have happened . . . could it? No, she decided without really deciding; she would not allow it to have happened. His reaction to her idea was an insult. That was it, plain and simple, and it rankled her.

"Oh for goodness sake," she snapped. She snatched back the ring from his hand to hold it between her thumb and forefinger. "They were two for $15.99, okay? It's not exactly the symbol of a lifelong commitment or anything."

"Actually, it is," he said softly. "It's a symbol for exactly that, no matter what it cost. Marriage is not something I have ever taken lightly, Georgia."

She looked up at him, unsure how to respond to his words, feeling scared and delighted and a tad peeved all at once.

"I can't wear this ring," he repeated.

Her lower lip quivered. She felt like a perfect fool, and a fool was a far more vulnerable thing than she ever wanted to be. She swallowed hard, but that action did not push down her anxiety. Somehow she found the composure to quietly say, "Well, if you won't wear it . . . "

"I didn't say I won't, Georgia. I can't wear this ring because I *can't* wear this ring." He pushed his ring finger forward until the band in her hand lodged just above his knuckle. "It's too small."

"Oh." This she could deal with. "Here. Let me see what I can do." She grabbed the ring, jerking and twisting at the same time.

"Uh, Georgia, that's my finger that ring is attached to."

"I know. Just let me try." She turned her body to gain leverage and began to work away at the thing. "Maybe we can stretch it out." Georgia twisted the ring harder.

"Ow!" Jett cried out, pulling his hand back in what must have been an instinctive reaction to her roughness.

The momentum of the two of them yanking with all their might in opposite directions took its toll as Georgia was thrown wildly off balance. The gravel crunched beneath her low-top sneakers, and her foot rolled to one side as wrenching pain shot up her leg, preventing her from stopping her backward motion.

Oomph. She landed squarely on her behind in a patch of lush weeds.

"You okay?" He rushed toward her.

"Got the ring." She held it aloft rather than admit she'd suffered any injury. "See? It stretched."

"You got it all right, but when you said you were going to stretch it out I thought you meant the ring, not my finger." He shook his left hand vigorously before holding it out to her.

Ignoring his silent offer of help, she closed one eye to peer at the ring. There was now a gap where it had once had an unsoldered seam. "Shows you how much you know. It worked."

"So it did." He took the ring, and apparently the hint that she would not need his aid, withdrawing his hand to slide the ring into place.

Pushing herself up, Georgia struggled to her feet. A faint but definite twinge of pain flashed in her right ankle, stopping her already awkward ascent mid-rise. Jett lunged forward, his large hands immediately under her arm.

"I'm all right. I just jiggled my ankle the wrong way a little. It would never have happened if I'd been wearing my cowboy boots."

She pulled her arm away from his gentle touch. "A little

rest while we drive on, and it will feel just like new."

Georgia started to stride back to the car. Though her steps were a bit uneven, she did all right until she made a reach for the door. Then her gait got out of rhythm, her ankle gave way, and she fell against the fender of the car with a quiet thud.

Apparently having learned his lesson, that she would not welcome any help from him, Jett strolled to his side of the car. He eyed her pose as she clutched the side mirror for support, one hand on the car hood. He clucked his tongue. He clawed his fingers back through the opaque mat of his darkly dyed hair, and a soft *scritch, scritch, scritch* accompanied his dry delivery as he nodded at her and said, "Yep, looks like that ankle is just like new already."

"Huh?"

"The way I see it, when your ankle was new, you were just a baby." He opened his door and, just before sliding into his seat, concluded, "You couldn't walk on it then any better than you can right now."

• • •

"You willing yet to admit your ankle hurts?"

Georgia would not give that man the satisfaction of responding the way he wanted. She hobbled through the crowd of people milling around the gift shop and vending machines at the front of Meramac Caverns, one of Route 66's first real tourist attractions and birthplace of the American icon, the bumper sticker. Behind her, Jett stopped at the cash register to pay for some trinkets he'd collected for his cousin's children.

Her shoulders were still hunched, her skin raised in gooseflesh after the perpetual coolness of the huge cave, and her sinuses were dripping from the dankness of the twenty-minute tour they'd just taken. Georgia trudged on, her eyes on the front door and her ankle throbbing. She only paused long enough to twist her neck so she could call out over her shoulder. "I'm fine. Really. Nothing to worry about. I'll just get back to the car now and elevate my foot for a minute—not that it needs anything therapeutic. I'm just being cautious."

Jett shook his head, his fingers buried in his hair just over his ear as he waited for his change. "Would it be so hard for you to take a little help from me?"

"I don't *need* any help—from anyone," she insisted, spinning around on her good foot to launch herself toward the exit.

"Here, allow me," Jett said softly, having crept swiftly up behind her to swing open the door.

Georgia halted. A family with one child in a stroller and another in a wheelchair moved past her through the door Jett held open. Then a gaggle of older women waltzed up, the front-runners of what looked like an endless stream of elderly people making their way from a chartered bus to the gift shop door. Georgia slipped out just before they reached the threshold, knowing they would keep Jett busy on door duty for a while.

One of the women pinched at her friend's short-sleeve knit top and whispered, "Doesn't that girl look familiar?"

Georgia's heartbeat picked up, and she limped as quickly as she could out to the front steps of the building.

Clamping her teeth together like a vise, she muttered to herself, "'See Meramac Caverns,' he says. It's all he talked about for the last hour. Every time he saw one of those black barns painted with a big ol' red-and-yellow sign for the place, he had to ask: 'Is your ankle strong enough?'"

She grabbed the wall and winced as she made her way along the edge of the simple building constructed over the opening to the cavern. "What was I supposed to say? 'No, I'd rather miss this classic sight, Jesse James's reputed hideout cave, because I'm a big baby and my ankle hurts'?"

Her flat-soled shoes shuffled over the edge of the top step as she gingerly tried to make her way to the car without drawing unwanted attention. She tugged at a curl of her wig, relishing the short-lived relief the movement gave her scalp. She'd had no idea a hairpiece would make her feel so claustrophobic . . . so . . .

"Wait up, Georgia!" Jett called out. "I can help you."

. . . so *agitated*, she concluded, though she suspected it was Jett and not the wig that had her feeling that way. The last thing she wanted on this trip was to find herself beholden to this man. She'd started out leading this expedition, and now she was limping along, barely able to contribute to the plan in any way. That did not bode well for the Double Heart.

"Georgia?"

"I do not require your help, thank you." She batted her hand over her shoulder and staggered onward.

"Whether you require it or not, you could certainly benefit from it. And I want to give it to you."

"No." Lunge. Shuffle. Lunge. "Thank you."

"Georgia!"

"I said, no, thank you." Shuffle. Lunge. Shuffle. She'd made it down the steps and now only had to navigate her way around the chartered bus that sat idling between the gift shop's entrance and the parking lot.

A handful of women in pull-on slacks and embroidered camp shirts waited while the last of their group struggled with an oversize handbag that had snagged on the open bus door.

If Georgia could just make it around the back of that bus,

she'd only need a few more shuffle-lunges, and perhaps a series of one-footed hops, to reach the car. Then she'd have the chance to sit and rest her aching ankle—and her battered ego, as well. Now if she could manage not to get hit by a car of frazzled vacationers . . .

She gritted her teeth. She drew in a deep breath of fresh air mixed with motor fumes coming from the long parking lot filled with travelers. She uttered a quick prayer that she could make it the rest of the way without falling flat on her face—or merely being flattened. "Please, Lord, just get me to the car. Please—"

"Stay right where you are. I'll be right there." It was not the voice of the Lord commanding her, but that of her persistent traveling companion.

"I said I don't need—"

Even Jett's thundering footsteps did not give her ample warning of what he had in mind. It wasn't until she felt his arm knock against the back of her knees and her feet literally lifting out from under her that she understood the man's intentions.

"Put me down!"

"Hang on."

"Put me down, I said." Despite her protest, her arms instinctively moved to wrap securely around his neck.

"Nope. Nothing doing. You can't walk on that ankle, so you'll just have to accept that I'm going to carry you."

She pressed her lips together, gearing up to howl out a crisp description of her feelings about that, but the hushed tittering of the nearby women made her breath stop in the back of her throat. From the corner of her eye she saw the women whispering and winking to one another. Obviously they thought they were witnesses to a lover's spat or . . . something.

Doesn't that girl look familiar? She bit her lip, recalling the words murmured just moments ago by another bus passenger. That memory, and the fact that Jett had actually cradled her in his arms, infused her plea with a quiet urgency. "I will not accept your carrying me. I am not a child. My ankle is fine. So put me down—now!"

Jett looked down into her face just inches from his own. "Why is it so hard for you to let somebody do something for you?"

Because I've never been able to depend on anyone to do that. That admission was still too dear, though, and came too close to revealing her weaknesses, for her to say aloud. Instead, she lowered her lashes in what she hoped showed smoldering defiance and turned the tables on him. "Oh that's rich, coming from a man who has other people to do everything for him."

"What is that supposed to mean?" He hefted her higher against his chest, securing his grip. When he did this, an approving giggle came from their audience as his reward. He ignored it, his entire focus on her. "Well?"

"It means just what it sounds like it means. As soon as we hit a little rough patch, you have to call your uncle-slash-lawyer to take care of things for you."

He scowled, displaying his confusion over that remark.

"And . . . and . . . " She had no real ammunition to aim at him, but she had to say something.

Georgia searched her mental list of the beefs she had with this man, most of which had disappeared as she spent time with him. Even as she tightened her grip around his neck and felt the beat of his heart quicken, she addressed the only real complaint she still had with this thoughtful, yet demanding man. "And you don't even buy those properties you profit from so you can build on them yourself. No, you grab them up to make them ready for someone else to do the real work."

"Ah, now I think we're getting a little closer to the marrow, aren't we? This is about the Double Heart Diner, isn't it?"

The mention of the diner plucked a chord in her, and she used that emotion to keep her from getting too comfortable in his arms.

"You were going to bulldoze—no, you were going to hire a crew to bulldoze the Double Heart Diner without so much as laying eyes on the place." Georgia ignored the prying eyes of the women who stood watching, mesmerized by their interchange. "What does that say about you, Jett Murphy?"

Jett ducked his head and started to walk toward the car, his fingers digging into her skin to keep his hold firm. "We'll talk about this in the car."

"We will talk about this when you put me down." She kicked her leg and made a pointed look at the black tar surface beneath them.

He leaned in close over her. "You are blowing our cover. This is not exactly how a honeymoon couple would act, now is it . . . *Lucy*?"

The Lucy reference got to her, and she settled down again, grudgingly.

"Your ankle is obviously the worse for wear from all that walking through the caverns, *dear*," he said loudly enough for the onlookers to hear. "Why don't you just let me carry you this last little bit, *sugarlips*?"

"Just put me down and I'll lean on your arm instead"—she clenched her teeth and gripped her fingers tightly into his taut shoulder, tacking on strictly for the benefit of the women watching—"*Honey dumpling*."

"Let him carry you, young lady," one of the women

called out. Her friends echoed their agreement.

"Yes, enjoy it while you can!" another offered. "You can walk on your own for the rest of your life. Might as well let him treat you like a bride now before the magic of the honeymoon fades and he starts yelling at you to hurry up or he's leaving without you!"

"Hear that?" Jett asked, his pleasure over her predicament shining in his eyes.

"Hear this," she shot back, too low for the others to understand. "I do not need your help. I do not want your help. I can take care of myself."

"And you hear this." His voice began hushed and amused but grew in volume and seriousness. "I may not have always done things for myself, but at least I've demonstrated an openness to change. And in case you haven't noticed, that's a lot more than you have done."

She swallowed hard at the on-target assessment.

"As for not doing anything, maybe you'll care to note that I am the one who has you in his arms. I didn't hire someone to come to your rescue on my behalf or consult an expert in the field of redheaded wildcat transport to do this job for me."

Now it wasn't just the chartered bus ladies staring at them. Whole families, some college kids, and people who worked on the premises stood gaping at Georgia, scooped up against Jett's chest. Even a few dogs—two on leashes, one in the back of a pickup truck with its tongue lolling out of its mouth—stared at them, as if waiting for Jett to sum up his tirade.

"Now if you'll just hold any criticisms of me and my way of doing business for a few minutes, *puddin' face,* I will show you that not only do I intend to continue this new, do-it-myself trend, I intend to carry you as long as you can't walk for yourself—even if it means I have to carry you all the way to Texas!"

He marched across the parking lot to the enthusiastic applause of most of the crowd, while Georgia felt a mix of panic, pride, anger . . . and something she could describe only as euphoria.

10

"So what's a nice girl like you doing in a place called Devil's Elbow?" Jett leaned back against the fender of the car while Georgia sat on the hood. They both looked out on the beautiful bluffs of the Big Piney River.

"Just another Route 66 roadie wanting to spend a little time with this piece of the past." She looped her arms over her raised knees and patted the toes of her shoes against the sun-warmed, blue metal hood.

"It's amazing, isn't it?"

"It is a gorgeous view, yes."

He shifted his gaze from the old steel truss bridge to the wonders of God's creation all around them. The air smelled of lush, green growth. The sky was dotted with billowy white clouds. At one time the peaceful serenity they now enjoyed would have been disturbed by the sounds of passing cars, radios blaring to be heard over the rush of the wind through the open windows—back in the days before air conditioning. If Jett closed his eyes and let his imagination run, the lure, the call of the open road, was still there. In years past it had been an invitation to progress and speed and excitement—to bigger, newer, better discoveries that lay around each new bend. Now, nearly deserted fragments of road, like the one that had brought them here, beckoned people back to a gentler time and urged quiet contemplation. With the interstate having been built around this stretch long ago, it now lay virtually undisturbed, except for visits by occasional Route 66 fans who sought it out.

In the distance Jett could make out the sound of the charter bus they encountered at Meramac Caverns. "You know, Georgia, I've been thinking about this whole Route 66 phenomenon. We've seen license plates from all over the country, and I swear back at the Jesse James Museum I heard people speaking German. I never realized how many people still sought out this old highway."

"Well, that's what happens when you don't get out of the old ivory tower now and then," she said in a faraway tone that echoed his own musings. She flicked a pale wisp of hair from her eyes. He still couldn't get used to seeing her as a blond, any more than he could get used to the almost constant itching of his scalp since his run-in with that irritating temporary dye. "At least back in my tower I could have washed this junk off my head."

Georgia's hand shot out to stop his arm before he could get in a really satisfying scratch. "No, you can't. You can't wash it out of your hair."

"You said I could. You said this stuff was temporary."

"You *can* wash it out; you just can't wash it out yet."

"I'd sure like to. My scalp is burning. My hair is dried out. It's driving me crazy."

"And you think this . . . this . . . thing is comfortable?" She put her hands on either side of her head and wobbled the wig back and forth. "We both have to make a sacrifice for the greater good."

"The greater good being saving your diner?"

"It's not *my* diner."

He tipped his head in a half-nod of agreement.

"But it is *your* deal." She wagged a finger at him. "And your reputation on the line. Me? All I stand to lose in this proposition is a dream and the last few slivers of my faith in humankind."

"Oh that's all."

She laughed. "Yet I'm willing to put up with a few hours of hot head in order to—"

"Did you just call me a hothead?"

She pried up the front of her wig just a smidgen to allow a little air circulation. "No, I'm the one with a hot head."

"Can I get you to sign an affidavit attesting to that? It might come in handy the next time one of your harebrained schemes gets us into an embarrassing fix."

The chartered bus, which just moments ago had rolled to a stop not far from them, let out a kind of mechanical sigh. The doors whooshed open, and the troop of older people they'd encountered at the caverns came spilling out.

"We'd better get going." Georgia scooted around to swing her legs off the edge of the car. "Before we have to play the happy honeymooners all over again."

"We wouldn't want that, would we?" He took her hand to help her down, whether she wanted him to or not.

She fell forward, but he caught her and steadily controlled her drop, allowing her to fall slowly until both her feet found the ground. Looking up at him, she wet her lips. "No, we wouldn't want that at all."

"Oh look, Elmira! It's the newlyweds!" one older lady cried.

"Who?" Another woman looked in the wrong direction.

"The newlyweds, Elmira. The ones we saw before. Remember, he said he was going to carry her all the way to Texas!"

"Oh!" The woman named Elmira, the one who had

advised Georgia to let Jett carry her, turned toward them and waved enthusiastically with both hands. "Yoo-hoo, newly-weds! Remember us?"

Jett gave a stiff wave.

Georgia offered the kind of greeting given by the Queen of England . . . from the back of a carriage . . . on a rainy day . . . only less enthusiastic. "Hi."

"We're just leaving now," Jett called to them, bundling Georgia into the passenger side of the car with swift efficiency. "Nice to see you again."

When he dropped into the seat and started the engine, Georgia asked, "You don't think their recognizing us will cause a problem, do you?"

"Yeah, I think we are going to get in a high-speed chase with a busload of sightseeing senior citizens. Maybe we can post some 'five-family yard sale' and 'early-bird special' signs as decoys along the way, to slow them down."

"Quit kidding."

"Okay. All kidding aside." He pulled the car around and headed back the way they had come, toward the interstate. "I really do not think that anyone cares about us or Campbell's accusations or our razzle-dazzle road show. I think that last night when we saw ourselves on that newscast in a strange city, we overreacted, as anyone would. I think that in the light of day, it seems excessive to even worry about it."

"You really think that?"

"I do and I'm going to prove it."

"How?"

"How far is it to Tulsa?"

"What's that got to do with—"

"How far, in hours?"

"Probably four."

"Hmmm. I don't think I can last that long." He scoured

his scalp with his curled fingers. "These mega truck stops along the way—some of them advertise that they have showers, don't they?"

"Yes. Some do. The really big ones. Why?"

"Just to show you how confident I am that no one is looking for us or will so much as notice us along the way . . . "

"What? What?"

"The very next big truck stop we come to, I'm going to wash as much of this stuff out of my hair as I can."

• • •

Georgia checked the door of the truckers' complex. She checked her watch. Then she checked the door again. She groaned her discontent from between her teeth, then repeated the ritual she had gone through at least ten times in the last thirty-five minutes.

How long could this simple hair-washing procedure take? For a moment she considered storming through those doors, past the snacks and souvenirs, magazines, cassette-tape displays, and automotive supplies, straight into those truckers' showers and—

She blinked. Well, even she wasn't that impulsive. She was almost, *almost*, that impatient, though, and the heat of the afternoon rebounding up in waves from the concrete parking lot didn't help her restless disposition.

Jett had chosen this place for its obvious amenities, but also because it looked like a good place for her to grab a soda, book, and snack to occupy her while she waited for him to take care of his hair. To Georgia, it looked like a good place to get seen by as many people as possible in one setting. Stopping there was not exactly the wisest action for anyone trying to conceal his or her identity. But then, neither was Jett's washing the dye out of his hair.

Wasn't that just like the rich and powerful? And Jett Murphy in particular! Having grown so accustomed to always having the best, and having it at his convenience, had spoiled him. Personal sacrifice was not a part of the picture for a man like this. Better just to let his uncle do a little— what had he called it, *damage control?*—than to suffer a little for a cause.

Well, she was made of sterner stuff than that, and she'd prove it. No matter how hot, how claustrophobic, how ridiculous her wig made her feel, she wouldn't give it up for something so fleeting as comfort. She'd play this out until the end or until there was no more hope that the situation would work out.

That's the kind of person she was: strong and determined. Her lower lip quivered and warm tears gathered on the rims of her sleep-deprived eyes. She was strong, she told herself. Stronger than a man like Jett could understand, and she'd show him that too. As soon as he showed up again, she'd confront him about his wishy-washy approach to the plan she'd recommended.

Georgia pushed down on the mesh and curls on her head as if pressing a ball cap low over her eyes. She laid aside the paperback she'd bought and stuffed the last of her chips, an empty soda can, and a candy wrapper into the paper bag she'd carried from the store. She scrunched down low in her seat and dared to peer out at her surroundings.

Sunlight glinted off the chrome-on-chrome of the eighteen-wheelers and flashed off the windshields of cars rolling past. The smell of diesel filled the air. The large, low building, painted white with blue-and-red trim, had signs in the tinted window promising lottery tickets, live bait, and home cookin'.

She checked her watch again, then took one more look

at the door. Just then it swung open and Jett Murphy stepped across the threshold. Her heartbeat leapt in her veins at the very sight of him with the afternoon sun highlighting the width of his shoulders and glinting off the silver crown of his gorgeous hair.

The dye she had so carefully selected promised it would slowly fade away with five or six washings. Jett must have scrubbed at his scalp like crazy until every last drop of the stuff—every semblance of his cunningly crafted disguise—had gone down the drain.

A slash of light cut across her face as sunlight reflected off the window of a passing car, creating the effect of a flash-bulb as the realization hit her: Jett had not only rid himself of every semblance of the disguise she had concocted, he had gone in that complex to systematically remove all traces of the help she had so cleverly given him. Swish. Glug, glug. Gone.

She felt like such a fool for not having realized it before. Everything this man did told her she could not slowly win him over. Despite his bold claims of being open to change, those changes never seemed to be in her favor or in accordance with her suggestions. This did not bode well for the diner or her efforts to get him to think differently about it. It did even less for the feelings she had been fighting against all day. This man was with her because it suited his design, not because he was open to her cause—or to her, personally.

Gulping down her explosive emotions, she scrambled out of the car, slung open the back door, and crawled inside on her hands and knees. With one swipe, she nabbed the "Just Married" poster Jett had thought would provide them the perfect cover. With that sign in her fist, she backed out, slammed the door, and came around to stand by the trunk of the car and wait for him.

The waffling sound the poster board made against her legs and the growls of passing engines made it impossible for her to hear whatever Jett shouted her way. Whether from the pumping of her adrenaline or thanks to the last two hours of rest, Georgia found her ankle no longer hurt. See, she told herself, she was strong and she did not need Jett's help. He, however, still needed hers.

She waved the poster board, brandishing it for him to read as he came up to her. She jutted her chin out. Her throat felt tight, but she still managed to speak. "It's because I thought of it, isn't it?"

His forehead furrowed. "What?"

"If you had hired me to come up with a part of the plan, if you could order me around and feel I was working for you, then you'd feel different about it, wouldn't you?"

"That would be different, of course, but—"

"Aha! I knew it." She slapped the poster to her side. "I knew it. You never wanted a partnership in this."

"That's not true, Georgia."

"Ha! Then why did you have to stop the whole trip just to negate—no, to totally *obliterate* my contribution to the plan? Tell me that, Mr. C-E-Oh-I-know-everything?"

"Slow down, Georgia." He held his hands up. "You're making my head spin."

"Oh-ho-ho, don't tempt me, Murphy."

He laughed. "Has anyone ever told you how beautiful you are when you're angry?"

"You think I'm beautiful now?"

"Yes, I do." He put his hand on her shoulder. Warmth radiated from the spot where his hand rested, but she would not give in to the soothing feeling.

"Well, if my anger makes you think I'm pretty, then you're going to think I'm a candidate for Miss Universe in a minute if you don't stop trying to change the subject."

He put his other hand on her other shoulder. "How can I change the subject when I have no idea what we are talking about?"

She held her breath, partly to fend off her reaction to his touch and partly to gather her thoughts. Did he really not know the meaning of what he'd done? How could he not? It seemed so clear to her. She lifted her chin as a visual aid to demonstrate her confidence in her conclusion.

"The subject—" somehow she managed to murmur, despite her heightened awareness of his nearness. "The subject is how you, by washing the dye out of your hair, completely did away with my part in our diversionary plan."

"I did?"

"Yes. You washed that dye out to rid yourself of my most important contribution to our success."

He adjusted his grip on her shoulders. "I washed that dye out because it itched."

"But—"

"I kept the ring on, you'll notice."

She glanced down. The inexpensive token, still stretched in a shape that hinted more at an oval than a perfect circle, remained on the ring finger of his left hand.

"And just for the record?" He stepped closer.

"Yes?"

"Your idea to dye my hair was not the most important contribution you have made to this crazy little entanglement of ours."

"It's not?"

"Not by a long shot." He moved closer still.

"Really?" She swallowed hard.

"Really," he responded in a conspiratorial whisper. "You've made a lot of contributions, including your unique insights, your even more unique transportation—"

She smiled at the mention of good ol' Truvie, which one of Jett's workers was even now driving toward Texas.

"Not to mention your quick thinking, your knowledge of the road—"

"And my boots."

"Oh we mustn't forget your boots."

"No," she whispered.

Whether it was something in her eyes or the catch in her voice, or perhaps the way her mouth lingered over the single word, Jett must have seen an invitation to proceed. He put his arms around her and drew her to him.

A lock of her fake hair fell into her eyes. He raised his hand to sweep it away, pushing it back with the other curls that clung to her temple and cheek. Georgia pursed her lips. Jett looked as if he wanted to say something but could not find the words. He moved his hand back to cradle her head.

Georgia felt a tug.

The gap of his ring had snagged in the coils of her synthetic hair. He tried to pull his hand free, his gaze still fixed on hers. She jerked her head to one side, hoping to jar the ring loose. The wig slid lopsided on her head. Jett started to struggle to free his ring but, proving that this was still a give-and-take partnership, Georgia intervened. Raising her hand, she whisked the wig away in one swoop, letting the poster she'd been holding fall against their legs. Jett easily pulled his hand away, capturing a few strands of phony hair in the process.

Georgia did not move away from him, but simply shook her head to unleash her natural curls.

"I like you better as a redhead," Jett murmured, just before he closed the final distance between them.

The kiss was chaste, yet infused with the promise of a

passion that lay beneath it. Georgia surrendered herself to it without thinking, giving herself over to the trust a woman must have for a man to allow him this kind of nearness.

The kiss did not last long, but she thought she would remember its impact for a lifetime. It was over as quickly as the flashes of sunlight bouncing off passing cars, and when she and Jett stepped away from one another, they both knew one truth.

Georgia knew it in her heart and she could see it in Jett's eyes. No matter what happened from this point on, neither of them would ever be able to go back to just being business partners. That kiss, fleeting as it was, had changed everything.

11

Are you sure we have time for this?" Georgia called out to Jett from her spot on the grassy grounds surrounding the Will Rogers Memorial building. The fierce wind whipped at her hair, tossing red curls with wild abandon.

Jett, who had stopped to turn and wait for her as she dawdled over the butterfly gardens, smiled at the sight. He inhaled the fresh summer air, raised his face to let the sunshine warm it, and offered a silent prayer of gratitude.

Thank you, Lord, for this good day. For this chance to see beyond my usual limited experiences. Thank you for the goodness of your gift of life, for good people, and most of all, for Georgia. No matter what happens from here on out, I will not regret having met her. Thank you for that opportunity.

"Hey!" Georgia reached his side and placed her hand on his arm. "Did you hear me? Are you sure we have this kind of time?"

He gazed into those trusting eyes glittering with happiness and nodded. "I'm sure."

"We still have to pick up your uncle at the Tulsa airport at six," she reminded him.

"Yes, but we saved quite a bit of time by taking Interstate 44 to bypass the Kansas corner Route 66 used to run through."

She started to say something, but he raised a finger to barely tap the tip of her nose and said, "I know. We cheated. We missed Graffiti Bridge. And even I am more than a little sad at not seeing Murphy's Restaurant. But we'll make up for it by spending a few more minutes here and going through Catoosa later so we can drive by that Blue Whale Amusement Park you were so intent on my seeing."

His argument swayed her. Or perhaps, he thought as his chest puffed up with a bit of masculine pride, she was still so affected by his kiss she didn't have the starch to argue with him anymore.

Whatever the reason, she pursed her lips, shook her head, then sighed. She extended her hand toward the entrance. "Then let's not waste any more valuable time gabbing."

"Time spent with you is never a waste, Georgia." He stepped up and pulled open the door for her. "In fact, I'd say I've learned more in the last twenty-eight hours I've spent with you than I did all year on my own." He caught her fresh scent as she passed.

"Really?" Her eyes shone, but there was a set skepticism around her mouth. "Like what?"

"Like the importance of getting out and seeing things for myself before I make a decision that will affect a lot of people."

The lines around her mouth softened.

"Like maybe I'm not as pleased as I thought I was with the way I've conducted my business and my life."

Her lips parted in what he could only describe as stunned awe.

This was getting too serious, he thought. If he didn't stop now he'd stand right here and confess the true depths of his emotions for her—even before he knew for certain what they were. If there was one other thing his time with Georgia had taught him, it was not to rush headlong into anything. He propelled her inside with his hand on her back and followed behind her. The door fell shut with a swoosh of air and a thump.

"I also learned in my time with you, Miss Darling . . . "

"Yes?" She turned those enormous, hope-filled, green eyes on him.

His heart melted. But since his mind had not turned to jelly too, he did manage to lower his head, grin like a rogue, and growl out, "I learned to duck, dodge, and just plain stay out of your way when that wacky redheaded enthusiasm of yours kicks in."

"Very funny." She tipped her nose up and flounced on ahead of him. "Maybe instead of dying your hair we should have just stuck a hard hat on your head. That way we'd cover the gray *and* protect against any damage I might inflict on you."

"Hmmm. Not a bad idea. Where do you think I could get a hard hat?"

"Don't worry. I think your head is thick enough to protect you."

Yeah, he thought, but was his heart as well guarded? Or would the lessons he'd learned in his time with Georgia Darling leave scars that would last a lifetime?

• • •

They'd walked the length of the large memorial museum, read the clips, and studied the exhibits in record time, mindful of their pressing schedule. At the end, Georgia held back a moment to catch her breath and collect her thoughts.

Since he'd kissed her, Jett had seemed awfully quiet—reticent almost, but at times animated and anxious. He acted . . . confused. Or maybe that's how he had been acting the whole trip and . . . maybe *she* was confused. She sighed.

Less than two days—that's as long as she'd known him. She'd known *of* him longer than that. But that knowledge included little more than the public bio of her company's CEO and, of course, her own assumptions about him based on his business dealings surrounding the Double Heart. But she'd known the real man such a short time. How, then, could she feel as strongly as she did toward him? She just wasn't the kind of woman to feel this way so quickly about a man.

What way? Her mind demanded an answer she did not have. She cared for Jett; she knew that much. Yet, with the unfinished business of the diner still between them, she just didn't see how it could progress beyond caring—or if it should progress at all.

She shut her eyes as if that could shut out the chaos of her thoughts and emotions. When she opened them again, she saw Jett standing by a display, his hand covering the lower half of his handsome face. The sight of him made her heart leap with the expectation of sharing the day with him, and at the same time it began to ache for all that could not be.

It was going to be a long trip to Texas, she thought. She plastered on a cheery smile, tucked her hands in her pockets to appear relaxed and casual, and strolled back over to Jett's side.

"What are you looking at?" She cocked her head.

"This display on the death of Will Rogers." Jett leaned in to read from the information placard. "Did you know he died in an airplane crash in Alaska with his friend—a famous pilot of the day—Wiley Post?"

"Hmmm. I vaguely recall learning something about that. I did a book report on Rogers in grade school. I don't remember any of the details though." She was making small talk, she knew. But if it helped her avoid her own feelings—the smaller the talk, the better.

"It amazes me." He shook his head. "I just don't know if I get this."

"What?"

"All of it. I just keeping marveling over the things we've seen on this trip—"

"Oh I thought you meant you didn't get something about Will Rogers."

"Well, that too." He shifted his feet on the cool floor. "I have to wonder about him when I read about this plane crash. What kind of man does that? Assumes that kind of implied risk when it isn't necessary?"

The question went far deeper than the idle chatter she'd hoped would occupy them. He was getting at something, and Georgia suspected that she had best let him work it out without trying to define it for him. "I'm not sure what you're saying."

"Well, look here: This was a man who could travel the world in the very best of transportation. Why hop in a little plane and take off for Alaska with a pal?"

"I'm sure he had his reasons."

"But why? Why do it at all when he could have just stayed home and been safe?" Jett shook his head. "You know, that's the kind of thing that I find myself asking as we drive along these pieces of Route 66. What compels that sort of behavior? What obliged a family back in the 1960s to pile into an un-air-conditioned station wagon, take off to see the country, and spend their hard-earned money at tacky road-side attractions? Why not stay home and send the kids off to camp instead? It would surely cut down on a lot of hassle and aggravation, not to mention the torture of hearing 'Are we there yet?' eight thousand times."

"I'd have given anything for a family to share a station wagon with, aggravation and all," she heard herself murmur before she could censor her gut response to the imagery Jett's tirade conjured up.

He looked at her hard, as if his speculative thoughts might now turn to her.

She gave an overplayed shrug and an underconvincing laugh. "So sue me. I happen to like roadside attractions, the tackier the better."

He grinned. "I'd be lying if I said that surprised me about you."

"I'm taking that as a compliment," she warned him.

"I meant it as one."

Her smile warmed with real sentiment.

He turned his head as if scanning their surroundings. "And that begs another question."

"'Where are the rest rooms?'"

He chuckled. "No. Where did all these people come from? Why did they come? Wherever we have stopped along the way, we've seen people who have purposely made the trek to these often way-out-of-the-way places. The guest books are full of names of people from all over America and even other parts of the world. Why do they do it?"

"It's a little bit of history. It's interesting. It makes a person feel something."

"Like what?"

Georgia shrugged. "I think it's a little different for everyone."

Jett thought about that for a moment. "But why do they go to these great lengths? Aren't there books and videos on the subject that cover it far better than most people can by trudging along on their own?"

"They want to *connect.*" Knowing this was the thing Jett needed to do himself made her emphasize the last word more than she might normally have done.

"With what?"

"With their memories, maybe. With their families. With the country's history and a kinder, more innocent time. With their sense of whimsy, with life, with each other"—she reached out to take his hand—"with themselves."

Jett's gaze sank into hers. His jaw tightened.

He wanted to understand what she was saying; she saw it in his eyes. He needed to understand it; she felt that in her heart.

She wet her lips and moved closer to him, her voice soft and intense, evoking an emotional, not physical, intimacy. "Some people see an expanse of highway as a metaphor for life. A lot of folks feel that way about the Mother Road. Surely you can see that: the seeking, the freedom—the longing to find for yourself what lies beyond your own safe little corner of the world."

He nodded. "There is something very special about this old road, isn't there? Something that's hard to put into words."

She gave his hand a squeeze. "Maybe you *can't* put it into words." He looked away, then directly into her eyes again. "But you feel it, don't you? You just get out here and drive and see these places and meet these people and you feel it. You do feel it, don't you, Jett?"

At those last words, his wistful expression shifted to one of impishness. "Aren't you supposed to read me my rights first?"

"Huh?"

"Hey, you think I don't realize this is one of those times when anything I say can and will be used against me in the court of private opinion?" He stroked her cheek with the side of his thumb. "If I start waxing nostalgic about the warm, fuzzy feelings this experience is giving me, I know it will come back to haunt me. Admit it, I'll find my words thrown back at me when we get to the diner."

"Well, 'thrown back' is harsh—"

"Okay, let's just say I'll find them sensitively repeated for my benefit. And yours." He wasn't angry. In fact, he seemed quite pleased with his deduction, and more than happy to tease her about it. "I'd expect you to use my own sentimental jabbering to gradually wear me down, then wheedle me into buying, renovating, and promoting the diner before sending the deed back to the current owner—all as an homage to the Mother Road and the lessons I learned on it. Am I right . . . Lucy?"

"Well, maybe you wouldn't have to send the deed . . . "

"Oh?"

"No. You'd probably want to make a magnanimous gesture like that in person."

He roared out a laugh.

She joined him, but with less fervor. She hadn't been kidding . . . not entirely. She did hope for some kind of sentimental or emotional connection that would reach Jett—one that would elicit from him a truly kind and decent act, for his own good and not just for the salvation of the diner. She prayed for him to start taking his life and business into his own hands, and to choose to do the right thing with both of them. That he could react to her suggestion with good humor, when just yesterday his temper would have flared at the very notion, gave her hope.

As his laughter died down, he wrapped his arms around Georgia and gave her a quick hug. "Okay, but until all that happens, why don't you tell me how you feel?"

"I feel fine," she muttered, though that was not the whole truth.

"That's nice. But I meant, tell me how you feel about the Double Heart Diner." He lifted her chin with one crooked finger and said in a deep, earnest tone, "Tell me about it and help me understand."

"We don't have time to stand here while I carry on about that." Georgia had to buy time, rebuild her defenses so that when she told Jett how she felt about the diner and Starla Mae and her experiences there, the telling would come from a point of strength, not from a whirlwind of emotional turmoil. "Why don't we get back on our way? When we're in the car, I'll try to explain it so even you can understand."

"Does that mean you'll use only small, simple words?" Pressing his hand to her back, he guided her toward the car.

"If that's what it takes. If necessary, I'll resort to charades or perhaps a short skit with sock puppets." She crinkled her nose at him, enjoying his infectious humor. "Okay?"

"Just so you get the message across. I really do want to understand the draw this place has for you. I want to know as much as I can about it before I get there—before I make my final decision."

● ● ●

Jett scanned the road ahead until he spotted the "Welcome" sign for Catoosa, Oklahoma.

Georgia had hardly spoken a word since they'd left Claremore. She explained her quiet by saying she was gathering her thoughts. And besides, she'd gone on to say, there was something she wanted him to see before she tried to explain her feelings about the Double Heart and others of its disappearing breed.

"That's it," Georgia whispered. "We're coming to the place I wanted you to see."

There, to their right, they saw a sign that read: "The Blue Whale Amusement Park."

"Pull over." She waved her hand frantically.

"But it's all broken-down and covered with vines, Georgia." He let the car roll slowly along, coasting up on the sight. "There's nothing for us to see here."

"Pull over, please? Just for a minute?"

"The sign says 'Keep Out or Eat Lead.'" From the safety of the now-halted but still-running car, Jett surveyed the decaying one-time tourist attraction.

His gaze roamed over a swampy pool of water choked by thick, green slime—stagnant yet alive with swarms of tiny bugs flying low to the water's surface. At the edge of the pond a large metal whale stood grinning, its open mouth once a play area or entrance of some kind.

With some imagination, he supposed, he could visualize scads of kids in '60s-style swimsuits, the girls' heads covered with those awful rubber swim caps, the boys with nothing more than the stubbled hair of a summer crew cut. He could picture them romping around the whale's mouth, diving from or lying on its back, and shooting down the slide jutting out of its side. He could hear them hollering, "Look at me! Look at me!" to big-bellied dads in Bermuda shorts and moms in matching shorts and top sets. He could all but smell the mingling of pond water with the suntan lotion that clung to their sunburned little bodies. In his mind's eye he watched as fathers carried back to the car little ones clutching giant-size pencils and back scratchers imprinted with the words "Blue Whale Amusement Park"—mementos of the day's fun.

Now the place lay in ruins. He blinked to make himself see it as it was now. One bulbous eye leered out at them from the faded blue form, and its jagged teeth—once white, he assumed—gave the poor old whale a maniacal appearance, which both compelled and repelled Jett.

"Eerie, isn't it?" Georgia asked.

Jett eyed a replica of an ark, its faded hull with a neat row of porthole-style windows along the side—once an oasis of cool diversion from the heat of summer travel, now seemingly cast adrift in a sea of weeds. He imagined the building probably had once rung with the cries of families: *Dad can I have a . . . ? Mom, did you see this? You kids go now because we're not stopping again until we get to . . .*

"Creepy—but somehow intriguing. You can almost see it as it was, but then how it *is* intrudes. It's . . . well, creepy." He glanced at the quiet area around them. "Who'd have ever thought that something like this was out here in the middle of nowhere?"

"It didn't used to be in the middle of nowhere, Jett. It used to be in the heartland of America."

"What happened?" he muttered.

"The interstate. More lanes, faster cars, affordable air travel, turnpikes, time." She shrugged. "The same thing that happened to this park happened to a lot of really amazing places after they decommissioned the Mother Road. Motels that are examples of bygone architecture are crumbling. Restaurants with personal service, silly slogans, and hearty food have been replaced by fast-food places. The Buffalo Ranch at Afton is gone now, as are so many others."

He set his jaw. "I thought there were people intent on preserving things like this."

"Some societies and associations are trying to do what they can. But loosely organized individuals lack the kind of financial backing they need to compete with developers and the realities of economic survival. How can they ever hope to make the kind of impact this calls for?"

"Okay, okay. Thank you, Ghost of Mother Road Past. I

get it. This is what you're fighting for by trying to save the Double Heart Diner." Jett put the car back in gear and started on, noting another abandoned site: a former "trading post" that had once prospered along the side of the road. "So the little guy doesn't stand a chance against the big guy. That much I knew already. Tell me something I don't know. Tell me why you're not asking me to throw my money at this place," he nodded out the window, "or at the Buffalo Ranch. Why does it have to be the Double Heart Diner? Why is that place the one you want me to save?"

Her gaze dropped to her lap, then she looked at him, her eyes softened by the glimmer of unshed tears between thick lashes. Her voice was quiet but strong. "They say that if you've lost your love or lost your way, you will find it again at the Double Heart Diner."

"Oh?"

"That's local lore." She folded her arms. "And just plain fact for me."

He sat up straight, leaning against the stiff upholstery behind his back, and fixed his gaze on the long, narrow road. "Tell me about it."

"I'm not sure where to begin."

"Why not begin where it all began for you?" he suggested. "Did your parents take you to the Double Heart Diner as a kid?"

She shook her head and did not look at him. "I don't have parents. That is, I did, but . . . "

Jett looked over and encouraged her with a brief touch to her cheek.

"My mother died when I was three. I don't really remember her, except for a cozy, safe feeling I get whenever I smell White Shoulders perfume."

"Georgia, I didn't know."

"How could you?" She shrugged. "My father tried his best to take care of me for a time, but he just couldn't do it. He left me with my grandparents and told me he'd be back for me as soon as he got a good job and a nice place for us to live. Once he got those, he wrote to tell me he couldn't afford to support me, but that he'd come home for visits whenever he could."

She told her story as though she were summing up someone else's life. But maintaining that level of composure and dignity took every ounce of character and stubbornness in that petite body, Jett could tell.

"Let me guess," he said, hoping to spare her from speaking the worst of it aloud. "Your father never did come for those visits?"

She shook her head. Her gaze locked ahead. "My grandparents did the best they could, I suppose, until their health began to fail and they put me in temporary foster care . . . "

" . . . that wasn't really temporary?" he surmised.

"It was temporary inasmuch as it was over when I turned eighteen." She clenched her jaw and swallowed so hard he could see the movement in her throat. She blinked away the tears that threatened to fall, then blew out a long blast of air between her lips. Straightening, she shook back her hair and smiled tremulously, still not directing her attention to him. "Anyway, I spent a lot of time watching TV and feeling like an outcast, even though my foster families were pretty nice."

"Is that when you found your affinity for Lucy Ricardo?"

She laughed. "Yes. They had reruns after school, and I guess I felt like I'd found my role model."

Her laughter broke over him like the dawn after a bleak night, and he welcomed it.

She shifted in her seat and, looking much less fragile than she had even a moment ago, faced him. "So about the time I was sixteen, I realized that if I ever wanted anything, I'd have to get it for myself—the way Lucy would. So I started looking for a job."

"Don't tell me you applied at a chocolate factory?" he teased, referring to a classic *Lucy* episode.

"Good one, but no. I didn't."

"You got a job at the Double Heart then?"

"Close, but I'll have to send you back a couple of spaces for making a wrong guess anyway. Thanks for playing."

"You mean you weren't a waitress at the Double Heart?"

"I applied there, but Starla Mae—Starla Mae Jenkins, who was then and still is the owner—wouldn't just give me the job. She insisted on speaking with my foster parents, caseworker, and teachers first."

"You're kidding."

"Hey, as a guy who takes his own business seriously, I'd have thought that would appeal to you."

"I guess when you put it that way . . . Maybe if she loses the diner I can find a job for Miss Jenkins running my personnel department."

She gave him a look that announced her determination to ignore even the possibility of that happening. "Starla Mae is good people, as we say in Texas. I think she sensed something about me and my 'problems.'" She paused to bracket the word with quotation marks slashed into the air with her fingers, as if to communicate she had no real deep-seated psychological problems he needed to consider. "Starla Mae wanted to tackle any difficulties right from the git-go."

"I see."

"Anyway, after she talked to all those people, Starla Mae flat-out refused to let me take a job waitressing in the diner. Refused!" Georgia shook her head as if she still could not believe the other woman's nerve. "But what she did do was

tell me to come around after school so I could do my home-
work in a quiet booth at the back. I didn't know it then, but
it was her way of looking out for me—of making sure I used
my head and got to college, rather than spending my whole
life on my feet, working for minimum wage and tips."

"That was nice."

"It was more than nice." She looked away again. "It was
the first time anyone seemed to really want me around, and
when she said I could come by every day, she meant it. For
two years I did exactly that, and she never once changed the
rules on me or went back on her word."

"So the diner became like a second home to you?"

"Well, I never considered myself someone who had a
first home. Maybe that's why it was so easy for me to pull
up roots and go to Chicago like I did—and why when I
started realizing that the diner was the only home I ever
knew and it was in jeopardy, it was so easy for me to resign
and leave again."

Jett had nothing to say to that. He had come to treasure
this woman, yet his plans threatened the only place where
she had ever felt wanted. Short of something utterly foolish,
what could a person say at a time like this?

"When my grades got good enough, Starla Mae let me
start waitressing. I was seventeen then, and I worked there
weekends and summers until I graduated from college. I owe
a lot to Starla Mae and the diner. She expected a lot of me.
She may look kind of kooky, but she really is one sharp lady.
She saw something in me that she knew could be developed.
After a while, she noticed my natural affinity for numbers.
She asked me to help her out with the books."

"She did?"

"By the time I was eighteen, I was getting paid to help
with the accounting as well as my waitressing, and I got

overtime for helping with taxes and inventory records and things like that."

"So you know firsthand what kind of revenue this place is capable of producing—or losing?"

Georgia stared at him a moment as if to tell him she was on to his game. "That was a long time ago," she muttered. "And my point is that I know what kind of good things this place is capable of generating because I am one of them."

He nodded.

"Starla Mae convinced some local people to write recommendations for me so I could get into college. My job at the diner and some grants paid my way through, often because I got tipped a little more than most waitresses would have somewhere else. That's the kind of patrons this place has. A minister and his wife who ate there every Sunday brought me into their church, and that helped keep me from being bitter or cynical about my situation. That adage about the diner certainly proved true for me, as I feel it must have for many other people. I did find my way at the Double Heart Diner, Jett, and it will just plain break my heart if *you* tear it down."

12

*T*hat's your Uncle Lou?" Georgia tried not to gape like a flounder at the stubby-legged man with the rolling gait.

"Yep. That's him. My father's only brother." Jett raised his hand to draw the man's attention.

"*He* is a lawyer?" She tilted her head as if looking at a computer-generated 3-D picture. Surely if she could just get her eyes to focus at the right angle or depth, the conglomeration of colors and patterns would merge to form one whole, cohesive image. "A lawyer who dresses like that?"

"Yep. Sean Louis Murphy: attorney-at-law by day, supermodel by night."

The man paused, trapped behind a couple herding a toddler and trying to juggle far too much carry-on luggage. He took advantage of that time to straighten his white straw hat, the kind Georgia had seen golfers on TV wear. The diamond in his heavy gold ring flashed, and the bold links of his bracelet fell half inside, half outside his blue, maroon, and orange striped sweater. His pale yellow polo shirt bunched at the collar until he lowered his arm and poked his hand in the pocket of his blue, maroon, and *green* checkered pants.

"Don't let the outfit fool you." Jett patted her back to assuage her doubts. "He's actually a very good lawyer."

"Then he should sue the guy who sold him that outfit."

169

She blinked her bleary eyes at the kaleidoscope of colors.

"I'll suggest that to him."

"Don't you dare." She seized his arm to hold him back. "I want to make a nice first impression on your uncle."

"You mean a nice *second* impression, to follow the one you made by writing that resignation letter calling his favorite nephew all kinds of names?"

Her throat closed. "He knows about that?"

"Sure." Jett laughed. "Does it matter?"

"Of course it does. This is the first time I've met any of your family, after all, and I want them to like me—" She cut herself off. She'd given away too much, assumed too much, said too much. It would take some creativity to back-pedal out of this without resorting to a bald-faced lie.

Fortunately for her, creativity was not a problem. "Sure, I want your uncle to like me. This is the man who is putting together the diner deal, after all, isn't it?"

Jett frowned at her.

Georgia laughed lightly and walked past him, heading in Lou's direction. Twisting her head, she said just loudly enough for Jett to hear her, "Besides, if all else fails, I may need to borrow some clothes from this man to create a new costume. He seems like a pretty good resource."

"Sure, if you want to escape disguised as a rodeo clown." Jett paused and held up his hand, his eyes dancing with amusement. "Oh wait, look who I'm talking to. I have a feeling you and Lou will get along just fine."

The couple in front of Jett's uncle finally collected their child and bags and moved on.

Georgia straightened her backbone and swiped her damp palm over her shirt sleeve, ready to greet Lou Murphy with a confident handshake.

"Hold on a second, Georgia." Jett's hand clamped down

on her shoulder. He did not try to physically restrain her, but the quiet urgency of his tone and touch made her hesitate, then turn to face him.

"What is it, Jett? Something wrong?"

"No, I just wanted to tell you something before either of us starts talking to my Uncle Lou."

"My, you look awfully serious." Her stomach clenched. She had said too much earlier. Her statement about meeting his family and announcement of her wish that Lou would like her had put Jett on the defensive. He wanted to put her in her place, to let her know that kiss or no kiss, theirs was still just a business partnership. The kiss had changed everything for her, but she could tell by the way he'd grown quieter with every mile since the Blue Whale that he was having second thoughts, withdrawing.

She squared her shoulders and anchored her feet, ready for the worst. "What do you want to tell me, Jett?"

"Everything," he whispered.

She blinked, trying to comprehend what he meant by that, even as her pulse quickened at his tender tone and expression.

"But the thing I need for you to know right now . . . "

She held her breath. It could be anything.

"The thing you need to know before Uncle Lou does, is that I've decided to drop this whole deal. The Double Heart Diner is safe."

* * *

"The Double Heart Diner is dog meat."

"Uncle Lou! You couldn't think of a better analogy for a diner than dog meat?" Jett tossed down the newspaper containing Rod Campbell's latest column, which his uncle had brought from Chicago.

"It's not that bad, is it?" Georgia snatched up the paper,

folded into quarters so that Campbell's picture smirked directly out at them. "Just a lot of sarcasm and speculation. He doesn't say anything about the diner. He doesn't say anything that gives away the details of the deal."

"He makes it pretty clear there is a deal." Jett tapped the paper.

"But obviously he doesn't know where or when it's supposed to happen, does he?" Georgia tapped her thumbnail to her teeth.

Jett glanced from Georgia's narrow-eyed look of pure concentration to his uncle's ruddy, bulldog face, then back to Georgia. Chuckling, he cocked his head and whispered, "If you're real quiet you can almost hear the wheels in her mind turning, can't you?"

Lou blustered out a laugh.

Georgia stuck her tongue out at him. "For your information I wasn't hatching one of my ideas. I was trying to get a glimpse of the big picture here."

"Better you than Campbell, young lady," Lou said. "He's just a couple of phone calls and one lucky tip away from putting all the pieces together."

"What if he does? Now that Jett isn't going to buy the Double Heart and tear it down, what does it matter if Campbell tells the whole world?" She plopped onto the bed.

Jett inhaled the stale odor of the hotel room he would share with his uncle while Georgia stayed across the hall. "The *whole world* happens to be a very big place, Georgia. And I told you before: Even if I don't buy the diner, that doesn't mean that no one will." He hated to burst her bubble, especially after his magnanimous announcement that the place she held dear would remain safe. But she had to know the truth of the precarious situation.

"The Padgett Group has a reputation, Georgia." Lou

placed his hammy hands on his round knees, rocking forward in his chair. "Once word is out that Jett is after a property—and that the deal is not yet sealed—that property suddenly becomes—"

"Hot," she supplied.

"Blazing," Lou confirmed.

"Someone else will try to buy it, just like Jett said before." She chewed at her lower lip.

For only a fleeting moment Jett recalled their kiss, and in that split second knew he would do whatever it took to help Georgia's cause . . . because he'd come to love old Route 66 and what it stood for, he rushed to tell himself, not because he loved her.

No. He did *not* love Georgia Darling. He couldn't. He glanced at her and his heart leapt. Could he?

She held up one hand. "Now wait one minute here."

It was like she had read his mind. *Wait. Stop. Think.* Could the seeds of real love have sprouted roots in such a short time?

"I'm wondering . . . "

That makes two of us.

"Jett's interest could draw others to bid on the diner. And since he's no longer buying it, they could get it handily. That may not be good for the diner or anyone." Her brows angled down over her stormy eyes. She gave her head a quick shake as if that would jar everything in place. "Hold on, here. Wait. I know this sounds convoluted, but I am absolutely sure I can get a handle on it."

That's where we part company, Jett thought. He wondered if he'd ever get a handle on his feelings for this woman or on how the events of the last two days had altered his view of his work and himself.

"Why can't you just announce that you're no longer

interested in the diner property?" Georgia snapped her fingers as if she'd solved the puzzle just that easily. "Beat any speculators to the punch? They won't want it anymore if you don't, right?"

"Wrong!" Lou's tone had all the delicacy and charm of a foghorn.

"The thing is, Georgia," Jett said more quietly, "I was interested in the diner because someone else wants to develop that land. My part in it was just to buy it cheap, get it ready, and pitch it to the new buyers at a profit." He cringed even saying it. What had seemed business-as-usual to him a few days ago now seemed so . . . He didn't know how else to describe it except as *unproductive*. Like so much of what his life had become, his work was just hiring people to do things so that others could hire still others to do something else.

And while he could argue that his involvement brought jobs and capital to various areas, he could not claim that it did much for his opinion of himself. His wasn't the kind of work a man could be proud of, that could make him feel he had left his mark on the world. It was not the kind of business a man would want to pass on to his children.

Children? Children had never been a part of Jett's thinking before. When had *that* scenario popped into his head? Children? *Children?* Not just any children, he suddenly realized as he tried to wrap his mind around the thought. Green-eyed, redheaded children. Wild things with brains full of bright ideas and smiles that would melt hearts.

He pushed his hand back through his hair. He could not let himself get carried away with the fantasy that he and Georgia could work things out enough to marry and have children. He had to keep his mind clear and fixed on the present.

"That's it!" Georgia clapped her hands together. "I've got it."

So do I, Jett thought. *I've got it bad, and I can't let it get in the way of what we are trying to do.* To conceal his feelings from his two companions, he decided to throw the focus of attention onto Georgia, who all but begged for it with her noisy proclamation.

"Oh no!" Jett ducked his head to level his gaze with Georgia's. "She has that look in her eyes."

"What look?" Uncle Lou's face wrinkled in deep folds as he studied Georgia.

"That look that says she just got one of her . . . um . . . 'inspired' ideas."

"Inspiration is good," Lou said.

"Uncle Lou, were you ever a fan of *I Love Lucy*?"

"Huh?"

"Never mind." Jett shook his head. "Suffice it to say that inspiration is good in normal doses. But when this gal gets a bright idea . . . "

Georgia's whole posture tensed, sending him a silent warning that his humor had begun to wear thin.

Jett grinned. "Let's just say it's best never to look directly at one of Georgia's brilliant ideas without protective eyewear."

Her lips twitched. "And rubber gloves," she added.

Lou's head moved back and forth like that of a cat following a Ping-Pong match.

Georgia tipped her nose up, but there was the definite hint of a smile under it.

"And knee and elbow pads," Jett murmured.

"And a hard hat." Georgia's smile blossomed on her full lips.

"Let's not forget that." He stared at her intently, warming

himself in the glow of her tender expression.

"Yeah, well, you guys, I'm getting a bright idea of my very own, and it ain't nothing about no diner in Texas," Lou muttered. "Which do you two want to tell me first? Georgia's idea or what's been going on between you since you left Chicago?"

"Nothing is 'going on,' Uncle Lou." Jett leaned back against the wall and folded his arms. "We just had a few mishaps—"

"And employed a few clever disguises—" Georgia interrupted.

"And made some hasty retreats—"

"—along the way."

"Yeah. I had to cut some checks to pay for one of them hasty retreats you two pulled off back home. The money you left only paid for part of the fun." Lou nodded slowly. "Don't tell me you've been doing that kind of thing all up and down the back roads of three states."

"We were just trying to get to Texas undetected," Jett said innocently.

"That's all," Georgia confirmed.

"Nothing going on between us. Over us, under us, on top of us, maybe, but not between us." Jett grinned.

"Yeah, right," Lou grunted. "The disguise part I like. In fact we need to keep up that part. But as for nothing going on between you two? I can see different."

"See? Where?" Jett tried not to notice how Georgia instinctively touched her fingertip to her lips.

"In your eyes. I seem to recall having the same kind of glint in my eyes once myself. Let's see, it was about forty-two years ago, when I met my darling wife, Cookie."

"Your aunt's name is Cookie?" Georgia asked Jett, clearly trying to detour the conversation away from his uncle's suggestion that they were becoming emotionally involved.

"It's my pet name for her," Lou explained, stroking his bald head the way pregnant women lovingly pat their bulging tummies. "On account o' she's so sweet."

"I thought it was because when she met you, she thought you were such a tease she decided to teach you a lesson and put a whole plate of homemade chocolate-chip cookies in your chair so that when you sat down—"

"That too." Lou held his hand up to quell the tale. "That too."

Georgia giggled and hugged her arms around her ribs. "I think I'm going to like this family."

Both Lou and Jett honed in on that remark.

Georgia's cheeks pinked up, and her hands flopped as she stammered to try to salvage the moment.

"I . . . I . . . Th-that is, I think I'm going to enjoy hearing about this family very much."

"You been telling her things?" Lou tented his fingers over his chest.

Jett started to speak, stopped, and began to shake his head, then halted that action too. "I don't recall."

"Did he tell you about my son, the minister?" Lou said to Georgia.

"No," she said quietly. "But somehow it doesn't surprise me that you'd have a minister in the family. There's a goodness in Jett that isn't taught at a fancy college and doesn't come with business acumen."

"Really?" Jett hadn't realized she'd thought that. Learning it now made his pulse thrum heavily in his ears.

"Really." She nodded. "That's one of the reasons I wouldn't hesitate to make the suggestion I'm about to make—because I believe that deep down, you really want to do the right thing."

* * *

"Give?" Jett choked on the word. "I still can't believe you want me to buy the diner, then just *give* it back to this Starla Mae Jenkins person. It's ridiculous!"

Georgia pulled free a red, white, and blue checkered shirt from the bag Uncle Lou had brought back from a quick shopping trip. Back in St. Louis, Lou had arranged for someone to drive Georgia's truck on to Texas. But since the driver was not personally acquainted with Truvie's personality quirks, it was not going well. Now, both driver and truck were stranded at a gas station on the edge of Tulsa. Georgia had insisted she could coax Truvie into making the rest of the trek, and Jett had insisted on staying with her, but Lou would not let them go out without some kind of disguise.

However unwisely, they'd trusted the fashion-impaired attorney with the task of picking out a few things guaranteed to help them blend in.

"The kinds of things people who drive trucks like Truvie might wear," Jett had called out to his uncle as he'd disappeared in search of a discount department store. Afterward, Georgia had told Jett that she thought he intended that as an insult. This did not improve her mood as they argued about her new plan to save her beloved diner.

After about an hour, Lou brought the new clothes back to the room, where she and Jett were still locked in debate over the issue. After just one look at their faces, he made an excuse Jett barely heard, leaving them to sort out the purchases—and their problems.

Georgia shoved a shirt in Jett's direction and headed for the bathroom to don a pair of animal-print pants and an oversize happy-face T-shirt.

"My plan is not ridiculous," she said loudly from behind the closed door. "It's generous."

"It's not good business," Jett shouted back, checking his shirt for pins before thrusting his arms into the sleeves. The faux pearl snaps popped as he fastened them over an orange-and-black Oklahoma State University T-shirt.

Georgia emerged wearing red plastic sandals. The dim room did nothing to lessen the glow of her gaudy outfit or her irritation. "Does everything have to be good *business?*" she asked, waving a polka-dotted, lime green cap she'd fished out of the bags. Its extended visor and backside bow gave it a baby-bonnet effect. "Can't it just be *good?*"

Jett looked down at his ill-fitting cowboy boots and shuffled them over the carpet. "I do good stuff all the time. I write checks to charity—sizable checks, even. That's good."

"That's also good business," she reminded him. "And it's just another case of you throwing money at a problem instead of getting personally involved."

She was right, and they both knew it. All he could do was shift his weight, reach out to grab the natural straw cowboy hat Lou had picked out, and jam it down low on his head as if to say, *Oh yeah?*

Yeah. She mimicked his action with her own hat, topping it with a one-handed crunch of her brim. "You can do this, if you really want to, Murphy. You could find a way."

"You really believe that, don't you?" Jett looked at her thoughtfully.

"Yes, I do."

"You believe not only that I can do it financially, but that I have it within me to make that kind of grand gesture." He spoke in a voice filled with quiet emotion. "That if you ask earnestly enough and appeal to my better side, I am the kind of man who would do such a thing."

"Yes," she said so softly that he saw it on her lips more than heard it.

He couldn't quell the smile that crept over his face. He hooked his thumbs in his belt loops and puffed out his chest. "I can't tell you how good it is to hear that, Georgia Darling."

"Why?" Her eyes clouded with wariness.

"Because it means that finally, after all we've been through, *finally* you are beginning to trust me."

13

He hadn't promised her anything, Georgia reminded herself. She went back over their conversation for the hundredth time since they'd left the hotel and made the trek to the gas station where Truvie and the driver waited.

It had been decided by all that Jett and Georgia would bring the truck back to the hotel and the driver would bring the car. In a show of faith in her ability to get her truck rolling, and to keep up the charade of them as an average couple, Jett had sent the driver on his way as soon as they reached the station where Truvie was parked.

The evening sky had begun to grow dark, and the busy streets that intersected at the station roared with the life of revved engines and radios blaring from open car windows. Occasionally, a horn would blast, reminding someone to move on when a light changed from red to green. The stream of cars would flow briefly, then stop, and the cars from the other direction would whoosh past.

Jett sat inside the truck cab, hand on the key, ready to turn it whenever Georgia gave the word. She leaned under the open hood, the thick smell of motor oil filling her nostrils even as the pungent vapors of gasoline stung her eyes. Her mind raced to keep the hectic surroundings, the job at hand, and her own jumbled feelings in balance.

An eager-faced attendant hovered nearby. He wiped his hands on a rag, stuffed that rag into his pocket, paced a step or two, asked about Georgia's progress—then repeated the whole procedure. He put Georgia in mind of an anxious expectant father, wishing he could help in some way with the delivery process yet knowing there was nothing to do but watch and wait.

Georgia squinted into the blackened engine, but her thoughts drifted back to her last exchange with Jett. He had not promised her anything. Then again, she told herself, he had not said no outright. He had called her plan ridiculous. But people often railed against ideas even as those ideas were taking root inside their heads. She had planted a seed in Jett's mind tonight. She knew it. Now she could only hope that seed would grow—and perhaps add a bit of fertilizer whenever the opportunity presented itself.

She gripped the ball-peen hammer in her fist and contorted her body to enable herself to reach just the right spot in Truvie's engine.

Ping. She gave the precise spot a resounding whack.

"Now try," she called to Jett from under the hood.

"What?" Jett's muffled reply came back.

"Rev it up!"

"You're giving up?"

Georgia rolled her eyes and groaned. She couldn't make herself heard, yet she was afraid to wriggle out of this awkward position just when she had managed to reach the exact spot she needed. Sometimes when Truvie showed signs of starting but wouldn't quite turn over, another quick tap would do the trick. She couldn't count on running over to give directions to Jett and getting back into place in time for that. Then she remembered the mechanic-in-waiting.

She twisted just her neck to look over her shoulder at the

attendant who had loaned her the hammer. "Tell him to try starting the truck now, would you, please?"

"Start 'er up!" the man bellowed.

The engine whined.

Georgia went in for the extra tap, but the motor died before she could act.

The whine resumed, then faded, never giving her the chance to apply the business end of her hammer to the trouble spot.

She gritted her teeth and issued another command to her helper, "Okay, tell him to hold off for a minute."

"Hold up!"

From the corner of her eye she could see the man slash his hand across his throat.

The whining did not resume.

The image flashed in her mind of Jett sitting in her truck, his capable hands on the wheel, listening to—and for once respecting without argument—her counsel. For one fleeting second she thought of yelling out the request for him to buy the diner and give it to Starla Mae.

"Concentrate, will you?" Georgia muttered to herself, trying to place her attention where it belonged, on the truck.

"Concentrate!" The attendant issued the order in no uncertain terms.

"No, not—"

"Concentrate on what?" Jett asked.

"I didn't mean him, I was—" Georgia climbed out from beneath the hood and peeled off her green sun hat. She'd worn it, even while she tried to work her mechanical magic on her truck, to hide her hair and shade her eyes. But now that the sun was setting, and given the work she was attempting to do, she figured it probably drew more attention to wear it than not to. She swiped at her damp brow with the soft crown of her hat, then ruffled the curls at the back of her head, savoring the cool breeze on her back.

Sighing, she slapped the hat against her leg and looked at the attendant. "I wasn't telling him to concentrate. I was just talking to myself."

"She was—"

She cut off his shout with her raised hand. "You don't have to tell him that."

"Oh yeah, right." The attendant cocked his head. "Hey, you look real familiar. Have I seen you somewhere before?"

Georgia's heart raced. She thought of cramming the hat back down on her head but decided it would be too obvious. "Um, no, not me. I'm not even from here."

"I don't mean from here—but somewhere like . . . TV or something."

Caught. Georgia's throat began to close. Uncle Lou had warned them that their pictures had been seen all over the area as the story gained notoriety. Most papers and telecasts played it up as a big joke: the important businessman recluse making a big scene in a crowded landmark restaurant. But that very fact had actually made more people pay attention to the story. If it had been done as a hard news piece, most people would not even have noticed. An anecdotal sound bite, however, and one that included very embarrassing pictures—*that* drew the average person's attention.

Apparently this man standing next to her was just such an average person.

Georgia jammed the hat down on her head, ignoring the stray hairs that stuck out all around its edges. Intent on not standing there and blurting out a lie, she drew in a deep breath and said, "Gee, that sounds pretty far-fetched, doesn't it? On TV?"

Then she practically dove back under the hood again.

Ping. Ping. Ping. Wham! Clang! Ping. She went after the engine with a vengeance. "Tell him to try it now."

As the attendant called out to Jett, Georgia whispered a quick prayer, "Oh, Lord, it's probably pretty selfish of me to ask you to help start a beat-up old truck when there are so many people in the world with real problems. But you know my goal is for a greater good. Help us, Lord, to get Truvie started so we can finish this trip and help Starla Mae and the diner. Thank you and amen."

Truvie whined.

Georgia held her breath.

Truvie coughed.

Georgia whaled at the engine with one last mighty blow. *Gong!*

Truvie let out a sputtering belch as if she'd been running on cabbage soup instead of gasoline, then she started up. Her motor hummed to life and growled with renewed gusto.

"Thank you, Lord," Georgia whispered beneath the bang of the hood slamming shut. She ran around the truck, still propelled by the fear that they'd been recognized. One quick nudge of the door and she was able to hop into the passenger seat. "Let's go!"

"Aren't you being a little—"

"He recognized me. Now go!"

Jett didn't need any more prodding than that. He jerked the truck into reverse and backed it up.

"Hey!" The attendant waved his hand.

"Hey, and thanks." Jett waved back.

Since they didn't owe the man any money, Georgia motioned for him to keep driving.

Jett obliged, guiding the truck in a lurching arch to the gas station's exit, where they were blocked by a line of traffic waiting for the light to change. When he stomped on the brakes, Truvie's engine gave a thundering shudder.

Georgia clenched her first, clumping up the faux wool seat covers.

Jett scowled.

"Hey! Hey, you guys!" The attendant began loping in their direction.

"He's not giving up very easily on this notion that he's seen you before, is he?" Jett lifted his head to check the rearview mirror. "Maybe we should just—"

"We should just go before he figures out why he saw us on TV and makes an even bigger scene. People are starting to stare at us already."

"We can't just go unless I crash into someone or Truvie sprouts wings. Either way that's bound to draw more attention than waiting our turn."

Truvie hacked and sputtered.

Georgia's pulse throbbed in her head.

"Hey, you TV guys! You people I saw on TV!"

Her heart stopped. It just stopped, she thought. But luckily for her—and Jett—her quick mind had not. Taking a swift visual sweep of the people around them in traffic staring at the commotion, Georgia knew she had to act fast.

Jett reached out to touch her arm. "Maybe they won't notice us."

Truvie growled louder, then louder, then . . .

Boom! She backfired.

"Hey, you TV guys!"

Georgia gasped.

People from every direction turned to stare.

This could not be happening, Georgia told herself. But it was happening, and she knew she had to stop it. She had to do something—anything—to hide their faces. She looked across the seat at the man she'd shared so much with already and knew in an instant what she had to do.

And so she did it.

She wasn't the type to go throwing herself into a man's arms and kissing him, but with Jett it felt so right. The action also could prevent almost anyone from identifying them, she reminded herself. That was the real reason for— *Forget it.* Her inner voice jeered at her feeble attempts to downplay her actions. The truth was that, while this was an excellent ploy for keeping their faces hidden, Georgia wanted to do it. She wanted to kiss Jett Murphy because she was in love with him.

Though her eyes were closed, Georgia sensed that the traffic light had gone from glaring red to cool green. Traffic just beyond them had begun to move. But neither she nor Jett moved to end their kiss.

A single knock on the passenger door made it fall open, and the attendant stuck his head in the truck. "Hey there, folks. Hate to disturb you but—"

Georgia slowly pulled away from Jett, wondering if her revelation about her emotions shone in her eyes.

"Pardon me for yelling at y'all like that, but you see, you've got my hammer."

"Your what?" Georgia blinked.

"When you finished up under the hood you took my hammer with you—by mistake, I'm sure."

"I did?" It was as if the man were speaking in a foreign language. She could not make any sense of what he was saying.

"The hammer, Georgia." Jett reached across to pick up the tool she'd laid on the seat and handed it to the man. "All the man wanted was his hammer."

"I wouldn't have made a fuss, but my darling wife gave it to me last Christmas." With a sheepish grin he tapped the

187

silver head into his cupped palm. "But then I don't suppose I have to tell y'all about that, do I?"

"About hammers?" She shook her head, feeling as if she'd just stepped off a merry-go-round.

"Naw, about love." The attendant laughed. "Why, anyone can plainly see you two know plenty about that already."

It showed. Georgia felt her cheeks blanch as she replayed in her mind the man's blatant claim. *Anyone can plainly see you two*—You *two?*

"You *two?*" she murmured, letting it sink in. Terrified, but hoping it could be true, she turned to Jett. "You too?"

"Me too," he smiled.

"Don't you think it's too soon?" She whispered aloud her own fears.

"Probably."

"Thanks." The attendant slammed her door shut. "Y'all drive safe now, y' hear?"

But Jett did not drive. He simply sat there with her hands in his.

"I've never known anyone like you, Georgia. You've just changed so many things in my life—my perspective, my expectations. You've helped me to laugh again and to be scared and mad and . . . and to want to be a better person, to be the kind of man you think I really am. Or can be."

"Oh, Jett." She bit her lip, trying not to start blubbering like a baby. So much had happened so fast, she didn't know what to think. She wasn't capable of thinking, only feeling. And what she was feeling, she tried to put into words. "When I first found out who you were, I wanted to just . . . just shake you. Then, I confess, I wanted you to like me, because the minute I looked into your eyes, I knew you were good and kind and patient."

"Patient? Me?"

"I know you reacted strongly to some of my ideas and actions, but you didn't belittle me for them. You even went along with a lot of them—more than most people would—and I don't think that was just because you were protecting your business interests. I mean, do you usually let your business partners tint your hair or wear a ring for them?"

He laughed.

"So yes, you are patient. And do you have any idea how long I've waited for a really patient man to come into my life?"

"Yeah," he put his hand to her cheek and looked deep in her eyes. "I've got some idea."

She leaned into his touch, her gaze searching his. "But it's all so sudden. How can we trust it? Maybe all the excitement has us confused."

"Maybe. I don't think so. But I understand the desire to be cautious." He kissed one of her hands.

She felt anything but cautious.

"Maybe we should agree to call it something else." He kissed her other hand. "At least until we're sure."

"Like what?"

"Like . . . I don't know."

She tipped her head. "Somehow, saying 'I'm in I-don't-know with you' isn't exactly the stuff of poetry."

"You have a point." He kissed both her hands. "If not 'love,' then maybe we can call it 'that feeling you get when you know that given enough time and the right circumstances it could blossom into love'?"

"It's a little long for a rhyme scheme, but I think it works for us."

"Good." This time his kiss came on her lips, light and quick. The he turned to steer the truck into traffic.

Georgia didn't think she needed the truck to get home

though. She felt certain that tonight she could simply float back to the hotel on those wonderful, albeit cautious, words.

It could be love.

* * *

Is It Love or Is It Larceny? The headline glared out at Georgia from the thin piece of fax paper in her hand.

"Nothing between you." Lou paced the length of the hotel room. "That's what you told me—that there was nothing between you."

Jett and Georgia exchanged glances. "We didn't know ourselves, exactly, until—"

"Well, you could have at least told me that someone had taken a picture of the two of you kissing! Especially one of you kissing while holding a 'Just Married' sign," the older man bellowed, making circles in the air with his thick arms.

"We didn't know about that either, obviously," Jett told him.

At first light, Lou had come pounding on their doors with a copy of the newspaper item that had been printed in Chicago the night before and faxed to him. Georgia had dressed in haste to attend what she thought would be an impromptu strategy meeting. It bothered her a little that by the time she got to their room, Jett and Lou had gone over the article and begun formulating responses without her input.

"Is It Love or Is It Larceny?" Georgia began to read aloud, her head cocked to see the words on the paper dangling from Lou's fingers.

Jett chuckled as if at a shared secret, hinting that they both knew which of the two was at work here.

Georgia's stomach lurched. Her chest felt tight. She struggled to maintain an even, objective tone as she read on. "When a prominent Chicago businessman and his former employee created a scene in a local restaurant yesterday, some people suspected he had stolen away with the young lady to keep her from revealing company secrets. This picture, snapped today at a Missouri truck stop, makes one wonder whether instead it is her heart he has appropriated."

"Huh." Lou shifted positions with his brusque response, jiggling the paper so she lost her place. Georgia didn't care. She drew in a deep breath of coffee-scented air, then let it out slowly.

"No point in reading on," Jett told her. "The rest is just a bunch of cockamamie conjecture and misquotes."

As if in agreement, Lou released the page he had been clutching between his thumb and forefinger. It swirled and somersaulted to the floor. "The thing is," he said, "it doesn't tip anyone off to the deal. Now as long as you can tell me that I'm not going to hear any other speculations, or see more photographs, or even have more bills for damages forwarded to my office, we'll be fine."

"Not as far as I know," Jett muttered, not like a kid being scolded but like a man deep in thought.

"Then it's okay." Lou clapped his hands together.

Georgia jumped at the sound.

"This looks to anyone who's interested like a merry chase pulled off by a couple of lovebird types." Lou's laugh blubbered from his lips. "No one can connect you two to the property in Texas. No one probably even noticed you along the way. Right?"

Georgia gulped.

Jett opened his mouth, cleared his throat, and finally said, "There was that busload of senior citizens, first at Meramac Caverns, then at Devil's Elbow."

"Two busloads of senior citizens?" Lou slapped his meaty hand to his cheek. "You forgot a little detail like two busloads of people who could identify you along the way?"

"Just the one bus," Jett corrected, his attention on Lou.

"They saw us twice." Georgia bent over and picked up the page, which she folded and slipped into her pocket.

"That's why we think they'd remember us."

She turned to Jett. "That and the fact that you carried me across the parking lot yelling about how you'd carry me all the way to Texas if you had to . . . "

"If you had just let me help you in the first place—"

"Well, if it happened today, I probably would!"

"You did what?" If Lou had had any hair left on his head, Georgia suspected he would now be tearing it out with both hands. "You yelled in a parking lot about going to Texas? Didn't you think that kind of thing might just be important enough to tell me?"

"Well, we . . . " Georgia bit her lip.

Jett fought to fend off a laugh but did not succeed.

"Is there anything else you two are keeping from me? Anything that might cause someone to connect you two with that Texas property?"

"Um . . . "

"Think hard before you answer," Lou warned. "Did you hand out itineraries with a big red star saying 'You are here' and arrows pointing out your destination? Entertain crowds at the highway rest stops with musical renditions of your adventures? Did you stop anywhere to get a likeness of the diner tattooed on your . . . on your . . . " Lou looked at Georgia, his face beet red. He blew out a long blast of air and concluded, " . . . on your biceps?"

"No, we didn't."

"Wait, Jett. What about that waitress?"

"You put a tattoo on a waitress?" Lou peered at them as though he actually suspected they might have wrestled some poor woman to the ground and done just that.

"No, but we did talk with that waitress at the Dixie Truckers Home."

"What's that? A retirement place for old truck drivers?" Lou asked.

"It's only one of the very first truck stops—on Route 66," Georgia explained. "And we told the waitress there about the Double Heart to gain her sympathy so she'd stall Campbell, who showed up asking questions about us."

"You think she'd remember you?" Lou groused.

Georgia tapped her feet together. "Um, yeah, I kind of think she would. See, I—"

"I don't even want to know." Lou put up his hand and shook his head. "Anyone else?"

Jett tipped his head back and scratched his chin as if making a grand tally. "Let's see: the bus full of senior citizens, the waitress, the gas station attendant last night. I think that's all—that we know about, of course."

"See? Only those few—and maybe whoever took that picture, if it wasn't someone on the bus tour," Georgia added. "That won't be a problem, though, will it?"

Lou smacked the heel of his hand to his broad forehead. Then he sighed and took her hand. "No, my dear, no problem. Will you excuse Jett a little while now so he and I can make a few calls and conduct some business?"

"I . . . um . . . " She'd come too far to be escorted out at that point. "Unless . . . "

"It's okay," Jett whispered. "It's just some things we have to take care of, a few contacts to make, things to check out. Give us half an hour, forty-five minutes at the most, then we'll be on our way."

"On our way?" A whirlwind of butterflies filled her stomach. Jett's answer to her question would tell her if he thought they were now headed back to Chicago or on to Texas. "On our way to where?"

"Well, I was headed to the Double Heart Diner. Did you have other plans?" He smiled.

She answered with her own smile, which rose from the depths of her feelings for this man. "Nope. Not at all. Going to the Double Heart suits me fine."

She started to turn, then paused. She had to ask, "Does this mean . . . are you going with my suggestion?"

Jett clamped his jaw down. He scowled. "Georgia, I can't talk about that now. I'm not in a position to talk about it, and I won't until the time is right, do you understand that?"

His tone was as hard as it had been the first day she'd met him, his expression closed off. Georgia felt she'd touched a nerve and wished she could ask more about it, to help him help her understand before she walked out of the room.

"Now I have to make some phone calls," he said, motioning toward the door with a jerk of his head.

Georgia's stomach knotted. In her mind she had known that Jett hadn't resolved what he would do about the diner. But now to feel so outcast, so dispensable, when the final decisions were being made confused and upset her. If only he'd let her in on it, let her at least hear what was going on. She started to ask him to do just that, but Lou trotted over to open the door.

"We won't be long, sweetheart," the older man said.

Georgia looked from the door to Jett.

He nodded and whispered, "Trust me."

She wanted to.

It surprised her to admit it, even silently, but she did want to trust Jett with all her heart. It had been so long since she had really wanted to trust someone, to believe a person would not betray, deceive, or just plain forget her in the desire to achieve his or her own goals. But she wanted to trust Jett not to do any of those things, and so she decided she would do just that.

She squared her shoulders. "I'll see you in a bit then. Looks like by late afternoon today, we'll be at the Double Heart Diner."

14

"That's it. It's over. There's no use in going any farther." With a sigh Lou clunked down the receiver of the hotel room phone.

"Let me call you back," Jett muttered into the mobile phone in his hand, then flipped it closed. "What are you talking about, Uncle Lou? What's over?"

"The diner deal. It's done." He slashed both hands waist-high in the air. "Kaput. Adios. A dead duck. Pffft."

"Could you possibly use a more exact description than 'pffft'?" Jett stuck out his tongue and mimicked the raspberry sound his uncle had just made. "What happened? Did someone else buy the diner out from under us?"

"Worse."

"Worse?"

"Worse."

"How much worse?"

"*Much* worse."

"Much, *much* worse?"

"The worst worse."

Jett placed his thumb and forefinger on either side of his nose and began to massage the corners of his eyes. "Could we try speaking plain English here instead of monosyllabic twenty questions?"

"Huh?"

Jett gritted his teeth. "Just tell me what is going on. Why is our deal to buy the Double Heart kaput, and what is the worst worse that made it happen? Start with that last question first."

"Okay." Lou patted his fingertips together. "The worst worse is that no one is going to buy the property that diner's sitting on."

"You mean no one else will bid against us?"

"I mean our developers are looking elsewhere."

"What? Did they cut a deal on another site?"

"As soon as the story broke and one bright fellow figured out you were after the Texas site, he had the jump on us."

"He's sweetened the deal for the developers to buy his property," Jett concluded.

"Sweetened it like honey-coated sugar cubes." Lou snorted. "A third party has already made the developers an equally competitive offer."

Jett quietly processed the new information.

"Secrecy was our best weapon," Lou continued. "We could have undercut any other offer by keeping the Double Heart deal under wraps until the last minute—bought the property at a rock-bottom price, got it ready, and turned it around for an attractive sum. Left the other guys scrambling to best *us*. But now that word is out, we have no leverage."

"And we're the ones who have to scramble."

"Like eggs in a skillet."

"Do you need to stop and take a breakfast break here, Uncle Lou?"

Lou laughed and shrugged. "We're in Oklahoma. Ain't that how people talk in Oklahoma? All colorful-like?"

"Well, you'd know about colorful." Jett glanced at the man's argyle polo shirt, plaid Bermuda shorts, black socks, and sandals. "But I'm not sure we can't still pull off the diner deal."

"We're too far behind, Jett." Lou shook his head. "We don't even own the property yet, much less have it ready, and they're already playing one-upmanship with each other. By the time we got everything ready down there and met their offers—forget about besting them—we'd lose our shirts."

"And that would be a bad thing?" He pinched at the sleeve of his uncle's bold shirt, then glanced down at the simple work shirt he wore courtesy of his cousin.

"Hey, I like my shirt," Lou grumbled. "What's wrong with my shirt?"

Jett shook his head, refusing to get dragged into a fashion debate when so much else was at stake. "Nothing. It's fine. And it's not important. What is important, however, is what we do next."

"Do?" Lou harrumphed. "What's to do? The deal bit the dust."

"It's not that simple and you know it."

"Yeah, yeah." Lou closed one eye and stabbed a finger in Jett's direction. "You like to play the big, callous tycoon, you do. But that ain't really who you are. You got a tender spot for the underdog in you, son."

"Like that's not a family trait?"

Lou laughed, and it half-sounded like choking. "So we make it a policy in our business never to go for the throat. Those are your orders, you know: Look for the win/win situation, not winner-take-all."

"I couldn't live with myself otherwise." Jett thought back to the fax page with its picture of him and Georgia kissing. "But if I don't buy that diner, what's going to happen to Starla Mae Jenkins?"

"Who?"

"The owner."

"Oh. Um, well, you know from reading your private reports, she has to sell. She's barely scraping by as it is, and the place is crumbling around her ears. One serious plumbing disaster, a roof leak, a piece of kitchen equipment that goes berserk and she's sunk. She'll lose everything. May even have to declare bankruptcy. With the money we were going to give her she could have at least bought a house, paid off her debts, set some money aside. And her kid brother—he's got a partial stake in the place—I'm sure he could use the money for something too."

"None of that's going to happen now." Jett sighed.

"None of the good stuff, no. It sure doesn't look like it."

Jett sank into his chair. "So my little escapade here has cost us a bundle and Starla Mae Jenkins . . . everything?"

Lou thought for a moment, his expression sober, then came across the room and placed his hands on Jett's shoulders. "Can I say how sorry I am, son?"

"Sorry? What have you got to be sorry for?"

"I did it. Did it all. From tipping off Campbell to egging him on in his chase."

"You?" Jett turned his upper body around, his voice almost raw. "You did that?"

"I confess, I did."

"But why?"

"For you."

"For me? How was any of this for me?"

Lou looked to the ceiling like a guilty kid trying to talk his way out of a trip to the woodshed. "I thought you needed to get out, to get your feet wet, to live a little."

No matter how hard he tried, Jett could not think of a comeback to that, so he simply glowered at his uncle and waited for him to go on.

"Sending you off, especially down what's left of old Route 66, seemed the perfect answer. And siccing Campbell on you like that . . . well, it ensured you'd keep going. I never thought it would ruin the deal. In fact, just the opposite; I thought it would cinch it."

Jett had thought as much himself or he'd have never taken off for Texas in the first place.

"So I am sorry. Guess I messed things up pretty good with my meddling."

Jett patted his uncle's arm. "It's not your fault. If only I had acted more responsibly . . . "

"You're saying you wish you hadn't gone?"

"Not on your life," Jett grinned.

"Because of the girl?"

Images of Georgia's face formed in Jett's mind. He saw her as she was when he first laid eyes on her, as she looked when he'd picked her up to carry her through the parking lot, then as she had been when he had kissed her last night. Yeah, it was because of the girl. He did not want to let her go yet—or let her down. Too many people in her life had already done that. He wouldn't be one more.

When he'd first seen her, he had sensed that Georgia Darling needed a hero. If it was within his power, Jett was now determined that he would be that hero.

"Yeah, Uncle Lou. It's because of the girl. And it's because of her that I know I've got to find some way to help out that diner—deal or no deal."

* * *

"What is taking so long?" Georgia muttered to herself, trying to peek at the room across the hall through her door's peephole.

The fate of the Double Heart Diner hung in the balance, and they were so close they could make it there in six measly hours. Why in the world was Jett dawdling now?

She knew why, of course. The kiss. And the photograph of that kiss. She brushed her fingertips over her lips. That one moment of abandon had changed everything. People in positions of power now knew that Jett was up to something. They were aware of his deal that was in the works. As she understood it, that could drastically affect the outcome.

How she wished she could be in on that meeting! She smacked her fist into her palm. But since it was largely her fault that they were in this mess—she'd told the waitress about the diner, created the scene refusing Jett's help, pulled the "Just Married" sign out of the car, kept a hammer that did not belong to her—she could understand her exclusion.

Anyway, this was her big chance to show Jett how much she trusted him. How he had earned her trust by his words and actions. *Trust.* What a perfectly lovely word, she thought. What a wonderful, amazing feeling it inspired.

She walked the length of the musty hotel room and picked up the fax sheet. She trusted Jett. She loved Jett. She smoothed out the paper, leaning over to look at the photo of their first kiss.

Is It Love or Is It Larceny? She flattened the page out on the cool surface of the room's wobbling table. She smiled. The memory came back as real as the crisp breeze from the air conditioner that rattled the paper beneath her hand.

Love and trust. Who'd have ever thought that a Lucy-wannabe without any family would end up loving and trusting a . . . a . . . She glanced down at the caption and read, " . . . prominent but reclusive Chicago businessman."

Georgia fell back into a nearby chair, the article in her hands. She glanced at the byline, a wave of gratitude washing over her that this time the name was not Campbell's, but that of a society writer she recognized from the paper's regular columns. Not hard-hitting enough for Campbell anymore, she thought, relying on Jett's opinion of the man to form her judgment. Given the cutesy nature of the photograph it only made sense that they'd give it to someone willing to give it the sappy write-up it warranted.

She smiled at the photo, slowly circling the words *Just Married* with her finger. In silent prayer, she thanked the Lord for all she had been given, then scanned the story Jett and Lou had prevented her from finishing earlier.

"Jett Murphy, thirty-nine, blah, blah, blah," she said as she skimmed along. "The Padgett Group, blah, blah, blah. No good deed goes unpunished, blah, blah . . . blah?"

She jerked up straight in her seat. Could she have read that right? Her heart thundered. Her throat went dry. Had Jett actually said that?

She searched the piece frantically for the spot where she had seen those blatantly sarcastic words. "'No good deed goes unpunished.' This, according to Mr. Murphy's secretary, will soon become the company's new motto."

Her mind spun. Her limbs felt numb and her cheeks hot. Either she was having a horrible allergic reaction to the ink on the paper or she had just slammed face-first into reality. She had been duped. Jett Murphy had let her lead him off on this wild goose chase as a . . .

"As a wild goose chase," she muttered between tightly grinding teeth. And all the while his secretary was back home, carrying out his orders and telling people this mean-spirited, mocking cliché.

"Wait now, Georgia," she told herself aloud, needing to hear something besides her own accelerating pulse echoing in her ears. "Wait one minute. You don't know that this had anything to do with you or the good deed you've asked him to do on behalf of the diner."

She forced down a painful swallow and turned again to the thin white paper. "When asked the reason for this new, unorthodox business creed, Murphy's assistant, Rowena Sorenson, the only one available for comment yesterday at his office, informed the caller that she could sum it up in two words. Two words that had been given to her directly by Mr. Murphy himself. What two words? A name, really. The name of the very woman he has now disappeared with, for what some have implied are dubious reasons: 'Georgia Darling.'"

If the initial information had made her feel sucker-punched, this last little tidbit was the knockout blow.

Jett Murphy had used her. He'd let her think the whole trip was her idea. He'd spoken to her of partnerships and much more, but all along he'd been in control. If she had any doubt of that, she only had to recall his rush to get her out of the room moments ago, his unwillingness to answer her question about the diner, the cool expression on his face when he told her there were some things he would not talk about with her.

Jett Murphy had been manipulating her the whole trip. Despite her naive efforts to keep it from him, he had found her weakness in her devotion to Starla Mae and the diner and had used that to distract and deceive her. Why else wouldn't he have told her about his secretary's remarks? She wanted to think that perhaps he had not known, but she suddenly recalled the phone conversation—of which she'd heard only Jett's side—in which he spoke of it to his Uncle Lou.

Tears sprang to her eyes. Still, she tried to convince herself one last time that this could not be true. What about the kisses? What about Jett's profession of feelings for her? And why would he and Lou tip her off to the truth by giving her the article if this was the way Jett really felt?

Kisses, she was old enough to know, were not commitments. And Jett had not said that he loved her. Instead he had chosen a very careful way of expressing himself: "Given enough time and the right circumstances it could blossom into love . . . " Georgia had been down this road before. And while she knew it could be love, she, even better than most people, recognized it could also be betrayal.

And as for the story, no one had given it to her really. She had just picked it up off the floor, probably without anyone noticing. Jett had told her it wasn't important for her to read it—going so far as to call it "a bunch of cockamamie conjecture" and full of "misquotes."

Georgia flexed her fingers over the paper, compressing it slowly into a ball, thinking that's how her heart felt. She crimped it tighter and tighter until she felt that all her tender emotions, especially those she felt for Jett, had been obliterated.

She staggered a bit as she stood, as though a weight had been dropped on her slender shoulders. While something in her wanted to confront Jett in person with all she had just discovered, she did not trust herself to face him without succumbing to her pain. She had given him her trust once. But her weakness—she would never show that to him again.

Silently, she prayed for strength. She prayed for insight. And she prayed that Truvie would start up quickly and quietly so she could slip away without anyone hearing her.

* * *

"Tell her what? That I knew Miss Sorenson had repeated my stupid remarks to callers, but that I chose not to share that information with Georgia because at the time I was convinced those remarks would probably prove true? Now there's a great way to regain her trust."

"I think it's a fine way to rebuild trust—the truth usually

is, son. But that's not what I meant. I think what you should tell her is just how much you really love her."

"Done it."

"You have?'

"Yeah, and you see what it got me." He waved the message the desk clerk had given him after Georgia did not answer her door. She had left the things Uncle Lou bought for her neatly stacked at the front desk with the phony wedding ring on top, and the clerk had scrawled out her parting shot on a piece of pink paper. Jett glared at it, then read aloud, "'No good deed goes unpunished. Thanks for the much-needed reminder.'"

"And she says this to you after you tell her how crazy you are about her?"

"The crazy part I think she could figure out from my actions, but I didn't exactly tell her that—"

"What *did* you tell her?"

"Look, Uncle Lou, she and I have only really known one another for a few days. That's way too soon to be—"

"I knew your Aunt Cookie for one hour—an *hour*—and I knew."

"You did?"

"I'm telling you, son: The minute I peeled one of those hot chocolate-chip cookies off the seat of my pants, I knew I had met the woman I was going to marry."

Despite his foul mood, that made Jett grin. "I knew Georgia was special the first time I saw her in that apron and plastic cap, her turquoise cowboy boots sliding all over the place as she randomly shoved that dish cart into the tables of perfect strangers . . . "

Both men paused to stare off into space for a few wistful moments. Then Lou abruptly cleared his throat, bringing them both back to the discussion at hand. "That doesn't answer my question though. What did you tell her?"

"I told her that given time and the right circumstances, it could turn into love."

Lou stared at him. "That's it?"

"Pretty much. You know my philosophy, Uncle Lou: Never give out too much information too soon—"

"In business, my boy. In *business*. But in romance? Me-oh-my-oh," Lou muttered, putting his whole hand over his face. "This is what you say to the woman you love? No wonder she ran off. What did she have to stay for? Talk to me like that, and I'd run off too."

"Promise?"

"Very funny, my friend." Lou batted his hand in the air. "The question now remains: Are you going after her or not?"

"What good would it do? You have to understand that Georgia is a person who does not give her trust easily. You have to earn it. I had just started to do that when her past impressions of me caught up with me."

"So you tell her that. She'll understand."

"No. Right now I think it would only hurt her again. Why would she believe me anyway? I have to win her trust again, starting all over—if she'll let me."

Jett ran his hand back through his hair. The ring he still wore on his finger scratched at his scalp. He lowered his hand and lightly stroked the inexpensive token with his thumb.

"The only way to win her back is to show her I can compromise again—to be worthy of her trust. To just chase her down and start unburdening my feelings would only muddle things up. I've changed a lot, but not enough for that. Besides, that wouldn't be fair to her."

"All's fair in love and war." Lou said it like he'd made it up on the spot.

Jett chuckled without humor. "Yeah, but sometimes it's hard to know the difference."

Neither of them spoke for a few moments. Finally Jett groaned and stretched his weary arms and legs. "Well, one good thing came out of all this, Uncle Lou. You got your wish."

"Did I?"

"Sure. You wanted me to take a more active approach to my life and my business, and that's what I've done. Of course, it didn't exactly turn out well, either professionally or personally—"

"Hey, maybe it hasn't actually turned out yet." Lou screwed up his face to one side, tapped his fingers together, then sighed. "Want we should call my son, the minister? He could maybe give you some advice, some guidance."

"That's okay, Uncle Lou. I actually already borrowed some good advice from a certain redhead on that. See, she told me that when she faces a big decision she always asks herself two questions. The first one is: What would God have me do in this?"

"And what do you think he would have you do?"

"What I promised Georgia I would do—see this adventure through to the end. Meet the people my decisions affect. Sit in the diner with Starla Mae Jenkins and try to figure out the best thing for all of us. I told Georgia I'd do that, and I won't go back on my word."

"Even though she's taken off on you?"

"If my honor and trustworthiness were based on how others behave toward me, then they wouldn't be worth much, would they?"

"No, not worth a plug nickel." Lou shook his head. "What's the second question?"

"Huh?"

"You said Georgia asks herself two questions. What's the second one?"

How would Lucy handle this? Just thinking it made Jett smile, but he doubted his uncle would understand the skewed logic and harmless good humor in it. He declined to answer with a shake of his head. "The question is not nearly as important as the answer, Uncle Lou."

"Which is?"

"Which is to take into account the old highway legend of the Double Heart Diner. There's this saying, you see, that if you've lost your way or lost your love, you'll find them at the Double Heart Diner." He hoped that was the way she'd said it. Though he wasn't sure, he felt he had the gist of it.

"So you going there to find your lost love?"

"Find Georgia? I don't deserve that. Maybe I can hope for the chance to patch things up with her someday. But I'm not doing this for her; I'm doing it for me. I'm going to the Double Heart Diner to find my way, Uncle Lou. That diner is still in trouble, and if I can do something to help it, then I have to do it. I can't sit back and let someone else take care of any of this now. I can't go back to my ivory tower. I'm ready to jump into my life again with both feet, and the best place to start is in the Texas panhandle."

15

Sometime before she reached Oklahoma City, Georgia knew she had to turn her truck around. Cowards left notes and ran, she told herself. In doing that, she'd shown Jett far more weakness than any teary-eyed confrontation ever would.

That's what she told herself as she filled Truvie's gas tank at a station planted between the parallel roads leading to and from Tulsa. But deep in her heart, she knew this was not a decision she should make alone. This was not a time to ask herself what Lucy would do either. Crunch time had arrived, and she had to ask herself what God would have her do. That was the only question that mattered now.

She squeezed the nozzle of the gas hose, ignored the chugging sound and the stinging fumes, and whispered, "Dear Lord, what a mess I've gotten myself into. Help me to understand what to do. I love this man, and now that I've cooled down some, I doubt that he intended to do this to hurt me. If only I had a sign. If only I knew for sure."

She bit her lip, trying to gather her composure.

"Lucy! Lucy, you come back here!" The words shocked her into interrupting her fervent prayer.

Georgia looked up to see a little redheaded girl running around a station wagon, clutching a toy tool belt in her hands, while her father called after her. A frazzled woman rounded the car on the child's heels tugging something along behind her—a little boy, wearing a hard hat! "Lucy, you apologize for your behavior right now. Then I want you two to hug and make up."

Georgia rolled her eyes heavenward and, grinning, gave a thumbs-up for what seemed a pretty clear-cut sign to her. "Not bad."

She watched as the family resolved their conflict, then paused to have a brief word with the child's mother. Afterward Georgia paid for her gasoline, climbed into her truck, and started it up. The morning sun shone down on the open roads that bracketed the station.

She wondered if Jett had even read her note yet. He and Lou were in heavy business negotiations, after all, and she'd been gone less than an hour. And if he had read her note, would he still be in Tulsa, or would he have started back to Chicago already? There was no reason for him to go on to the Double Heart, after all, if the deal was dead and Georgia had gone ahead on her own. She thought of the young mother's admonition: *"Apologize for your behavior right now. Then I want you two to hug and make up."*

Smiling to herself, Georgia wrangled her stubborn, sputtering pickup around and pointed it back the way she had come. She couldn't pretend anymore. She wanted to look Jett in the eye and get this resolved. She would never forgive herself if she didn't at least try.

• • •

"Toll road or Route 66?" Jett tapped the neatly creased rectangle of a map on the seat next to him. The toll road was the fastest. It didn't take the jagged path that had once been the Main Street of America. It bypassed the small towns along the way.

But Jett sort of wanted to see those towns. No, he *needed* to see them. He'd set out to gather information on Route 66 that would help him with his decision, and he wasn't going to give that up now. If he stayed as close as possible to the decommissioned highway, he noted from looking at a travel guide he'd picked up with the map, he'd see plenty. The book suggested the famous round barn in Chandler, the Cowboy Hall of Fame in Oklahoma City, and the new Route 66 museum in Clinton. It might take longer to go that way, Jett realized, and he wasn't sure if he could take the time to stop at any of the attractions, but he could use the extra time to think.

Besides, he thought as he started up the rental car and headed off solo to finish the adventure, Georgia would probably take the old route, and given Truvie's penchant for breaking down and Georgia's way of getting up close and personal with the occasional tree, he wanted to be able to come to her aid. She'd probably pitch a fit if he tried that, of course. But the very notion of her stranded on an often-deserted stretch of old road made him shudder. Old Route 66 it was, then—or as close to it as possible.

He drove away from Tulsa, his mind spinning with thoughts. The ones about Georgia he tried to set aside. Those were fruitless and only distracted him from the things he could actually do something about.

He thought of his work instead. He'd never before seen firsthand how his work affected people. He'd always tried to choose his projects wisely—those that provided a win/win situation as Uncle Lou had said. But he'd never actually gone and found out for himself how the other "winners" in the deal might feel. He wondered about going back to his old way of doing things after this. *If* he could go back.

Driving down the quiet stretch of road, with the sun on

the vast plains, he pondered *how* he could go back to his work at all and what he could do to change things for the better if he did. It was not as though they needed him. His philosophy of hiring the best and remaining detached while they did their jobs had paid off financially but had virtually cut him out of the picture. That approach had had a similar effect on his private life. But when he met Georgia, he'd found someone who needed him. When it came to the diner, only he could step in and do what had to be done.

To have a purpose, to step up and tackle a job *himself*: He had forgotten how wonderful and fulfilling that could be. As his mind leapt ahead to the diner and what he might do to help it, he began to let the two thoughts merge. Georgia had said once that he was beginning to think like her, and heaven be praised, Jett thought, that might just be the truth.

● ● ●

"He's gone *where?*" Georgia's voice broke into a squeak mid-question.

"That diner you two were originally headed for, my dear." Uncle Lou set his suitcases down with a clunk in the hotel lobby, then placed his white straw hat just so on top of his gleaming bald pate. "If you'd gotten here fifteen minutes later, I'd be gone myself. My taxi to the airport should be here any minute."

"B-but why?"

"Well, much as I like your general area of the country, Miss Darling, I gotta get back home. My business, my children, my grandchildren, and my sweet Cookie are all in Chicago."

She blinked at him, wondering if his purposefully evasive act was meant to protect Jett or to punish her for hurting his nephew. Probably both, she decided, studying the fierce set of Lou's jowly jaw.

"I meant why did Jett go on to Texas?" She wondered if she looked as meek as she felt. For some reason, whether because of Lou's age or the fact that her own rash behavior had humbled her, Georgia had no problems showing her vulnerability to Jett's uncle. She sniffed and blinked back the tears in her eyes. "I thought when the deal hit a snag he'd be on the phone, trying to salvage it. And after I'd gone, I figured if he went anywhere it would be back to Chicago."

"Well, he didn't. According to him, he told you he'd look at this diner firsthand."

"He did." The words stopped in the back of her throat like a rush of wind stealing her breath. Jett had said he'd look at the diner, but she'd assumed that he would feel no need to make good on the promise now that things had gone sour between them and with the deal. Why would he bother—unless, of course, it was because he was a man of his word?

"If my nephew said he'd go to Texas to personally clap eyes on this eyesore, why wouldn't you expect him to do just that?"

She ducked her head. Her voice grew thin. "Because not everyone does what they say they will."

"Jett does."

She stared down at her shoes. "I . . . I realize that now."

"You do?"

"Yes."

"That's why you came back?"

"Yes."

Lou stuck out his plump lower lip, sucked his teeth, scratched his nose with his bent knuckle, then coughed. "Well, knowing that you understand what a good fellow my nephew is, and knowing that he handled this whole thing like a fool who's too afraid of his own feelings to act right, I guess it wouldn't hurt for me to tell you . . . "

"What?"

"Then again, I have mixed in far too much already." He stroked his chin.

"So what will a little more hurt? I say mix away!"

He raised an eyebrow. "Maybe I should just repeat something Jett himself told me."

She wrung her hands. "What's that?"

"Something about if you've lost your love or lost your way, you'll find them at a certain diner."

"Jett told you about that?"

"Yes, he did."

"When?"

"Just a few minutes before he took off for the Double Heart, and you know what?"

She wet her lips. "What?"

"If you want to prove that little adage true, my dear, you had better get going there yourself."

16

*D*ing. *Ding.*
"Order up!"

Starla Mae blinked and shook her head as if she'd just awakened from a trance.

Jett sat up, realizing his stomach had begun to growl. Luckily, it seemed that the order he'd finally convinced Starla Mae to take—somewhere between telling about the Meramac Caverns and the Blue Whale—was ready.

"That'll be your burger." Starla Mae popped her gum. "Be right back, hon."

"Hold up, Starla Mae. Don't go until you sign this." He pushed forward the heavy white napkin he and Starla Mae had been writing on as he'd retold his tale of the race down Route 66.

Starla Mae's bracelets jangled as she picked up the napkin, looked it over, then placed it squarely down on the counter and inked out her name in large, fanciful swirls.

"There you go, sugar." She extended her hand to him.

He took it and gave it one firm shake. "Thanks."

"Thank you, doll face." The waitress with a heart of gold gave him a wink, popped her gum again, and spun away to get his meal.

"Now you." He gave the napkin to Elvis, who began

scribbling away on it. "And you're sure this'll hold up in a court of law?"

"Written agreement, signed by all parties, no one under duress. Should do 'er. But if you want to contest it, at least wait till I have my degree and can defend it myself, huh?"

For an instant Jett pictured the hunk-a hunk-a burning lawyer facing off in the courtroom against Uncle Lou. He laughed, then shook his head and clapped a hand on the back of Elvis's shiny black jacket. "I don't plan on contesting it at all."

"Thank you," Elvis muttered as he shook Jett's hand. "Thank you very much."

"No problem," he said even though he felt as though he had a world of problems bearing down on him. Where was Georgia? And why hadn't she shown up yet? Jett checked his watch. He'd been in the Double Heart about an hour but it seemed a lifetime. He sighed.

"Women, huh?" Elvis leaned both forearms on the counter and gave a sneer. "Can't live with 'em, can't—"

"Can't check into the Heartbreak Hotel to get away from them," a woman's voice broke in.

Ka-ching. The door fell shut, but Jett did not have to turn around to know who had just walked in. He would recognize that voice anywhere.

"Seems to me I can't get away from one particular woman no matter what I do." He swiveled three-quarters of the way around on his stool.

She was here. Georgia was here! His heart soared. He wanted to jump up, wrap his arms around her, and shout out a big "Yahoo!" Somehow he managed to rein in that impulse. He'd lost her once; he would not do anything that might scare her off again. "Not that I *want* to get away from that woman."

"You had your chance for that." She dropped the bag she'd carried in, lowered her chin, and looked up at him. "And by coming here, Mr. Murphy, you blew that chance!"

"Why? Because you think I fulfilled some local adage about people who've lost their love or their way ending up right here?"

"No." She gave her head the tiniest shake, causing the neon lighting to glint off those impish red locks of hers. "Because you fulfilled your own promise—the one you made to me to come and see the diner for yourself."

"I see." He turned to completely face her, his hands folded in his lap to keep himself from reaching out to touch her.

She stepped forward. "A man who keeps his word, who tries to do the right thing—I'm not letting a man like that slip out of my life without kicking up a fuss."

He raised one eyebrow at that.

She was now close enough for him to see the green of her eyes in the dimness of the diner, to see the hint of blush on her cheeks, to smell the sweet scent of her skin and of those awful lambskin seat covers from Truvie the truck. She wet her lips and stepped so close she was only an arm's length away—a distance she clearly expected him to bridge. Georgia looked at Jett, waiting for him to meet her partway.

"And, honey, you know me." She batted her lashes and lowered her voice. "When I kick up a fuss—"

"It's some fuss." He smiled. Unable to contain his feelings any longer, he reached for her and took her hands in his. "Not the kind of thing a man is likely to forget either. If you doubt that, just ask my heart."

She laid her hand on his chest. "I don't doubt it. Not for a minute."

He pulled her fully into his arms.

"And I don't doubt *you*, Jett—not for a minute." She nestled into his embrace, her face upturned. "You've more than proven yourself to me. I'm so sorry I judged you harshly because of my own fears instead of coming to you to find out the truth. I only wish I knew how to make it up to you."

"I know exactly what to do about that."

He kissed her. But it was more than a kiss, it was, to him, another promise. Moving back, he whispered that promise. "I love you, Georgia Darling. And even though in most people's books it's too soon to be sure of that, I promise you that whenever you're ready to say it back to me, I will still love you. Do you believe that?"

She nodded. "I love you too."

"Wow, two promises fulfilled in as many minutes! You've gotta hang on to me now."

"Forever," she whispered.

Around them, the diner crowd broke into applause. As they pulled away from each other, Jett saw Starla Mae Jenkins dab at her eyes with a paper napkin, and he did a quick double take to reassure himself it wasn't the one she'd just signed.

He laughed and hugged Georgia close again. "Now all we have to do is settle everything else we've been arguing about these last three days—"

"Wait!" Georgia jerked back out of his arms, her hand up. "Before you say another word, I have something for you." She opened the bag she'd dropped when she came in and plunged her hand inside, withdrawing something vivid yellow.

"What's . . . ?"

"It's a hard hat!"

It was, indeed—a child's hard hat, but a hard hat all the same.

She offered it to him. "It's just my little way of saying that if you're brave enough to hazard the trip to Chicago with me, I'm willing to go back. To leave Texas."

He smiled, pivoted on the stool, and looked at Starla Mae. He pointed to the napkin. "May I?"

"It's all yours, and I mean that."

"What's that?" Georgia looked from Starla Mae to Jett.

"Just a little business document Ms. Jenkins and I drew up tonight, with the help of a soon-to-be law student named Elvis."

Georgia's eyes shifted again as she studied first one, then the other. "What kind of business document?"

"Well, let me just say this." Jett waggled the napkin in the air. "We can go back to Chicago if you want, but it'll be a doozie of a commute to work each morning."

"Work?"

"At my diner."

"*Your* diner?"

"Mine and Starla Mae's."

Starla Mae leaned across the counter to put her hand on Jett's shoulder. "We're partners. He's found a way to save the diner, honey, and to give me a little nest egg. Bought out Elvis's shares so he can go to law school too."

"B-but . . . you're moving to Texas?" Georgia blinked.

"At least until we've got the diner renovated and back on its feet. I've got some great ideas for bringing in business."

"You? Now *you're* the one getting ideas?" Georgia's eyes grew enormous.

"Hey, I learned from the best," he teased.

"But what about Chicago? What about the Padgett Group and your family?"

"The way I've set up my business, I can run it from anywhere. And we're just a short flight away, really."

"Airline tickets are such an expense though. It's not like you could go back all that often—"

Starla Mae gave out a little hoot of laughter. "Georgia, honey, the man can afford the price of the ticket. Land's sake, child, don't you think he can't buy a whole plane if he gets an itch to?"

Jett shrugged. There was no use in arguing with the truth.

"Oh . . . yeah." Georgia bit her lip. Then a sudden brightness flashed across her features. "Hey, that's an idea! I could learn to fly and we could get these big banners advertising the diner, and—"

"Whoa!" He reached over to grab her to him. "Let's hold off on that concept a while." He twisted in his seat to explain over his shoulder to Starla Mae. "I've seen her *drive.*"

"You'll get no argument from me, partner. I've seen her *truck!*"

Jett laughed. "Heaven help us all! The last thing this place needs is a big old flying Truvie sputtering over our heads!"

"Ha-ha." Georgia gently pinched his cheek. "But you are right about one thing."

"What's that?"

"Heaven has helped us through all this—and I'm truly grateful for it all."

"So am I, Georgia Darling." He kissed her forehead, her nose, and then her lips. "So am I."

Epilogue

Three months later

"So you're going through with it?" Lou pursed his lips, swiped his wrist across his sweat-dampened brow, and glowered at Jett.

"Yep."

"No hesitations? No reservations?" Lou pushed down his straw cowboy hat with the Mexican hatband to shade his eyes.

Jett blinked, secretly grateful for the reprieve from seeing the late summer Texas sun glare off his uncle's bald head. He sighed. "No hesitations or reservations. Not a one."

"You're sure? You're absolutely sure?"

Jett opened his mouth to reassure Lou yet another time, but it was Georgia's voice that resounded at him from across the Double Heart's parking lot.

"Hey, hey, hey! What's this now? Are you trying to talk Jett out of the wedding, Uncle Lou?" She shaded her eyes with her hand, but that did not dim her brilliant smile.

"Well, I should hope to say not!" Lou adjusted the silver longhorn head that decorated his black-and-white braided leather bolo tie. "Marrying you, sweet Georgia girl, is the only thing this big lug is doing that makes any sense to me."

"Does that mean you've forgiven us for not wanting to have a big wedding?"

"What's to forgive?"

"It's just that your family is so big and Jett has all these business contacts that would expect to get invitations, and I only have Starla Mae and Elvis—"

"And Truvie." Jett pulled his bride-to-be into a hug. "Let's not forget Truvie."

"Are you kidding? I'd have had to have Truvie be my maid of honor." She laughed.

"Then I am glad you two decided to elope now, then have a big, Texas-style reception after you get this . . . this . . . " He made bold, circular motions in the air in the general direction of the diner. "This *place* all fixed up again."

"That's what he can't believe I'm going through with: the diner renovation," Jett explained.

Lou shook his head. He tucked his thumbs beneath his hand-tooled belt with the name Lou on the back. His silver-and-gold belt buckle the size of the diner's lunch platter winked in the unrelenting sun. "Are you sure, son?"

Jett nodded. "I'm sure. We've already got the kitchen, the plumbing, and the wiring taken care of. Now we just need to spiff up the interior a little, then tackle the exterior and restore the Double Heart to its former glory."

"Former glory?" Lou yipped like a kicked dog. "This dump? No offense, Georgia, honey. I know how much this place means to you. But even you have to concede that a greasy spoon in the shape of two valentines—one pink, one purple, and I ain't even sure which one is which—well, the word 'glory' don't exactly leap into one's mind."

Jett and Georgia both laughed.

"Anyway, we're all set to begin the rest of the renovations this fall," Jett said. "Starla Mae and Elvis have already taken some time off to help him get ready for law school. He's still off on one of his Elvis gigs—there were a couple of those he didn't want to give up, it seems. But now that Starla Mae is back . . . "

Jett grabbed Georgia's arm, then slid his hand down to hers and lifted it up to plant a kiss on her delicate fingers. "It's our turn to take some time away for a quick wedding and an extended honeymoon before we have to get back to work—that is, if we ever come back."

"First thing you've said in a while that made any sense at all," Lou grumbled. "If I were you two, I'd want my honeymoon to last a lifetime."

Jett never took his eyes off Georgia. "Who says it isn't going to, Uncle Lou?"

Georgia's cheeks, already rosy from the heat of the day, turned a deeper shade of scarlet. With a twinkle in her eye that would do her favorite TV redhead proud, she smiled and whispered, "That's one promise I'm going to make sure you live up to, you know."

"Count on it," he murmured just before his lips came down over hers to seal that bargain with a kiss.

Look for the next book in Annie Jones's
Route 66 Series!

CUPID'S CORNER

Available May 1999

Cupid's Corner, Kansas, earned its title of "Hitchin' City USA" during the glory days of old Route 66, when it once hosted a record sixty weddings in fifty-eight days. Now the city has been all but forgotten, and Mayor Jenny Fox hopes to revive her beloved hometown with one all-out attempt to break their own record. This year, between July 4 and Labor Day, she will do everything possible to see their tiny town stage a whopping sixty-six weddings—and she is not going to let anyone get in her way, least of all the compelling new editor of the town paper, Joe Avery.

Joe has his own ideas about the town, the event, and—most of all—the stubborn but lovely mayor. He'd like to get to know her better, but their jobs, the wedding chaos, and Jenny's insistence that she is not interested in love or marriage complicate his plans. The return of a man who left Jenny at the altar, now a big city doctor who can't forget his once-intended, may stop the presses on any romantic headlines Joe hopes to make.

Records, reporters, reunions, and romance—one thing's for sure, it's going to be a memorable summer in Cupid's Corner.

If you enjoyed *The Double Heart Diner,*
check out Suzy Pizzuti's *Say Uncle . . . and Aunt!*
The following is an excerpt from Pizzuti's
first book in the Halo Hattie's Boarding House series,
available in bookstores now.

1

"Are you . . . uh, oh . . . are you going to . . . ," Julia Evans stammered uncertainly, ". . . be all right? Oh, dear . . . can I . . . help . . . ?" Grimacing, she rushed forward to offer Mrs. Hattie Hopkins her arm as the elderly woman proceeded to lurch up the porch stairs. "Mrs. Hopkins? Uh . . . can I give you . . . some help?"

As she hovered at Hattie's back, Julia trailed the boarding-house landlady up the steps, her arms outstretched, ready to catch this tiny dynamo should the need arise. I . . . uh . . . okay, I guess you . . . have it under control. I'll just stand back . . . here."

Oblivious to Julia's concern, Hattie swayed wildly and snagged a porch post with the hook of her walking cane. Regaining her balance, she continued her precarious trip up the steps, never once breaking her informative monologue.

". . . and the house was built in 1864—or was it '65? Gracious sakes," Hattie twittered with laughter. "I can never remember . . . and of course, back yonder are the rose gardens and gazebo. Nice place to sit, on a midsummer night, yes, my, my, my. Lovely view of the lake, don't you know. In the fall the trees really put on a show. It's stunning, I'm telling you. Well, you'll see for yourself in a few weeks. October is always spectacular, I say."

Once they had safely reached the top of the steps, Julia dropped her arms and allowed her gaze to travel slowly around the front porch as Hattie—owner and proprietress of Hattie Hopkins's Boarding House—continued to lead her on an interesting, if somewhat wobbly, tour of the facilities.

Covered with corbels and fish scales, spindles and spokes, and an abundance of ornate gingerbread from a bygone era, the aging Victorian reminded Julia of her own grandmother's house. Only Hattie's place, sitting atop a gentle hill at the edge of a lake in McLaughlin, Vermont, was even lovelier. It was uncanny how at home Julia felt, considering how far away from home, and her grandmother's house, she actually was.

"Well," Hattie warbled, "that's the whole place, inside and out. Come on back inside and tell me what you think," she instructed, beckoning Julia with a shaky wave of her cane.

Julia followed Hattie into the quaint parlor and perched on the springy, buttoned-and-tufted loveseat the little land-lady indicated. From the smell of lilacs and lemon furniture polish to the way the afternoon light filtered through the voluminous lace curtains, from the porcelain knickknacks to the musty old books, yes, and even the elderly woman who slowly settled onto the antique settee across from her—everything reminded Julia of home. Of family. "I love this place," Julia breathed.

Yes, she decided firmly. She would take the room, regardless of what it looked like.

"You love his face . . . hmmm." Hattie bunched her lips into a thoughtful wad as she pondered Julia's words. "Oh! My, my, yes. Why, thank you, dearie. Yes, I love his face too."

A puzzled frown marred Julia's brow. Whose face? Had she missed something?

The elderly business owner waved a gnarled finger back at the black-and-white picture of a smiling man on the fireplace mantel. "That's my dear late husband, Ernest. Ernie went to be with the Lord about ten years ago, and I'm sure he's up there having a fine time chasing the angels around till I arrive to cuff him upside the head. Hee-hoo-hoo-hoo!" Sapphire-blue eyes twinkling, her laughter yodeled up and down the scale. Tucking a snow-white tendril back into her droopy bun, Hattie sobered slightly. "I surely do miss him."

"Oh, I can imagine," Julia murmured. Brows arched, she attempted to keep track of the erratic conversation.

"So," Hattie trilled in her birdlike falsetto as she slowly grasped a stack of papers that had been lying on the coffee table and moved them to her lap, "are you going to take the room?"

Julia nodded. "Yes, ma'am. As soon as possible. In fact, the sooner, the better." As often as she had been transferred on her climb up the corporate ladder, Julia didn't have much in the way of personal effects. Everything she owned was crammed into her car, now parked at the curb. Though Julia considered renting an apartment right away, Hattie's boarding house seemed like a much less complex, much less lonely, answer to her housing needs. For now, anyway. After she'd had time to discover McLaughlin's rental possibilities, she would undoubtedly move again. Until then, Hattie's place was surely a godsend. "I hate to disrupt your Sunday afternoon, but I'd like to get settled today and explore the town tomorrow. So, if it's all right with you, I'd like to move in right away."

"Oh, no, don't worry, I haven't given the room away. Now then," Hattie fingered the delicate cameo broach at her throat, "when will you want to move in, honey?"

Julia blinked. "Uh, right away," she repeated, "if that's

okay." Smoothing her skirt over her knees, she smiled expectantly.

"Not today?"

"Oh." Not today. Hmm. Was the old woman asking or telling? In the short hour she'd been here, the conversation had taken more turns than a spinning ice skater. Perhaps it would be easier to work within Hattie's schedule. "What would be good for you?"

Looking pleased, Hattie nodded. "Ah, yes. Well, that's just fine."

What? What was fine? Julia studied Hattie's sunny face for a clue. "Um, Mrs. Hopkins, what exactly is, uh, fine?"

"Good. Good, then it's settled." Reaching forward, Hattie patted Julia's stocking-clad knee. "Breakfast begins at 6:30 every morning. You're on your own for lunch, and I start serving supper at 6:30 every evening, except for the Lord's day. Sundays after church, we all lie around, eat sandwiches, play games, and rest. In the afternoon, everyone is on his own." Peering at Julia, she winked. "Just remember 6:30, and you'll be fine."

Okay. Six-thirty is mealtime. That much she comprehended. Julia smiled and gave her head a slight shake. This was certainly the answer to her prayer, she thought gratefully and heaved an internal sigh of relief. Being transferred to a new city was always such a hassle. Having dinner prepared every night was a bonus she hadn't counted on. "That's really lovely."

"Oh yes, we have laundry facilities in the basement." Hattie tapped her orthopedic shoe on the hardwood floor to emphasize her point.

Julia cocked her head. Laundry? Now they were discussing laundry? Well, good. That had been her next question.

This was perfect. Aside from the rather frustrating style of Hattie's conversation, Julia was sure she'd stumbled into a little piece of heaven. And even though her new landlady at times seemed a bit dotty, Hattie was a doll. Julia loved her already.

"Hattie!" a male voice bellowed from the top of the basement stairs at the end of the hallway. "Hattie? Where are you?" The insistent hollering continued to fill the parlor.

Ignoring the ruckus, Hattie extended toward Julia the rental agreement that had been lying in her lap. "Now then. If you will just sign here, dear," she chirped, pointing to the dotted line at the bottom of the page.

"I think someone is calling you, Mrs. Hopkins." Julia inclined her head toward the doorway as she scribbled her name at the bottom of the agreement.

"No, I'll fill out the rest, honey." Hattie smiled placidly.

"Hattie!"

Julia looked up in surprise as a young man carrying several overflowing baskets of laundry stumbled into the room, leaving a trail of socks and underwear as he went.

"Hey, Hattie, Rahni left a bunch of stuff in the dryer again," he said, shouting at her. Then he noticed Julia. "Oh, hi," he said, lowering his voice and smiling appreciatively. "I'm sorry. I didn't know Hattie had company." Turning, he deposited the mountain of clothing in front of the fireplace, his smile fading to a frown.

Gesturing to the laundry, his voice rose again as he announced loudly, "Rahni forgot the laundry again."

Startled, Julia clutched uncertainly at the overstuffed arm of the small loveseat.

"Bonnie forgot the sundries again?" Hattie frowned. "I will speak with her."

"The laundry!" he shouted, then turned and grinned at

Julia. "Rahni is an exchange student who helps out around here with the cooking and cleaning when she's not in class learning English."

"Bonnie is from the Midwest," the beaming landlady put in.

"Middle East," he corrected, biting back a smile.

"Don, dear, this is Beulah."

"Hi, Beulah." Smiling easily, the handsome young man moved to Julia and extended his hand. "Nice to meet you."

"It's, uh, Julia," she murmured as his large, warm hand enveloped hers. "My name, that is—Julia." What was her last name? Oh, yes. "Evans." Mercy! Julia thought, her heart picking up speed as she stared up into his mischievous green eyes. He sure is cute. "Nice to meet you, Don."

"Sean," he corrected with a wink, lowering his voice to a normal level. "Sean Flannigan. Nice to meet you too. You've probably noticed by now that Hattie is a little hard of hearing."

Hattie smiled benignly at the two as they conversed.

"Ahhh, so that's it," Julia murmured, returning his smile.

"Sit, sit, sit, Don," Hattie ordered. "Don is a director of films over in England." Beaming, she motioned for him to squeeze in next to Julia on the minuscule loveseat.

"Rooms," Sean murmured as he took his place next to Julia. "I'm director of rooms for the New England Inn."

Julia could feel a warmth radiating from him and couldn't be sure if it was from his lanky body as he wedged it into the remaining space on the tufted loveseat or from the light of his compelling personality. Something about Sean was simply irresistible.

Clearing her throat, Julia tore her eyes away from his and studied her shoes in embarrassment. Could he tell she was blushing? How silly. He couldn't read her mind. He couldn't have any idea how appealing she thought the little cleft in his chin was. His thigh rested lightly against hers. Swallowing, she tried shifting away to allow him extra room, but the ancient springs beneath her legs thwarted her best efforts, making it uncomfortable to rest anywhere else.

"The New England Inn? Ah, yes," Julia nodded, attempting to bring the erratic timpani of her heartbeat under control and exude a cool, sophisticated demeanor. "I love the New England Inn. I stay there quite often when I travel on business," she said, finding herself staring at the small cleft in his chin. Julia quickly looked away. Goodness. She was practically sitting in his lap.

"Yes," Hattie interjected happily, following the gist of the conversation, "Beulah is a nurse."

"Nursing-home medical equipment," Julia whispered for Sean's benefit and glanced up at the dimples that created deep crevices in his cheeks. Have mercy! They were sitting so close his face was nearly out of focus. Fighting the lumpy cushions that held her captive, she leaned slightly back and continued. "I work for Gerico Industries. We sell medical equipment to . . . ahhh . . . nursing homes." Her gaze traveled over his nose, across his cheekbones, over his slightly unruly, chestnut-colored hair, back down his forehead, and finally collided with his glowing, green eyes.

He certainly wasn't handsome in the classical sense. So, considering she didn't know him from Adam, what on earth was it about him that made him so . . . interesting? No, Sean Flannigan wasn't just another pretty face, but his rugged good looks coupled with the twinkle in his emerald eyes made him an attention grabber. The quiet strength he exuded was also very compelling.

Eyes darting in confusion, Julia looked away and struggled to don the mask of professionalism that had gotten her this far in her career.

"In that case," Sean deadpanned, "next time I'm injured or bleeding, I won't bother you, Beulah."

"Not unless you want to see me faint, Don," Julia returned.

Sean grinned. "So. You're moving in?"

Clearing her throat, she wondered briefly if he was married. No ring. Not that it mattered to her, of course. She was simply curious. At this point in her increasingly successful career, Julia didn't have time for regular social relationships, let alone the romantic variety. A long time ago she'd made up her mind to follow her career path instead of the paths of the heart. It had been a good decision. Already she was senior vice president of the sales division of Gerico Industries and only twenty-seven years old. She'd lived in almost every state on the East Coast so far and had traveled extensively on behalf of her company. She had no regrets. In respect to her career, she'd been blessed.

"Yes," she said, proud of the cultured note she was able to inject into her voice. "I think this boarding house will suit my needs as I get the lay of the land, so to speak. It's close to my new office and to shopping. I just arrived here in Vermont. I was transferred." She exhaled slowly. "Again."

"Oh yeah. I've been transferred a time or two myself. Always seem to end up back here though." Sean's lopsided smile was empathetic. "Well, that's great. Welcome to McLaughlin."

"Thank you," she murmured, trying to ignore the little tingles that danced down her spine at his kind words.

"Need any help moving in?"

His voice was like chocolate, rich and smooth. Julia

decided she could listen to him recite the greater McLaughlin area phone book all afternoon, it was so soothing.

"Oh, no," she demurred quickly, once again catching herself staring in a most unprofessional fashion. Generally, Julia's heart didn't go all atwitter this way at a mere offer of assistance. "I don't have much to move, being transferred so often and all . . . just a suitcase or two and some light boxes." It was important that she travel light. Surely she would be transferred again before a year had passed. She sighed. Relocating was always so bothersome.

"Don," Hattie trilled, "when you have a moment, give Beulah a hand moving, will you, dear? Her room is next to yours on the tower side." To Julia she said, "Don's always loaning me his muscles."

Julia's eyes bounced to the biceps that bulged beneath the fabric of his ratty football jersey.

"You heard the lady," Sean said with an easy grin. "I guess you're stuck with me."

"Oh. I . . . well. Okay then." Secretly pleased, Julia focused on her hands and tried to keep her growing attraction in its proper perspective. She didn't know anything about this man. Maybe his easy countenance and affable charisma were simply part of an act. She glanced up into his eyes. Hmm. No. Some gut feeling told her that Sean was a genuinely nice person.

"Here, Beulah," Hattie warbled, plunging her hand into the valley of her generous bosom—where Julia noticed that the older woman tended to store various items—and extracted a key ring. She removed a single key. "This is yours. Run up and make sure the door is unlocked before Don begins bringing your things in from the car."

"Thank you." Julia took the key and attempted to stand up. Unfortunately, wedged as she was so tightly between

Sean and the arm of the little loveseat, she merely succeeded in becoming more acutely aware of her new neighbor's solid build. "I'll just . . . uh . . . run up and do that," she huffed and smiled.

Once again, she leaned forward, gathered her momentum, and attempted to stand. With no luck.

Face now crimson, Julia gripped the overstuffed arm and tried to gracefully work her way out of her slot without inadvertently touching Sean's firm thigh any more than absolutely necessary.

"Ooph! I . . . uh . . . ha! . . . ," she puffed, inching her way forward on the springy cushions that tended to work against her best efforts to leave.

Darting a quick glance at her new neighbor, she noticed he was—much to his credit—trying not to grin. The telltale crimson flush that stained her cheeks now crawled to her neck and left her entire head feeling as if it were engulfed in flames. Her groping feet barely touched the floor, and she felt like a high-centered car revving her engines but going nowhere fast.

Waving an airy hand, she strained to appear graceful. "Excuse me," she murmured in what she hoped was a well-modulated, breezy tone of voice—and not the grunt she suspected it was. Clutching at the hem of her skirt, she tugged it back down around her knees as she alternately worked her hips back and forth. She felt like a complete and total idiot.

"Of course," Sean said, leaning over to his side of the loveseat in an effort to give her more room. Creaking and popping, the springs in the cushions responded, creating a dip in his direction that suddenly sent Julia sprawling against his side and pinning one of her hands beneath her. Mortified, she dared not look up.

Time suspended for a moment as she wondered what to

do. Other than the shoulder her cheek was now flattened against, there didn't seem to be a single thing she could grab hold of for a boost. Slowly, she brought her eyes to his. His brows were arched in surprise.

"Uh . . . ha! Oh, dear," Julia warbled. Now don't go and get all flustered, she warned herself, attempting to exude an attitude of carefree abandon. "I'm so sorry," she chirped, gripping Sean's arm with her one free hand as she tried to find purchase on the floor for her airborne feet. Oh, this is just awful, she thought wildly.

"I'm really sorry," she apologized again, her legs flopping about like the tail of a freshly landed fish. Gracious! Some impression she must be making. She'd only just met him, and now here she was, trying to tear the sleeve off the poor man's shirt.

"No problem," he assured her as the grin he'd been holding in check finally split across his face.

Eventually, they managed to sort themselves out.

"Oh, thank you," Julia said. She could feel Sean supporting her lower back with his hand as he helped her over to her side of the seat. "Thank you," she repeated, battling her way to her feet. Once standing, she pushed her skirt back down around her knees and patted her falling chignon back into place. Her cheeks still felt like twin spots of molten lava.

"Any time," Sean assured her in that chocolate voice of his.

Taking a giant step back, Julia fought a burst of hysterical laughter as she darted a glance at the nearest exit. "All right, then," she said with a lilt to her voice. She laughed brightly, hoping to belie her mortification. "I'll just go unlock the door, then I'll . . . be back." Unless of course, she died of embarrassment before she could return.

"I'll be here," Sean assured her.

Turning, Julia waved good-bye then promptly bolted into a tottering wall of buttons, military bars, and medals.

Will this hideous embarrassment never end? she wondered as she slowly peered past a pair of wire-framed bifocals and into the quizzical, watery-blue eyes that stared back at her from the surprised face of the ancient man she'd almost knocked to the floor. Wispy gray hair sprouted crazily from his spotted and balding pate, and his sagging lips opened and closed rhythmically, reminding Julia of a goldfish.

"At ease!" the aged commander commanded, his thin, reedy voice cracking as he reached out to pat Julia on the arm.

"I'm so sorry." Julia's apology was breathless as she backed into the parlor to make way for the older man.

Nodding, he continued to stare at Julia for a moment as if trying to remember where they'd last met; he thoughtfully sucked and clicked his ill-fitting dentures, then giving up, shuffled into the room. Shoulders stooped under the weight of a good century on this earth, he stopped in front of Sean and waited.

Sean shot a glance at Julia, who still hovered near the doorway. Blushing as he attempted to maneuver his lanky frame from the depths of Hattie's man-eating loveseat, he grunted, "Good afternoon, Colonel, sir," as he finally found his feet. Coming to attention, he crisply saluted.

Pleased, the Colonel returned his salute and nodded. "At ease," he rasped, then slowly turned and smiled. "Afternoon, Hattie," he said and cackled dryly. Swinging his gaze back to Julia, he hiked a curious brow. "Afternoon, miss."

Uncertain as to whether she was expected to salute this superior officer, Julia lifted her hand to her brow, scratched a little, and decided to let him do the interpreting.

"Hello." Straightening her spine, Julia brought her hands stiffly to her sides.

Sean's dimples exploded into bloom. "Colonel," he said, crossing the room to stand between Julia and the older man, "I'd like to present our newest boarder, Julia Evans. Julia, this is Colonel Milton Merryweather."

"So nice to meet you," Julia murmured.

"Likewise," the Colonel said with a bob of his head and an illusive twinkle in his pale-blue eyes. Snatching his gaze from her face, he unsteadily surveyed the rest of the room. "Anyone seen the Ross sisters?" At the blank faces that greeted his question, he shook his head. "I told them thirteen hundred hours," he muttered as he fished his timepiece out of his coat pocket. "They'd never have made it in the army."

At this ominous pronouncement, a throbbing ballyhoo down the hall filtered into the parlor.

"Have you lost what's left of your senses? I'm simply telling you it's not proper at this station in life, Glynnis!"

"Who says?" a snappy voice replied.

"Are you trying to get us thrown out of the senior center?"

"Really, Agnes, you are such a kill-joy."

"I am not-t-t-t!" the first voice shouted, mindless of the fact that her words carried farther than a foghorn on an ocean liner.

"You are too!"

"Why? Because I do not think you should consider a swimming costume that reveals the midriff? Especially a midriff that looks as if it could use a good ironing."

There was an audible gasp. "I beg your pardon! I'm in fine shape. Besides, I'm not planning on wearing it to . . . to . . . to church!"

"Not yet, you're not! I don't care, Glynnis. Call me a pooper and start the party without me."

Suddenly the Ross sisters rounded the corner and came sternly toward Julia and Sean as their argument continued. "The senior waterobics class would never withstand the shock." Raising a finger, the first sister—Julia quickly figured out it was Agnes—gestured at the Colonel. "Oh, he's in here. Come on, Glynnis," she screeched as though the other woman were a half-mile away instead of following closely behind her. Agnes beckoned to her sister with one of her long, bony arms.

"Oh, here you are," Glynnis twittered girlishly, spotting the Colonel and pushing in front of her elderly older sister.

"I'm precisely where I should be," the Colonel hollered, then coughed and wheezed for a frightening minute. "It's . . . thirteen hundred hours." He flipped open his watch and held it open to prove his point.

"You see," Agnes said with a smug look at her elderly younger sister, "I told you thirteen hundred hours was one o'clock, not three o'clock."

"You did not."

"Glynnis, I distinctly remember . . ."

Hattie smiled blandly as the sisters squabbled.

Deciding to interrupt before Monday arrived, Sean stepped between the bickering ladies and charmed them with his smile. Julia watched in amusement.

"Oh, hello, Sean, dear," Agnes groused. The frown lines between her brows furrowed. The slighter and more digni-fied of the two sisters, Agnes still had a commanding pres-ence that Julia feared could be formidable when the situation warranted.

Glynnis, taller, plumper, and most obviously—by her clashing clothing choices—less concerned about style than her sister, laughed flirtatiously and patted Sean's cheek.

"Miss Agnes and Miss Glynnis, I'd like you to meet our newest boarder, Julia Evans."

"Well, hello," Agnes sniffed. The older woman slowly about-faced, taking several dozen tiny steps, and squinted up at Julia through the thick lenses of her trifocals. "Do you play bridge? We are looking for a fourth . . ."

"Actually," Glynnis crabbed, correcting her sister, "we are looking for a third too. Sean, do you play?"

Sean took a step back toward Julia, and they exchanged befuddled glances.

"I—" Julia started to say.

"You know, Miss Glynnis, bridge was never one of those games I learned to—" Sean began, but before he had a chance to reveal his hopelessness at the art of bridge, a large, black Doberman pinscher came bounding into the parlor.

Ears back, teeth bared, fur at attention, the dog sniffed the air.

Terror-stricken, Julia unconsciously reached out and clutched Sean's strong arm.

"Nobody move!" came a harried and breathless shout from down the hallway. "Sweetpea! Stay! Sit, boy!"

Eyes wild, clothes rumpled, and hair standing on end, a man swung around the doorcasing and into the parlor. Sweetpea, an ominous growl emanating from deep in his throat, crouched low and surveyed the room's terrified occupants.

"Freeze!" the man needlessly instructed the frozen faction and, holding his palms up, slowly inched his way toward the dog.

"Please what, Brian, dear?" Hattie wondered. Obviously not having heard the dire instructions, she laboriously made her way to her feet.

Swinging his head in Hattie's direction, Sweetpea bared

his teeth. Saliva slowly dripped from the animal's jowls. Eyes narrowed and filled with suspicion, the dog crouched low, and it seemed to Sean to be eyeing Hattie's jugular. He was sure his heart had stopped beating.

"Sh-Sh-Sean?" Julia whispered, paralyzed with fear.

Sean covered her fingers with his own. As he mentally sized up the animal, he rolled his eyes and could only hope that he wasn't going to have to resort to mortal combat with this devil dog.

"Don't worry. It will . . . uh . . . ," Sean swallowed, ". . . be okay," he asserted manfully under his breath to Julia. Yeah. Right, he thought, moving slightly between Julia and the dog. Everything would be okay, provided this devil's spawn didn't rip out their throats before he could remember his basic karate. Unconsciously, he began to pray. Oh, Lord. Oh, Lord. Ohhhh, Lord. Hellllpppp!

"Hattie!" the dog's compatriot hissed. "Don't move! And whatever you do, don't make eye contact with the dog. That will only serve to incite him."

Julia tightened her grip on Sean's arm as five pairs of eyes shot to the floor.

Adjusting her glasses, Hattie peered into the dog's eyes. "Well, of course you can invite him in, Brian, dear," she warbled and clutched her cane for balance. "Hello, darling puppy. Come here." She held a shaky hand out to the dog's viselike jaw.

Everyone gasped.

"Nice doggy," she crooned.

As if in slow motion, the dog leaned forward and tentatively sniffed Hattie's fingers. Then, apparently deciding she was to his liking, Sweetpea flopped docilely at her feet.

A collective sigh of relief filled the air.

Moving purposefully toward the dog, the man who'd been chasing him slipped a muzzle over his mouth and deftly fastened the buckles. Straightening, he cast an apologetic glance around the room.

"Sorry if he scared you. We were in the middle of his first session when he decided to . . . uh—the dog began to thrash in an attempt to cast off the unwanted muzzle."

"He went AWOL!" the Colonel cried with a look of disdain at the crazily swaying dog. "Look out, Ryan, old man; he's going ballistic!"

Leaping forward, Ryan barely managed to keep one of Hattie's vases from toppling over. "Uh . . . yeah," he panted, "but I can . . . promise you . . . it won't . . . happen again."

Clipping a leash on Sweetpea's collar, Ryan tugged the violently flailing dog to his side. Anxious to regain his freedom, Sweetpea growled and strained against the leash.

Ryan grunted, attempting to maintain his balance, "I'm . . . s-s-sorry for . . . uff! . . . the bother. Sit, Sweetpea!" he roared. "Stay!"

In an effort to soothe the alarm he saw in her eyes, Sean patted Julia's hand as it still clutched his arm. "Ryan, I'd like you to meet our newest neighbor, Julia Evans. Julia, this is Ryan Lowell."

Though rather disheveled, Julia could tell that when Ryan wasn't chasing renegade dogs, he was a handsome man. Although not, in her humble opinion, as handsome as Sean. Tall and dark, he exuded a certain kindness and sensitivity that Julia responded to immediately.

"Nice to . . . meet you," Ryan huffed as Sweetpea proceeded to circle his legs, tightly winding the leash around his knees.

"Nice to meet you too, Ryan." Julia glanced up at Sean,

then at Hattie. Adjusting her glasses, the landlady gazed fondly at Ryan as he grappled with the hyperactive and decidedly unhappy Sweetpea.

"Brian works with dogs from the Colombian rain forest," she told Julia with pride. "The poor things seem to have an inordinate amount of problems, for some reason. Must be the humidity," she mused, oblivious to the whirling dervish at her side.

"Actually," Ryan grunted as he struggled to disentangle the leash from his legs, "I'm a . . . canine behaviorist." Arms waving in broad circles, he fought to remain upright and tossed a feeble smile at Julia. "And, uh . . . most of my dogs . . . are . . . sit, Sweetpea! . . . from . . . right here in McLaughlin. Sometimes . . . as far away as . . . Montpelier or Barre, but mostly right around here. SWEETPEA! SIT!" Having issued the order, he dove to the floor and pinned the writhing and growling Sweetpea beneath his body.

Seemingly used to such unusual behavior, the little group in the parlor relaxed and began to make small talk among themselves.

Julia sent a questioning look at Sean.

"Dogs are pack animals," he explained with a shrug. "Ryan tells us that pinning the dog with the . . ." He frowned thoughtfully, "What do you call that hold, Ryan?"

"Alpha s-s-stronghold," Ryan panted.

"Oh, yeah. The alpha stronghold. Anyway, this shows the dog who's boss."

"Oh," Julia said dubiously.

Sweetpea issued a vicious snarl from somewhere beneath Ryan's chest.

"Well, ladies," the Colonel said to Agnes and Glynnis as he impatiently clicked and sucked at his dentures, "if we are going to make it to waterobics, we are going to have to march."

Amid much dissension and hullabaloo, the Ross sisters each took a proffered arm and proceeded to battle for the Colonel's attention.

"I've got a new swimming costume," Glynnis informed him as they shuffled into the hall.

"It's disgusting," Agnes snapped.

"Why, Agnes! What a meanspirited thing to say!" Then to the Colonel, Glynnis groused, "I think she's jealous."

"Of what?"

"Of my new swimsuit. And my new bathing cap. Next to me, she'll look positively frumpy."

"Better a frump than a strumpet. Colonel, you should see the undignified thing she stretches on over her addled brain. All that gaudy fruit. Carmen Miranda wouldn't have been caught dead in such a getup."

Their voices faded as they argued their way to the front door.

"It is not gaudy."

"Yes, it is!" reverberated down the hallway until the Colonel herded them onto the porch and slammed the door behind him.

Once Sweetpea was suitably subdued, Ryan rose to his feet and dusted himself off. "All right then," he said with a quick peck on Hattie's temple, "I have to get back to work myself." With a sheepish smile at Julia, he bade everyone good day and was summarily yanked into the hallway by the dog.

The room was silent for a moment as Hattie, Sean, and Julia stared after him. Julia glanced around, shifting awkwardly from foot to foot as she groped for something to say.

"Well, Julia," Sean's voice finally broke the hush, "the only person—aside from Rahni, our exchange student—that you have yet to meet is Olivia."

Julia smiled weakly. "There's another one?"

Sean grinned. "Don't worry. Olivia is very quiet. No pets either."

Heaving a grateful sigh, Julia glanced at the key in her hand. "Okay. Well, I suppose I should . . . you know . . . go open my door." Waving the key in a little circle, she took a tentative step back. She looked both ways before she ventured into the hallway and then turned. To Sean she said, "I'll be back in a moment to unlock my car if, you know, you still want to help."

"I'll be right here."

His eyes stayed on the empty doorway for a moment after Julia had eased herself out of the room.

"Nice girl," Hattie informed him, snapping him out of his reverie. "You should invite her out on a date, Don. She's single. Twenty-seven years old. Never been married." The old woman narrowed her gaze at him.

She's single? he thought jubilantly, feeling Hattie's hawk-like gaze studying him. He tried to look blasé. Yes! He'd wondered about that, considering she wasn't wearing a wedding ring and all. Playing it cool in front of Hattie, he decided he'd wait until he was alone to do a little end-zone victory jig. Carefully, he filed this information away in his mind, where he hoped it would someday come in handy.

ASK FOR THESE OTHER BOOKS FROM
A TIME FOR LAUGHTER...AND ROMANCE
AT YOUR LOCAL BOOKSTORE!

Suzy Pizzuti
Halo Hattie's Boarding House Series:
Only God could take hard-of-hearing Halo Hattie's fervent prayers for the wrong things and make them right!

#1 Say Uncle...And Aunt: Sean Flannigan and Julia Evans, two high-powered executives, are suddenly on baby-care duty and unexpectedly fall for more than the baby.

#2 Raising Cain (and His Sisters): Olivia Harmon is struggling to heal after a tragic loss. Only the arrival of Cain and his sisters can bring her out of her shell again! *Available June 1999.*

#3 Saving Grace: Everything Grace touches or tries turns out badly. That is until she meets Ryan Lowell, the handsome bachelor who helps her realize that with God's help, anything is possible. *Available June 2000.*

Shari MacDonald
The Salinger Sisters Series:
Meet four sisters, each of whom has her own escapades while falling in love.

#1 Love on the Run: Cat Salinger wants one thing: the big new ad account. Her chief competition (and major distraction in the love department), Jonas Riley, proves to be more than Cat bargained for.

#2 *A Match Made in Heaven:* Lucy Salinger is a fantastic match-maker. But will she find the cute new doctor a wife—or keep him for herself?

#3 *The Perfect Wife:* After her husband divorces her, Felicia begins a new life. But her new male housekeeper cares for her more than she dreams! *Available October 1999.*

Barbara Jean Hicks
The Once Upon a Dream Series:
Fairy tales retold in modern times!

#1 *An Unlikely Prince:* A professor rents a quiet cottage in a distant town to accomplish his writing goals. Little does he know that his lovely neighbor is running a day-care center for seven imps!

#2 *All That Glitters:* Spunky Cindy Reilly has a disagreeable stepmother, an eccentric "fairy godmother," and one too many princes. Pilchuck's very own Cinderella story. *Available June 1999.*

Book #3; Coming in February 2000.

Annie Jones
The Route 66 Series:

#1 The Double Heart Diner: Georgia Darling's mission seemed simple: Save the Double Heart Diner. But things have become more complicated since sophisticated Jett entered the picture. She likes him, maybe too much, but it's clear she can't trust him. Can she save the diner—and her own heart—before it's too late?

#2 *Cupid's Corner*: The fiesty lady mayor of a small Kansas city on a stretch of forgotten Route 66 is trying to reestablish its title of Hitchin' City USA by staging a summer marriage-a-thon. Will the mayor and the winsome new editor of the local paper find themselves with their own irresistible itch to get hitched? *Available October 1999.*

#3 *Lost Romance Ranch*: Built by a broken-hearted cowpoke years ago, the once famous dude ranch is now the subject of legal wrangling. When a separated couple is sent off on a treasure hunt along Route 66 to see who will win ownership of the land, can they find the love they've lost along the way? *Available June 2000.*

DYNAMIC, EXCITING, AND EFFECTIVE—
FIND OUT HOW MUCH YOU CAN DO TO END RACISM

- Dos and don'ts of using nonracist language
- Toys, dolls, reading material, music, videos, and activities for children that will help reinforce positive images of all ethnic groups
- Interviews you can conduct with community leaders
- Vital signs you can assess to determine if an institution is racist
- Steps you can take using your personal computer
- What you can do if you feel your rights have been violated in employment, housing, public accommodations, or education
- How to organize, publicize, and run a civic event
- What the Universal Declaration of Human Rights of the United Nations can tell you

. . . and much, much more

WE *CAN* ALL GET ALONG

QUANTITY SALES

Most Dell books are available at special quantity discounts when purchased in bulk by corporations, organizations, or groups. Special imprints, messages, and excerpts can be produced to meet your needs. For more information, write to: Dell Publishing, 1540 Broadway, New York, NY 10036. Attention: Special Markets.

INDIVIDUAL SALES

Are there any Dell books you want but cannot find in your local stores? If so, you can order them directly from us. You can get any Dell book currently in print. For a complete up-to-date listing of our books and information on how to order, write to: Dell Readers Service, Box DR, 1540 Broadway, New York, NY 10036.